MARY L/

BIRDS OF
THE STORM

MARY LAY

First published in Great Britain in 2023
Mary Lay Stories

Copyright © 2023 Mary Lay

A CIP Catalogue of this book is available
from the British Library

ISBN 978-1-7396653-5-7 (Paperback)
ISBN: 978-1-7396653-4-0 (e-book)

Cover and layout design by Chandler Book Design
www.chandlerbookdesign.com

Self-published by Mary Lay Stories
www.marylaystories.com

Printed in Great Britain by
TJ Books, Padstow, Cornwall

For Ray

CONTENTS

1

AWAKENING

At the beginning of 1927, a hurricane developed in the Atlantic Ocean. It made landfall on Friday the 28 January in the south-west of the United Kingdom and continued north-east across the country leaving a trail of devastation, injury and death in its wake. Caroline Munhead was woken by the noise at a little after two in the morning and couldn't get back to sleep. She lay for a while listening to the wind and rain roar around the apartment building in Cheltenham where she and her father George lived. Every now and then the noise intensified, followed by a crash somewhere nearby. After almost an hour, she got out of bed, wrapped her dressing gown around her, shuffled her feet into her slippers and went to the kitchen to make a drink of cocoa.

Caroline's father heard her movements and as he was also unable to sleep, he joined her in the kitchen.

"Would you like some cocoa too? I can add some more milk without leaving us short for breakfast."

"Yes, if we have enough." George rubbed his hand over his face and went into the sitting room. Their apartment was on the third floor, at the top of the building. There were six apartments in total, two on each floor on either side of the central staircase. George stood at the large window and looked out into the night in the direction of The Park opposite. It had always been just The Park, where others in Cheltenham had more distinctive names. He had not put on the central room light, thinking that he might be able to see better what was happening outside without it.

Caroline brought in the mugs of cocoa and gave one to her father. They stood in silence for a few moments, both looking out at the trees that were being torn and twisted by the wind and lashed by the rain. The Park had been laid out some fifty years before as public garden, with some mature trees retained to give areas of shade and substance. Cheltenham was a town with an abundance of trees and several parks created for the inhabitants of the previous century to promenade. As the pair watched, a bolt of lightning illuminated the view and Caroline frowned.

"I'm sure there should be more trees standing than that."

"This wind has probably brought one or two down. I heard some tiles crash on the road a while ago. I hope they are not from the roof here." As if to illustrate his comment another crash came through the howl of the wind to their right which sounded very much like a roof tile.

They sipped their cocoa. The streetlights cast yellow pools on the scene before them. A large tarpaulin danced and flapped its way along the road, trailing the ropes that had optimistically been used to secure it to something further up the street. It momentarily wrapped itself around the trunk of one of the street trees before being peeled away again by the wind and carried off further down the street. Its progress was obscured by a sudden deluge of rain against the window, as if someone had thrown a bucket of water at it. Caroline jumped at the force of the water.

"I've never known a storm to be so noisy before!"

"But we have never been up so high in one before, my dear. We are also on an exposed corner of the building. Our house before this was much closer to its neighbours. We would not have noticed the wind as much."

They had lived in the apartment for only nine months. Caroline's mother had died the year before. George had decided to salve his grief by moving himself, the then twenty-two-year-old Caroline, and their maid Annie, from their dark Victorian semi-detached house near the railway station to the sleek, bright, modern apartment. Their old home held too many memories, both of his wife Elizabeth and also Caroline's elder brother Freddie who had been killed in the final days of the Great War.

Much had changed over the previous year, both materially and in Caroline's own consciousness. She was now on the cusp of another change; she would be twenty-three in three weeks and shortly after that had arranged to spend a month by herself in north Somerset. She intended to see how the area suited her, and to decide whether to make the move more permanent. Her two friends, Helen and Tommy, lived in Minehead so she would not be entirely without connections in the county.

George finished his drink. "I must try and sleep. It won't do to be late for work."

Caroline took his empty mug. "I'll stay here for a while. I don't think I could go back to sleep with this racket going on."

The Munhead's maid, Annie, lay awake in the bed she shared with her husband Jacob in their new house. She too heard occasional slates crash into the street, but the trees that lined the new 'Poets' corporation housing estate of Milton Road, Tennyson Road, Byron Road and Shakespeare Road were all small and recently planted and would do no damage to the houses. Jacob snored quietly beside her. Annie wondered how he could sleep through the storm. She assumed it must be because he worked so hard in the coal yard which he would one day inherit from his father. Jacob had been diversifying since the coal miners' strike the previous year had left them perilously close to bankruptcy. While his father continued to oversee the coal delivery rounds and sales from the yard, a portion of the space was now filled with timber and builder's ironmongery which Jacob was responsible for. It had been a wise investment and several builders in the town now had accounts with Jenks & Son.

Annie was relieved at, and proud of her husband's success. After four months of marriage, she was almost certain that she was now pregnant. Her days of being the Munhead's daily maid were coming to an end, but she would wait another month or so before she said anything, just to be on the safe side. She would be sorry to leave her position. The Munheads had been very good to her and her relationship with Caroline, only two years her junior, was much more of a friendly one than servant and mistress. The wardrobe that stood opposite the foot of her bed had come from the Munhead's previous house, as had a few other pieces of furniture, and George Munhead had bought both Caroline and Annie bicycles when the family moved to their new apartment. Annie got out of bed and went into the small bathroom between the main bedroom and what would become their child's room. Now she was awake, she might as well go down to the kitchen and stoke the small black boiler ready for when Jacob woke for his breakfast.

In the Lewis' terraced house near to the gas works, Caroline's ex-workmate Lottie slept soundly next to her equally slumbering husband Eric. They would both wake in an hour; she to go to her job in the canvas sewing room at the Sunningend engineering works near the railway station where she and Caroline had met, and he to his shift as trainee police cadet in the town centre station. Lottie and Eric had been married a month longer than Annie and Jacob, but no children were as yet on the horizon. They were being especially careful in that respect as neither of them wanted to hinder Eric's aspiration to complete his training and be posted to a station somewhere in the county. They hoped such a position would come with a house, and only then would they consider starting a family. For now, they slept in the second bedroom of Lottie's parent's house.

In the smallest bedroom of the Lewis' house, Lottie's older brother Bob was wide awake and worried. Not for the house he was currently living in, but for the little house he had bought with a mortgage the previous year and had spent much of his free time since then repairing. Bob and his father, with occasional help from other men at the gas works had put in new windows, repointed the back wall and the chimney, and replaced almost half the roof slates on the little end of terrace house in Blacksmith Lane, Prestbury, a village on the northern edge of Cheltenham. It had been his dream for years to own a house there, keep chickens and tend his garden, and more recently have Caroline Munhead installed there as his wife. He had achieved the house; he would have the chickens as soon as he could move in (which he hoped would be in a month or so now that he was ready to start furnishing the place) but installing Caroline had been put on hold indefinitely. He wanted no other, but knew she was not interested in settling down to married life. He was determined to wait for her, forever if necessary.

Laying in the single bed and listening to the storm rage across the rooftops that night, Bob couldn't help being worried for his own little house. Would the chimney survive? Would the tree to the side of the house stay upright? As soon as his shift ended on Friday afternoon, he would take the tram to Prestbury and find out.

The storm had already been raging for some hours in north Somerset. The sea at Minehead boiled and grasped at the buildings along the seafront and swept into the town flooding the basements and lower floors of several houses. Boats were tossed up against the harbour wall, causing substantial damage and sinking three small cruisers and a fishing boat. The lifeboat had been called out twice to assist other fishing boats racing the hurricane home to port, thankfully with no loss of life.

Helen and Tommy Gersen-Fisch were both awake, in their separate rooms in the large house that they rented overlooking the newly laid out Blenheim Gardens. They had married for convenience as neither were interested in the opposite sex. However, they cared deeply for each other and Tommy's involvement with Christopher Hawkins, a tutor at Exeter University, had if anything brought them closer together. Both of them also were very fond of Caroline. Helen and Caroline had been school friends, keeping in touch by letter along with Midge, the third of their little group.

Helen sat up in bed and lit a cigarette. She was used to storms, having grown up mostly in Plymouth when not at school in Cheltenham, but this was like nothing she had heard before. She could see the brass hands on the bedside clock pointed to twenty minutes past three. Closing her eyes as she inhaled and exhaled the smoke, Helen noted with irony that only a year ago she would have been begging to stay out on the dance floor at this time of night, and not begging for the noise to stop so that she could get some sleep. She needed to be fully alert later on Friday at the Minehead Town Council meeting. She was determined to gain a seat on the Council at the next election and was attending as many meetings as she could to observe her opponents in their natural habitat.

Tommy was also awake, hands behind his head and bedclothes in disarray across his body. He had not slept. The approaching storm had kept him indoors the previous day, depriving him of the exercise he needed to tire him enough to fall asleep unaided each night. He would walk the headland, artist materials under his arm and over his shoulder, or drive deep onto Exmoor and spend hours wandering the valleys and open countryside, painting in his increasingly abstract way. Thoughts of Christopher came unbidden. Try as he might, Tommy could not forget the man. He got out of bed and sat at his desk. Taking a sheet of paper from the drawer, he began another letter to Christopher that would end up in the waste-paper basket.

Midge Frampton was already half-way through her day with the African sun beating down on her while the hurricane trampled across her home country. She and Marie-Claire Anju were copying hymn lyrics onto sheets of rough paper ready for the following Sunday service. They worked in companionable silence, feeling they were at last beginning to do the Lord's work after several months of cooking, cleaning, washing and mending for the men of the mission in their compound. The service on Sunday would be a large one, the compound being opened to the surrounding communities. The Bishop of Mombasa would be attending, and there was talk of Tanganyika separating from the Diocese and becoming a Diocese in its own right.

Midge missed her home in Berkshire, and her four brothers, one of whom was also in Tanganyika but at a different compound. Making friends with Marie-Claire, and improving her rusty French in the process, had helped Midge settle into Africa and life in the compound. She enjoyed the animals she saw as she travelled on the carts to and from the marketplace in Dodoma. She did not enjoy the unsanitary conditions of the compound, but Midge was stoical and realised that complaining would not improve the situation. Her engagement with the mission would be for another eighteen months and she was sure she could endure it.

In London, the city did not sleep. Dance clubs and bars were filled with young people drinking and enjoying themselves while outside thunder rumbled ominously, and lightning began to illuminate the sky to the west. Elsa House, photographer, and her lover Bobby (Roberta) Richardson were celebrating a successful exhibition at the gallery Bobby had opened the year before.

"Do you think your friend Caroline will send us any more of her work before she goes to the West Country?" Bobby sipped her champagne and waved to an acquaintance who had just entered the club.

Elsa drew on her slim cigar and blew the smoke away from Bobby. She was dressed in her usual jacket, shirt and trousers, her hair slicked back from her forehead.

"I think she is unlikely to be sending any more nudes, for now at least. She simply doesn't move in the same circles; the Cotswolds are not the liberated heart of the country."

"Such a pity, I could sell them all ten times over and still have a waiting list. Couldn't you find her a model? What about young Peter?"

Elsa snorted. "Peter? Don't be ridiculous. His talents are in management, principally the management of my clients and commissions and not as a male model for your salacious patrons."

"I knew you'd say that. I was teasing you darling. Though he does have the frame that many of my patrons would admire in charcoal, oils or any other medium." She sipped her drink again. "I can always find a buyer for her more traditional works, but the money is in the nudes."

"Perhaps the good people of Somerset will be less inhibited than their Cotswold cousins."

"We live in hope."

Back in Cheltenham, Reverend Philip Rose, his wife Mary and their young daughter Angelica (who was also Caroline's Goddaughter) were all in the adults' bed in the Vicarage of St Mark. Angelica had fallen asleep in between Philip and Mary, and neither dared move and wake her again just yet. Mary was pregnant with their second child, her third pregnancy, due around Easter. She lay on her side facing Philip, and he lay facing his wife, her black face in shadow but clear against the white cotton bedding. Philip reached up carefully and stroked her face. He never tired of looking at the contrast of his white skin against her darkness. Angelica whimpered in her sleep between them, and Philip froze until he was satisfied she would not wake.

"I will take her back to her cot in a moment." He whispered.

"You'll be careful when you do your visits in the morning, there will be branches and broken tiles on the roads."

"It's as well that I have a bicycle and not a car."

"But in this wind, you'll be blown off your bicycle. I think you should walk." Mary's lilting Bristol-Trinidadian accent sounded sleepy.

"We'll see how it looks when it gets light. You've no need to get up when I do. Let me take Angelica back to her cot and I will sleep in her room for the rest of tonight."

Mary murmured her ascent and Philip began to carefully move off the bed.

Caroline put the mugs in the kitchen sink and went back to her bedroom. She had noticed light coming from the apartments below, escaping from the gaps between pulled curtains. Being on the top floor, the Munheads rarely pulled their curtains in the sitting room. She thought that most of Cheltenham must have been woken by the wind and rain that night.

On the ground floor, Agatha Kettle, an elderly spinster from London, took her warm milk back to her bed and decided to read a few pages of her current novel. She was not concerned about the storm outside, knowing the risk of flooding was minimal and having the security of the two apartments above her for protection. In the other ground floor apartment, Rebecca Monk lay in bed awake. She was not concerned by the storm either; she was concerned at the whereabouts of her husband Michael. Since Christmas he had begun to stay at the barracks on a Friday evening rather than travelling home from Brize Norton where he taught arial reconnaissance to young pilots and navigators. Or so he told her, she thought bitterly. They had moved from Oxford after his affair with a telegram operator became public knowledge, the girl making a scene in front of several senior officers at the base. He had kept his job of course, and the girl had been transferred to somewhere in Kent, but Rebecca had insisted that they must move to a new town where nobody knew his history. And now she simply could not believe him when he told her that he was working later on Fridays and that it was more practical for him to return home on Saturday mornings instead.

The apartment beneath Caroline and George's was still empty after the optician Vaughan Rickard had taken Caroline's newly-married neighbour Florence away to his parent's house in Norfolk. Florence had aborted a pregnancy with serious consequences for her health, and had refused to return to her husband Josiah, the owner of Curzon's Exotic Plant Nursery near to the railway station. Vaughan had fallen head-over-heels in love with Florence, despite declaring his intention of marrying Caroline to her father George only a few days earlier.

Across the landing, Captain McTimony slept peacefully after an evening of whiskey and cigars with a friend from his old regiment. The taxidermy and collection of Indian and African masks and statuary that decorated his sitting room were lit up with every flash of lightening like a scene from a horror film.

The apartment opposite Caroline and George's on the top floor was currently rented by the widow Galina Ivanova Bassett, but she was not at home. Caroline had noticed that Galina recently spent Thursdays to Saturdays away somewhere. The music that often crept under Galina's apartment door was absent on those evenings now, and Miss Kettle had told Caroline that Ferris, the doorman at the apartment block, arranged a taxi to collect Galina and take her to the railway station on Thursday afternoons.

"Perhaps she is concluding her business in London." Caroline had suggested.

"Perhaps she is. Or perhaps she is resuming her social life. It must be so difficult for her to have lost her husband at still such a young age."

"She told me she deliberately wanted to live somewhere that she was unknown, so one would assume her friends will not be in Cheltenham."

"That would explain the suitcase." Miss Kettle closed her little mouth tightly, as if she was fighting hard the impulse to embellish her theory further.

Edward Ferris, doorman and porter for the apartment block at Norwood Court, The Park, Cheltenham, had been asleep in his small house behind the Bath Road parade of shops. A crash and splintering of wood and tiles, above the howl of the wind, woke him with a start. For a moment he lay in bed, dazed and confused. Then he heard shouts through the thin wall that separated him from his neighbours. He dressed quickly and hurried downstairs, into the back yard. A large tree had fallen diagonally across his neighbour's roof, missing his own by inches. Part of the wall above the rear window had been smashed in, and the window itself was a mass of broken glass and splintered wood. The cries of the family who all slept in that one bedroom could be heard above the wind. It was a shared house, with three families having a bedroom each and a fourth in the front room on the ground floor, all of them sharing the kitchen and the outside lavatory.

Ferris looked around for a ladder finding it difficult to see in the dark and rain. There was often one propped up against the house on the other side of his but that night it was not there. He went back into his own home and out through his front door into the street. Others were coming out of their houses despite the storm. Some were pointing at the tree now lodged in the roof of Ferris' neighbour's house.

He shouted to a man he knew to get a ladder, that the family were trapped, and they needed help.

It took some time to find a ladder, then get it into the back yard and up against the wall. Several men helped Ferris by holding the ladder in place while he climbed up. He placed an old coat over the broken window to stop the family from being cut by the glass. Then one by one, he guided first the distraught children, then the shocked parents out and down the ladder with him. He was thankful that all of the inhabitants could climb down under their own steam. His bad back (the result of a fall caused by a sack of dried fruit at the bakery that had been his employment for many years) would not have allowed him to carry any of them. Another neighbour took the family into their home to dry off, while Ferris and the men returned the ladder to its owner.

Wide awake now, Ferris decided to make his way to Norwood Court and see if any damage had occurred to the apartment block under his care. He changed his clothes, put on his raincoat, decided against taking his bicycle, and set out again into the night. Turning into the wider Bath Road, the wind stopped him in his tracks and made him gasp. He was already soaked through, his wellingtons beginning to fill with rainwater. He battled on, occasionally clinging to a lamp post when a particularly strong gust of wind buffeted him and threatened to send him sprawling backwards. The journey that would normally take him ten minutes on foot that night took him almost twenty-five minutes. By the time he arrived at Norwood Court he was exhausted, wet and cold, but also relieved to see only one or two roof tiles on the gravel driveway in front of the apartment block. There had been several more trees either completely uprooted or with their upper parts resting at precarious angles on railings and across roads on his route.

He let himself in through the glass entrance door with its curved brass handle in the Deco style – careful not to let the wind wrestle the door from his grasp – and unlocked his little office which took a small portion of what would otherwise have been Miss Kettle's apartment. He lit the paraffin heater he kept under his desk, removed as much of his clothing as would preserve his dignity, and put his little kettle on the primus stove to make some tea. The clock on the wall said a quarter to four. Then the electricity went out.

Caroline had not been able to get back to sleep despite the cocoa. She lay in bed waiting for each new crash and creak of severed tree limbs to reach her above the noise of the storm. At six o'clock she rose again and found the switch gave no light in her room. For a moment she thought it was the bulb itself which had blown, but on trying the light in the hallway she realised it was a power cut. There must be more trees down around the town she thought. With just enough light from the gas-powered streetlamps to see by, Caroline placed two eggs in a pan of water to boil on the smaller of the two gas stove rings and cut two slices of bread to be buttered. She and her father had never been great breakfast eaters, but he insisted that they have something however small and not wait until mid-morning when suddenly their stomachs would growl with hunger. She heard George go into the bathroom for his ablutions and went to look out of the small window in the dining area.

It was still dark and would be for another hour and a half, but she was sure now that more than one tree had been felled by the storm in The Park across the road. Power cuts were not unusual, and stubs of candles set onto old saucers around the apartment were kept for just such events. Ferris had also topped up their two oil lamps just before Christmas, and Caroline retrieved one and set it on the dining table, lighting it with a spill from the gas stove ring.

Over breakfast, George expressed his concern for Caroline should another such storm sweep in from the Atlantic while she was staying in Somerset.

"But I won't be on my own, Father. I'm sure Mrs Harding's house is quite out of reach of the sea, I seem to remember Dunster being a few miles inland with the railway between it and the coast."

"Are there no trees in Dunster?"

"Oh, I hadn't thought of that. I suppose there must be. Really though, I'm sure I will be perfectly safe there."

"There is still time to change your mind, perhaps postpone until later in the year." He knew she would not.

"That would be quite rude I think, having already paid Mrs Harding for the full four weeks. She might then have to put someone else off later to accommodate me. No, I shall still go. And if it comes to it, I shall find some way of getting to Minehead and impose on Helen and Tommy."

George finished his tea and wiped his mouth. "Yes, at least they will be nearby." He looked at his watch. "I should leave now. The trams won't be running if the electricity is off across town and some of the staff might have difficulty getting in on time. If you venture out today, I should leave the bicycle at home."

George was the manager of the Cheltenham branch of the Cheltenham and Gloucester Benefits Building Society. It had prospered under his authority, and now employed six clerks at their office in the High Street. George oversaw most of the mortgage applications himself and had cautiously approved Bob Lewis' to buy the house in Prestbury. His circle of work acquaintances was large and not insignificant, stretching across the Home Counties and as far north as Leeds.

These were not friends; the Munheads had not been regular hosts mainly due to Elizabeth's prolonged illness and mourning for Freddie while Caroline was in her teens. If she were asked, Caroline would be hard pressed to name more than two or three people she would consider to be her father's true friends.

He had, however, remained part of the congregation at Christ Church, a short distance from the Spa railway station. It was here that George headed first as he left Norwood Court. His route took him around The Park (prudence and darkness dissuaded him from taking the more direct route across it), through Tivoli and Lansdown. There were trees with their limbs hanging down in front gardens, resting on telephone and electricity wires, and one or two more through rooves. Tradesmen were attempting to go about their business, with their horses picking their way around the detritus of the previous night. The wind was still strong – too strong for an umbrella – and George had to hold on to his hat for much of his journey.

Christ Church stood with its severe grey façade impervious to the hurricane. The door was open; George found two families huddled together in the pews being provided with tea and biscuits by the sexton's wife. She explained that one family's chimney had blown down and taken much of the roof with it. The other family had been living in the basement of a building near to the river Chelt which had flooded. George listened politely for some moments before excusing himself and pressing a few coins into the sexton's wife's hand for the provision of more refreshments should any other parishioners require relief.

From Christ Church George walked along Overton Park Road and into the town centre. More trees were down in Montpellier; one across the tram lines was being dismembered

by a gang of men with a huge two-handled saw. Many of
the buildings there had either flat or very shallow apexed
rooves, but nearer the town centre and around St James
railway station the factories and housing were of old and
poorly maintained Victorian stock. Many of these had gaping
holes in their rooves where tiles had been peeled off by the
wind, and two were missing their rooves completely. Men
were struggling with a large tarpaulin to cover one of the
holes, but the wind was proving more than a match for their
strength and patience. George was glad to reach his office
and lit the small fire in the grate to provide some light as
well as heat to dry his outer clothes.

Caroline stood for some time at the sitting room window
watching the sky gradually lighten. The clouds were still dark
and rain-heavy, the wind still howled, but she fancied not
quite as much as it had over night. She had been thinking
about her father's concern for her stay in Somerset. Was she
being too reckless? After all, she had only Mrs Harding's
sister as a recommendation. Mrs Frobisher was a member,
as Caroline was, of the Cheltenham Women's Section of
the Royal British Legion, her son being an invalid after the
war. She had given Caroline her sister's address and told her
that her sister would be happy to come to an arrangement
for four weeks. Caroline had written, and then spoken to
Mrs Harding using the telephone in Ferris' office. She was
reassured by the woman's soft almost purring voice and the
promise of a bathroom to herself for most of her stay.

George had decided to have a telephone installed in their
apartment as Caroline was using Ferris' with more regularity.
The engineers were booked for the following week, and
Caroline was determined to telephone Helen as soon as
it was working. It was equally reassuring to Caroline that

she would be able to contact her father if anything should require it while she was away.

As she looked out of the sitting room window, a crow took flight from one of the trees across the road. It threw itself up into the arms of the wind and seemed to revel in the way it twisted and turned in the air before swooping low to the ground and landing on the sodden grass below. Caroline saw it call out in its rattle-stick caw, as if to encourage its fellows out of the trees. She felt inspired by the bird's bravery against the stormy conditions.

2

VILLAGE LIFE

Dunster railway station was indeed sandwiched between the Bristol Channel and the gently rising land, mostly tree-covered, that hid the village of Dunster and its castle from view for much of the year. The station porter stacked Caroline's two suitcases and her carpet bag on to a trolley and wheeled it through the ticket office and out to the taxi. The taxi driver trod on his cigarette and opened the passenger door of his motorcar for Caroline to get inside. She was pleased to do so as the fog that had obscured her view for much of her journey was thicker here and the air felt cold. Caroline had wondered if she might have to stay at home unable to travel, as hot on the heels of the January hurricane arrived widespread snow for the beginning of February. It had cleared by her birthday on the eighteenth, for which George had given her the new sturdy suitcase now in the rear of the taxi. But here she was heading up the lane towards the village and a month-long exploration of north Somerset.

Caroline had spoken to Helen the week before and agreed that she would call on them in Minehead once she had got her bearings. She was arriving on Tuesday 1 March and planned to send Helen a postcard saying to expect her the following weekend. Three days would surely be long enough to explore her new surroundings.

The taxi drove carefully up the lane after crossing the wider road that led along the coast to Minehead, and Caroline began to see the village emerge through the mist. It appeared to be a single wide street, leading up to the church and the castle a little higher, and then winding around to a mill and more houses before petering out into farmland again. They passed a peculiar, thatched structure with eight thick oak beams supporting the roof and rumbled over the cobbles until the taxi came to a halt outside a house next to the White Hart Inn in West Street. The house was white-washed with its door and window frames painted a dark red.

Celia Harding kept a clean house. It had been her home since her parents had died of the influenza within two weeks of each other in 1918 and would have been her marital home had her fiancé Edgar returned from Passchendaele. She knew she was one of many in a similar situation. Her older brother Edward had married and moved away to Yeovil. Her sister Joyce, older than Celia by ten years, had moved to Cheltenham with her husband. Their son had at least returned from the front but had given much of his face and upper body along with his senses to the War. Celia had suggested that Joyce and her son William move back to Dunster and live with her, but Joyce had decided to keep William in surroundings that he recognised.

That left Celia at the age of twenty-eight with a four-bedroom house that had once been two cottages. She joined the growing ranks of guest house proprietors and thoroughly enjoyed looking after her visitors. She baked, she cleaned, she did all of the laundry; there was never a still moment from dawn to dusk. She advertised occasionally in respectable publications such as *The Lady* and *Woman and Home*. She preferred to have female guests but would never turn down a male visitor if she had a room available. Her main rule was not to accept those who wished to find long-term accommodation. Celia liked to air the bedrooms and give them a thorough clean between guests and after three or four weeks of habitation she found the cleaning required far too much of her energy to achieve the finish she prided herself on. She had made an exception for Caroline, having been reassured by Joyce that the girl was from a respectable family.

Celia had been watching from the window in the bedroom where she intended to place Caroline and trotted down the stairs when she saw the taxi approaching through the fog. Caroline paid the driver while Celia took the suitcases inside, and then followed her host into the narrow entrance hall and from there, to the sitting room. She was given a large iron key to the front door and was informed the door would be bolted at ten o'clock each night without exception. Caroline nodded her approval. She could smell beeswax and lavender and every surface gleamed despite the dim light through the small-paned window.

"Now you're here I'll light the fire, then we'll get you settled in your room, and I'll make us some tea. I do all the cooking for my guests, so you must let me know if there is anything you don't like. We had a chap a few weeks ago, I served him steak and kidney pie three times before he told me he didn't like kidney. He'd eaten every scrap, mind you!"

"I can't think of anything in particular that I don't like Mrs Harding, although I much prefer tea to coffee if that's not too much trouble for you."

"No trouble at all, my bird. Now as I told you, I have one other guest for the rest of this week and after that it will be just us two. Mr Cartwright is a historian. He has been writing about our church. Spends all day there, looking at the records and talking to the vicar." Celia Harding took a box of matches from the mantlepiece and lit the paper in the grate. It glowed as she blew on it a few times, then the flames caught the dry kindling and after a few moments the coal on top slumped inwards and began to send smoke up the chimney. Celia placed the fireguard around the grate and led the way up the stairs carrying Caroline's suitcases.

Left alone in her room, Caroline unpacked, hung up her clothes, and pushed the empty cases on top of the wardrobe. She tried out the bed, which had a metal frame and springs underneath a substantial mattress and was covered with a pink candlewick bedspread. The room was at the front of the house; she would have a good view of the street when the fog lifted. Caroline hoped there would not be much noise from the patrons of the public house next door.

Over tea and crumpets that Celia toasted on a long fork in front of the fire, the two women got to know each other. Caroline had already explained the basis of her visit to the county, but Celia was interested to hear about life in Cheltenham and in particular of the damage inflicted by the hurricane in January. In turn she described the social activities that Caroline would find in Dunster and the surrounding villages. Saint George's church bells would ring out on Sunday morning and Caroline would be welcome to join the congregation. The strange construction Caroline had seen at the entrance to the village was known as the Yarn Market reflecting the area's heavy dependence on sheep and their fleeces. Caroline was fascinated by Celia's way of calling her 'my bird' rather than the more usual 'my dear' and wondered if it were a common quirk of the area.

As they sat and talked, the room grew dark with only the fire to see by. The sound of a key in the front door roused Celia. She collected up the tea things and disappeared into her kitchen to prepare the dinner. Mr Cartwright was an elderly gentleman with a bushy grey beard and thick eyebrows. He wore a long raincoat which he hung on a peg in the hallway and a felt hat which gave him a striking appearance. Entering the sitting room, he introduced himself to Caroline, and then took out a tobacco pouch and pipe to smoke before his evening meal. Caroline was warm and comfortable in the armchair and decided not to retire to her room. The sound of the fire crackling and Mr Cartwright's regular sucking on his pipe were soothing and the next thing she knew was Celia gently nudging her arm to say that dinner was ready in the dining room.

The fog was still wrapped around the village when Caroline went down to breakfast the following day. She had been undisturbed by the pub customers and had slept well in the cosy room. Mr Cartwright was just finishing his bacon and eggs. He greeted Caroline brightly and asked her plans for the day.

"I thought I might have a look around the village, I noticed one or two shops in the High Street on my way here. Just a boiled egg please Mrs Harding."

Cartwright sat back in his chair. "Yes, today would be a good day to see Dunster as it really is, because tomorrow is market day, and the High Street will be filled with sheep pens."

"Really? That sounds exciting, I've never been to a live-stock auction before."

"Just keep your hands down, else you risk coming away with a flock of your own!" Cartwright chuckled.

"Will you be continuing your research?"

"I will. I fear I shall run out of time here, so many documents and records to investigate and only two more days to do so."

"You are leaving on Friday? Where is home for you Mr Cartwright?"

"Yes, I take the train back to Portsmouth on Friday morning. It has been a thoroughly enjoyable stay here, but my publisher insists that I return and commit my findings to print. You may be familiar with my earlier works on the Norman churches of Hampshire and Medieval church carvings in Suffolk?"

"I'm afraid not, but they do sound fascinating. I shall look out for a copy."

"If you would care to leave an address, I would be delighted to send you a copy of each."

Caroline thought her father would appreciate the subject matter and agreed happily.

As the clock on St George's church tower struck fifteen minutes past ten, Caroline closed the front door behind her and set off for the High Street. Being used to the rumble of trams, trains and more recently cars around her, the quiet of Dunster was eerie. As it was so close to the sea, Caroline had expected to hear the raucous call of seagulls or perhaps a mellow cooing from pigeons or doves in the trees. A black cat stretched along the top of a low wall and disappeared behind it as Caroline approached, but that was the only sign of life as she walked towards the corner where the entrance to the castle opened, and the High Street began.

The village inhabitants, Caroline imagined, must all be very busy inside their homes with cleaning, mending and other industry. Whisps of smoke rose and curled away from the chimneys, and in places the thatched rooves dripped with moisture from the fog. At the castle entrance the first sign of human life appeared. A young man leading a fine chestnut hunter out from the stables and up towards the castle. He tapped the side of his cloth cap in acknowledgement when he saw Caroline and she smiled in return and wished him a good morning. The horse snorted and tossed its head but was willing enough to be led.

In the High Street the first shop Caroline came to was a small tobacconist and stationer. Despite the new telephone being successfully installed in their apartment, Caroline had agreed to write to her father on a weekly basis as she had before when staying away for more than a few days, rather than finding a telephone in Dunster to use. Mrs Harding had of course offered the use of hers, but Caroline still preferred to write. She noticed a rack of picture postcards just inside the shop door and decided to call in on her way back and purchase one for George and also one to send to Helen.

For the next hour Caroline went into almost every shop in the High Street, introducing herself to the proprietors in each. She had been asked if she knew three separate relatives who lived in Gloucestershire and realised quickly that she needed to have a response ready to the question, 'What brings you to Dunster?'. The idea that someone from the cosmopolitan hub of Cheltenham might actually want to live in a village on the edge of Exmoor seemed absurd and faintly suspicious to most people, particularly a young woman on her own. It was only when she reached a bookshop near to the Yarn Market that her reply of, 'I am looking to find a permanent home here', caused the listener to regard her with serious interest.

"Here in the village or in the general area?" Daisy Clare put down the newspaper she was reading and took off her glasses to see Caroline better.

"I don't really know yet. I suppose it depends on what is available, and the terms of course."

"Forgive my directness, but how would you support yourself? There is very little employment to be had in this area unless you are willing to live in Minehead."

Caroline was willing to forgive, though she was somewhat surprised to be asked. "I have a small income, and there is the possibility of selling some of my paintings."

Daisy held out her hand. "I'm dreadfully sorry, we seem to be doing this all round the wrong way. My name is Daisy Clare, Miss, and this is my bookshop. I do a little printing as well, no one could survive on selling books alone here, and I write poetry though mostly for magazines rather than anthologies these days. How do you do."

"Very pleased to meet you, Miss Clare." Caroline shook the woman's hand.

"Do call me Daisy, Miss Clare sounds so schoolteacher-ish! Are you staying at The Ram?"

"No, with Mrs Harding in West Street."

"Oh, you'll be well looked after there, Celia is a treasure. If you are interested in our sleepy little village, you would be most welcome at the Women's Institute. We meet on Thursday afternoons, generally while the menfolk are in the pub after market. We also have a small Women's Section, only recently formed, they meet in the upstairs room at The Ram on a Tuesday at seven. Then there is choir practice on Monday evenings at St George's, and if you play bridge, I can probably rouse a couple of other players for an evening. Only if you're interested of course, please don't feel obliged." Daisy looked down at her desk, which doubled as a shop counter, a little embarrassed. She knew she was talking too much, being too forward as her parents and teachers had so often said, but she couldn't help it. Meeting someone new, someone who would be staying for more than a day or two, was such a rare treat.

"I do play bridge, although I have only recently learned." Caroline couldn't help smiling at the slightly awkward woman in front of her. Daisy wore wellington boots and a tweed skirt to her calves, a floral blouse that tied at the neck and a sweater made from thick brown yarn that was a little too long in the arms. She reminded Caroline of Midge, except Daisy was a good ten years older. "And I am a member of the Women's Section of the Royal British Legion at home, so I would be interested in attending the meetings here if I would be allowed, or the WI."

"I can introduce you, if you'd like to come along to the WI tomorrow. We're having a demonstration of whorl spinning and it will give you an opportunity to meet some more of the locals."

They agreed to meet at the bookshop at two o'clock the following afternoon, and Caroline left feeling that she had made a friend. Daisy sat down at her desk again and said to the silver tabby cat that had appeared, "She seems a very nice young woman, Gladstone, I do hope she decides to stay. She says she's a painter." Gladstone yawned and proceeded to wash his hind legs.

A painter, thought Daisy to herself. She had known another painter, some years before. A German named Udo, who had pretended to be Dutch and had spent a month in the village before someone discovered his secret. One of his secrets, thought Daisy with a wistful smile. She still had two pairs of Udo's socks in her chest of drawers, knitted, he had told her, by his grandmother in the Black Forest. It had sounded so tantalising, as Udo had also been.

Thursday dawned elsewhere, but in Dunster the fog gave way to drizzle and the sound of water trickling along gutters and gullies. Caroline had learned that the livestock would start to appear around the Yarn Market from eight in the morning and was keen to observe the activity. Mrs Harding assured her that the market happened every Thursday, and as a consequence most of the shops closed at lunchtime so that socialising and outdoor business could be conducted.

"But if there are more people in the village on Thursdays, one would have thought the shops would stay open and make the most of the trade." Caroline pondered over breakfast.

Mr Cartwright helped himself to another slice of toast. "Typically, it is the one day of the week that families are able to be together. Those who have come in from the farms all around get to see their siblings and cousins who moved here for employment. Farms rarely sustain multiple offspring these days, and many are tenanted in any case and wouldn't necessarily be passed down."

"I see. So, it is not church on Sundays that brings families together, but sheep on Thursdays."

"Country people are rather different to those of the town."

Mrs Harding poured more hot water into the tea pot. "The school gives the children a half day also. The old school master, Mr Patton, always said we were unteachable on a Thursday on account of the noise from the market."

"I did wonder how the Women's Institute came to meet in the schoolhouse."

"I'm not sure what this afternoon's talk will be worth, though I don't want to be uncharitable. I should think most of us know how to whorl spin."

"What exactly is a whorl, Mrs Harding?"

"It's what you spin fleece with when you have no wheel. I suppose you wouldn't have seen one before. I learned when

I was on my Granny's knee, though I haven't needed to spin for many years now. You'll enjoy the talk I expect, my bird, if you're not familiar with the subject."

Caroline wasn't entirely sure how one would spin fleece even if one did have a wheel, but it seemed an interesting prospect and she was looking forward to meeting more of the village residents.

Borrowing an umbrella from Mrs Harding, Caroline retraced her steps from the day before to the High Street. She was surprised at how it had changed overnight. Where the day before it had been an almost deserted plane of cobbles, now it was a jumble of carts, hurdles arranged in pens, sacks of animal feed, and straw. As she got closer the smells and noises grew. Not only sheep but pigs, chickens, geese and ducks, a pair of young heifers and a large bull, sheep dogs and braces of rabbit and pigeon strung by their legs and hanging upside down from one of the hurdles. Caroline was used to seeing meat hanging in the butchers' shops of course but seeing them alive and all together was a novelty. Men in oilskins and heavy serge suits with their hats and caps pulled down on their heads stood alone, in pairs and small groups. Many were smoking, some drank from stone jugs despite it being still early in the morning. Caroline struggled to make out any of the conversations as to her ears the men mumbled and drawled and rolled all of their words into one.

One area of the Yarn Market had been reserved for the farmer's wives to display their produce. Here Caroline viewed eggs of various sizes and colours, bread in traditional loaves as well as rolls and fancier plaited and scored styles. Butter in small and large pats wrapped in greased paper, cream and milk in urns, jugs and bottles. Great wheels of cheese were stacked on one trestle table with rind the colour of granite. Others were smaller and wrapped in what looked

like spinach leaves, but which Caroline was informed were
nettles. She was tempted to purchase a little of everything
but settled on a hot water crust pork pie, a small jar of spiced
apple and pear chutney and some of the nettle-wrapped
cheese. The wives were as unintelligible as their husbands to
Caroline's ears, but with smiles and pointing on both sides,
she achieved her aim. Turning away from the cheeses, she
came face to face with the groom she had seen with the
chestnut hunter the previous day.

"Good morning, Miss. Watch you don't drop those." His
face was weathered even though it was early March, as if he
had spent every one of his twenty-nine years out in the sun.

"Good morning. I should have brought a basket, but I
didn't expect to purchase anything."

"Can I carry them for you? My business is done, and I'm
heading back to the stables now."

"Thank you, Mr?"

"Jack."

"Thank you, Mr Jack."

"No, Jack is my first name, Jack Herridge." He took the
food from her.

"Oh, I'm sorry, Mr Herridge. Jack." Caroline blushed.

They moved through the crowd of the market, around
the pens until a crash made them stop and look to see what
the commotion was. A large black pig had pushed over one
of the hurdles and a pail of milk that was standing near-by
while its new owner was talking to the auctioneer. Men with
boards quickly surrounded the animal and goaded it back to
the pen, while others made to repair the hurdle and secure
the animal inside. Nothing could be done for the milk, but
a pair of Border Collies made short work of clearing it up.

Away from the bustle of the market, Caroline felt able
to speak and be heard.

"That was a handsome horse you were leading yesterday."

"Beacon. He's darkened over the years, but he was almost golden when he was a foal. He's got a stubborn nature."

"And you look after him?"

"I do. And the rest of the stable. Got a couple of lads who help, but it's mostly me."

"Are there many other horses?"

"Not as many as there were in Father's day, but Old Andrew keeps a couple of hunters, a couple of cart horses for the estate and the polo ponies. He doesn't ride the polos now of course, keeps them for his friends to ride out. Fine horses they are."

"Old Andrew?"

"Andrew Maxwell Fines. Lord of the manor. Only visits occasionally now, stays mostly in Tiverton, but comes over for the polo."

Caroline was aware of the sport, as Cheltenham also had a polo club at the foot of Cleeve Hill between Cheltenham and Prestbury. She had never been to watch but had read reports in the *Chronicle* of the large, and by all accounts wealthy, crowds that did so. As they reached the start of the castle drive, Jack asked, "Would you like to meet the horses?"

"Could I? That would be wonderful."

They turned off the main street and walked down an incline to the stables. The distinctive smell of leather, saddle soap and horse grew pungent; Caroline almost put her hand up to cover her nose but then decided it could appear rude. There was little light inside the stable block. It took a moment for Caroline's eye to adjust. Then she saw a row of low stalls were on one side and a row of larger enclosed stalls on the other. Through the centre a gulley ran, Caroline presumed to make cleaning the stalls easier. Jack placed Caroline's purchases on a shelf just inside the door and beckoned her forward.

"Joffrey here is the other hunter." Jack stood by the door of one of the large stalls and a black horse pushed its head through the gap. Jack gave it a broken carrot and rubbed the horse's nose. "The cart horses are both out, Knibbs is collecting milk from the estate farm. But these two," he moved on to the other large stalls, "these are the polo ponies. Sultan is the bay, and Balthazar is the black. Both a bit bad tempered at the moment, they need a decent run out." As if in agreement, Sultan kicked against the wooden stall wall and snorted loudly. Caroline took a step back, then shook her head and stepped forward again. Jack grinned. "Not used to being this close?"

"Not really. We have delivery horses in Cheltenham of course, the Jenks have one that pulls their coal cart, but these are larger and more spirited."

"Joffrey is calm enough, I took him out earlier." Jack indicated that they should go back to the first stall. He unbolted the door and talked quietly to the horse to move him back from the entrance to the stall so that Caroline could get in as well. She stood in the doorway.

"Here, give him this." Jack produced another broken carrot. "Hold it on your hand, keep your fingers and thumb flat. He can't see your hand, so he won't know if he's eating you or the carrot. That's it."

Caroline giggled as the horse's soft muzzle flapped over her hand and gently took the carrot from her. "Can I stroke him?"

"Yes, just move slowly as he doesn't know you. Give his neck a pat, tell him he's been a good lad."

She did as Jack suggested. Joffrey seemed to approve, his ears twitching as he stood still.

They left the horse and bolted the stall door behind them before walking towards the daylight again. Caroline retrieved her shopping from the shelf.

"They are lovely animals, thank you for showing me."

"If you rode, I'd suggest you take out Sultan or Balthazar, they never get enough exercise and the lads find it difficult to handle them. It's hard to keep them in good condition, but I think they'll be alright for the next match. It's at the end of this month."

"You ride the hunters?"

"Yes, two or three times a week. In between they're just turned out into the paddock. You're welcome to see them any time, the lane there leads down to the paddock and the polo field beyond. Do you have much further to go? I can carry those for you again if you like."

"Oh, no, I'm staying with Mrs Harding just along there. Thank you though."

"Staying long?"

"A month. I have friends in Minehead. I'm thinking of moving to the area."

Jack looked away from Caroline, back down towards the Yarn Market. "It's a quiet place. Good to come back to when you've been away."

"Have you been away?"

"Ireland, during the uprising. I thought they'd send me to the Front, but they had other ideas, they sent most of our horses there instead."

"My brother Freddie," she swallowed, it still hurt to say the words out loud despite the lengthening years, "he was killed at the end of the war. In France."

"I'm sorry to hear that."

They stood for a moment, both with their thoughts elsewhere. Then Caroline said, "Well I should be getting along now. Thanks again for your help."

"If you're staying a while then I'm sure we'll bump into one another again." Jack smiled.

"I expect so. Goodbye!"

Caroline turned and headed off along West Street. What an interesting man Jack was, she thought as she walked. There was something about him that reminded her of Freddie, his self-containment and easy-going nature. Someone useful to have around in a crisis she thought.

Mrs Harding was happy to take the provisions into the cold store, and they shared the pie for lunch. She told Caroline more about Jack Herridge, how his father had been groom to the Fines before him, and how they had both wept in the street when the army took the horses into service for the war. Mrs Herridge had been employed in the castle; the family had always lived in the area.

"He's not courting anyone either, as far as I know." Mrs Harding said with a sly smile.

"Mrs Harding, I am not here to find a husband."

"No, my bird." She replied.

Daisy Clare locked the bookshop door behind her and stepped out onto the High Street. The drizzle had stopped, and the clouds had receded a little so that the castle entrance could be seen from where she stood. She put the key into the pocket of her coat. As she did so, she heard the muted meow of a cat. She looked around, and spotted Gladstone inside the shop, sitting on the floor just behind the door. Daisy unlocked the door and let Gladstone out.

"How did you get back inside? I was sure I shut you out in the yard." The cat sat down again and looked through half closed eyes at the remaining farmers putting away their goods. "I do hope Miss Munhead is on time. I rather feel she will be, don't you?"

The cat continued to look in the opposite direction.

"Of course, she might have changed her mind completely. Or even been invited somewhere else. But I'm sure she would have called in to let me know. Unless she did when I was making tea. No, I would have heard the door. She'll be here."

Gladstone turned and looked at Daisy.

"I know, I'm being silly. I simply can't help it. People do let one down so."

"Miss Clare!" Caroline called out as she came around the side of a cart and saw Daisy at her door. She smiled, slightly amused at Daisy's appearance. Her coat was a man's long waxed raincoat; on her feet were the wellington boots again with thick stockings, the hem of her tweed skirt was coming down on one side, but the most striking thing was her hat. Not for Daisy a fashionable cloche like Caroline wore. On Daisy Clare's head sat a dark blue felt hat with a wide brim, very similar to Mr Cartwright's. It was pulled at a jaunty angle almost covering one of Daisy's eyes (which were behind her glasses once again), and her black shoulder-length hair was starting to frizz and curl in the damp air.

"I hope you haven't been waiting long," Caroline held out her gloved hand in greeting for Daisy to shake.

"No, hardly any time at all. And Gladstone has kept me company." She noted Caroline's blank face. "Gladstone, my cat. There he is..." she turned to point. "Oh, he's wandered off. Cats do that, you know, and then appear again at the most inopportune moments. Do you like cats?"

"I don't dislike them, but we've never had one as a pet. Or a dog, or any other animal."

"I would feel very alone without Gladstone. Shall we get on our way? It's just along the lane there."

They set off together, Daisy chattering on about nothing in particular. Caroline guessed that it was a nervous habit, and that Daisy would not want the conversation to flag for fear of being thought boring. It suited Caroline to walk and listen, and to make appropriate acknowledgements every so often. She had learned the trick at her mother's Thursday afternoon tea parties when the conversation would ebb and flow around her. They walked along a narrow lane and came to a school building set a little way back from the road. There was a small, grassed area to the side of the building for the children to take their exercise, and a cobbled path that led up to a bright red wooden door that stood open.

Daisy introduced Caroline to several ladies of the village and the surrounding farms before the Secretary called them all to order. There followed an entertaining two hours where the ladies were treated to an excellent demonstration of spinning, followed by the general business of the Institute and the appointment of a sub-committee to arrange the Easter bonnet parade. Tea and cake were consumed, Caroline was asked repeatedly if she knew cousins and other relatives who lived 'up the line', and *Jerusalem* was lustily sung by all.

While they had been inside the school building, the rain had stopped, the clouds lifted, and a bright sun was causing the thatched rooves to steam gently. Caroline left her coat undone; Daisy steadfastly pulled her hat down on her head and thrust her hands into her coat pockets.

"I must say Daisy, that was a very interesting talk. I'd never considered spinning yarn before. I've only recently mastered knitting, but I feel enthused to try my hand at making my own yarn as well."

"Do they have sheep in Cheltenham? You would need a supply of fleece."

"Of course, it's not London. We might not have them roaming the streets like you do here, but we do have them. Ours have longer fleeces than the ones here though. I suppose they are different types."

"Breeds. Yes, there are many different breeds, some developed for their fleece and some for their meat. Did you feel the sample Mrs Brewer had with her? It was rather greasy. I think I would still prefer to buy yarn from a wool shop than make my own."

"Do you knit?"

"Oh yes. I make most of my own clothes. It's such a bore to go to Minehead just for a sweater or pair of socks. There used to be a dressmaker here in Dunster but she moved away a few years ago. One can still purchase items from the iron monger of course, this coat was a bargain!"

"Very practical."

"Certainly. And if you don't mind my saying so Caroline, you will need to invest in a pair of wellingtons if you are staying here for any length of time. Your shoes are lovely, but the mud will ruin them."

Caroline had come to the same conclusion after noticing several of the ladies at the WI sporting rubber boots. The following day she began her further explorations of the village by purchasing a pair in the ironmonger's shop. She did not need to wear them that day, however. The sun did its best to get spring into motion. Thatches continued to steam in the warmth, birds sang hidden in hedgerows and from fence posts, and in the distance, cows lowed, and sheep bleated. After taking her wellingtons back to Mrs Harding's house, Caroline decided to walk to the sea.

She knew it was just beyond the railway tracks. The two-mile walk down to the station from the village was pleasant and Caroline congratulated herself on dressing in a light cotton blouse and skirt under her sweater and overcoat. She had been undecided about wearing a hat; it seemed to be required for the WI meeting but a number of women at the Yarn Market had been hatless and hadn't appeared to cause a breakdown in the social fabric of the village. After several minutes Caroline had decided against the hat but had resolved to purchase a new straw hat if the opportunity presented itself.

By the time she reached the railway, she had been passed by just two cyclists, two riders on horseback, and an elderly gentleman leading a very large bull by a rope threaded through a ring in the beast's nose. Caroline had stepped as close to the hedge as she could as the bull passed her, wary of its rolling eye and large horns. The gentleman had tapped his hat in her direction and kept his steady pace. As Caroline went on her way, she considered her own reactions of the past forty-eight hours to the menagerie of animals she had encountered. She had been around horses of course, as many of the deliveries to her home had arrived on carts drawn by them over the years, but sheep and cows were things of picture books. She had not realised just how big they were, or their unpredictability. When they simply arrive on a plate or hang in the butcher's window, their nature, behaviour and husbandry are inconsequential.

Caroline was still pondering the subject as she crossed the railway tracks. The lane here was narrower and vegetation grew in the centre with ruts either side from numerous cartwheels. Rounding a bend, the Bristol Channel was suddenly visible as an expanse of grey-blue, flat and silent in the morning sun. Caroline walked until the lane became low sand dunes with tufts of marram grass doing their best to stop the sand crawling inland or out to sea. There was no one else to be seen.

Once on the firmer sand, she walked west for some minutes along the high tide line studded with small pebbles and shells. Then she sat, legs out in front of her and hands behind, and watched the tiny waves creep in and out as if whispering to each other secrets from far away shores. Had she ever been so completely by herself? She could not remember a time. The sensation of sand between her fingers brought back memories of Max. She fancied she could smell his cigarette smoke and shook her head. Helen had been right; Caroline must forget all about married Max, forget how their attraction had been consummated so quickly and briefly on his final night at the artists' retreat in St Ives the summer before. Forget how his injuries from the war had been so easy to ignore by the way he had made her feel even without touching her. No one else would ever be Max, and she must not measure each man up against his memory.

Dusting the sand from her hands, she noticed a boat in the distance, so far out on the water that it shimmered in the haze. That was something else she had never done, she realised. She had never been on a boat. Perhaps she should make a list of things, to give herself some focus instead of simply aimlessly drifting from one experience to another. She would do so when she returned to Mrs Hardings' house, with things both mundane and fantastic, to see how many she could cross through that year. A boat trip. Riding a horse. Catching a fish. Driving a motor car. Tommy had said he would teach her to do that if she decided to make her new home in the area. She wanted a purpose, some direction. She missed her brother Freddie so much at times like these, he would have had suggestions.

Caroline closed her eyes for a moment and brought Freddie's face to her mind's eye. It was becoming more difficult to do so now, after 8 years without him. As she saw him, he turned and pointed to the east. She opened her eyes again with a frown. The boat had drifted eastwards but was still as far out as before. She rose to her feet, brushed herself down and turned to retrace her steps. When she reached the section of dune where she had climbed onto the beach earlier, she stopped and looked up at the headland that rose on the eastern end of the beach, stretching out into the channel. Something glinted in the sunlight at the top of the promontory.

3

FURTHER EXPLORATIONS

"Darling Caro! Come in, come in. You brought your overnight bag? Excellent. You can leave it there; Mrs Rich will take it up presently. Come through into the drawing room." Helen released Caroline from a hug and ushered her into the room that looked out over Blenheim Gardens. "Tommy is out, as you might expect on such a glorious day. We don't expect him to return until it gets dark, but he has not forgotten that you were arriving today."

"How is he? How are you both?" Caroline pulled at the fingers of her gloves as she sat on the settee opposite her friend.

"We are as we ever were," Helen smiled, her face indicating the layers of meaning in her response. "Tommy is still writing those infernal letters to Christopher in the middle of the night. One doesn't read them of course, they are in shreds in the waste-paper basket most mornings, but I do wish he would draw a line under the affair. Ahh, Mrs Rich, you are an absolute treasure!"

Mrs Rich, the Gersen-Fisch's daily housekeeper, entered bearing a tray of tea things. Conversation paused as she arranged the items on the low coffee table, then withdrew.

"So, tell me all about Dunster."

"It is a rather contained village, where everyone appears to know someone on a nearby farm and also 'up the line' as they call the rest of the country. Mrs Harding is a dear, I am sure I have put on half a stone in weight already and I shall be the size of a house by the end of the month. It has a castle and a folly tower that I haven't managed to walk to just yet. Oh, and I have made one or two acquaintances already."

"Really, already? Do tell." Helen handed Caroline her tea.

"A lady who owns a bookshop in the village, Daisy Clare. She introduced me to the local Women's Institute crowd, and we had a talk about spinning yarn."

"Fascinating!"

"It was actually, though I know it's not your thing."

"And the other?"

"Other what?"

"Other acquaintance. You said two." Helen now watched her friend intently.

Caroline looked at her shoes, then lifted her head and looked directly at Helen. "The castle groom, whose name is Jack Herridge. I met him at the Yarn Market and he showed me the horses in the stables. And I can read your mind Helen, he is devoted to his horses."

"I am sure he is. I am not going to tease you about him darling. There will be many such acquaintances I am sure while you are staying here."

"And how are you settling in to Minehead society?" Caroline deflected the attention on her own affairs.

"I have my eye on a seat at the next Town Council elections later this year. The ward is not this one unfortunately, it is on the other side of town, but I have it on good authority that the present councillor intends to step down. I am being seen in all the appropriate locations and have become a regular correspondent in the local newspaper. I have also joined the Primrose League, on Mother's suggestion."

"How exciting for you! Will there be hastings?"

It took a moment for Helen to understand. "Hustings, dear heart, not Hastings. Not exactly. One is required to speak at public meetings, but the real work is done by influencing the right people and their friends in the town. Of course, being a woman, there are still so many to convince of my capabilities. I may canvas a few notables in the ward itself, but the rest is down to association."

Caroline didn't really understand politics, particularly at a local level, but she knew it had been Helen's plan for some time now and was happy for her friend that her efforts seemed to be on the verge of reward. She had been eligible to vote in local elections, though had not always done so. Caroline felt she would need the guidance of her father if she were to vote in anything that would have country-wide repercussions, should the chance ever arise.

After lunch the women strolled around Blenheim Gardens, admiring the daffodils regimented in the flower beds. Clouds had arrived overnight, and the sun was regularly obscured by them. The wind had also got up and brought a chill from the east, as if determined to remind the inhabitants of north Somerset that it was still only the beginning of March. Despite their hats and coats, Helen and Caroline were happy to return to the house after an hour's exercise, their cheeks pink from the wind.

Tommy, as predicted, parked his car outside the house as dusk was falling and unloaded his artist equipment. He apologised for not being at home to welcome Caroline and explained that he had been working on capturing a particular view the day before and wanted to finish it before the weather turned. He seemed energised if a little dishevelled, his shirt untucked at the back and his waistcoat unbuttoned. Tommy took out his handkerchief and mopped his face.

"Are we eating in or out tonight?"

"I thought out, unless you have a preference." Helen noticed one or two flakes of crushed dried leaves on Tommy's collar and brushed them away with a frown.

"Out suits me fine if it suits you two. I'm sure The Plume will find us a table. I'll go and change."

Helen's eyes followed him out of the drawing room, then returned to Caroline.

"There is something going on. I don't know what; I almost don't want to know, but it will gnaw away at me if I don't find out."

"With Tommy? Do you think he could have made a new friend?"

"I do hope so. If only to put this business with Christopher to an end once and for all. But let's not concern ourselves with it this evening. Let's go up and get ready."

Caroline stayed with Helen and Tommy until Monday and caught the 11:05am train back to Dunster station. As always, she had enjoyed seeing them both, but there was an unspoken tension present that had at times made her a little uncomfortable. Tommy had been extremely good company throughout her stay. They had discussed his art and locations he thought she might be interested in painting, and both agreed to meet up again in a week to spend a day on the moor.

Arriving at Dunster railway station, Caroline decided to forgo the taxi ride up to the village and carried her small case up the lane on foot. She felt a sense of relief to be back in the quiet of the countryside after the bustle of Minehead. There were very few people out on the High Street. Gladstone sat outside the bookshop door, surveying his dominion with half-closed eyes. Caroline continued on the opposite side of the street and as she turned the corner into West Street where the castle drive began, she heard the whiney of a horse in the distance. It came from the side of the castle drive in the direction Jack had told her the paddocks were located. Caroline resolved to take a walk that afternoon to see where the horses were turned out.

"Did you have a good time with your friends?" Jack was walking towards her across the grass on the opposite side of the post and rail fence. He was leading Sultan on a long rein while one of the stable lads cantered Balthazar around the paddock.

"How did you know I'd been to see friends?" Caroline leaned her arms along the top fence rail and smiled.

"Mrs Harding mentioned it at church. I think she was missing you, or perhaps was hoping to show you off at St George's."

"I shall attend church next Sunday. I thought you only rode the hunters?"

"I do, I'm too big for these two. Edgar has already put Sultan through his paces. He can hang on, though he's not got the skill of a professional player to get them to twist and turn the way they need to in a match."

"Did you say there would be one at the end of this month?"

"Yes. There's a team visiting from India. We've been told they'll be staying at the castle for a week, their horses are coming down by train from Aldershot."

"They bring their horses all the way from India? Is that good for them?"

"Not this time, these horses were brought over by the army last year. The Indians will just be riding them while they are staying here. I believe they have other matches elsewhere before they return home."

"It sounds terribly exciting."

Sultan snorted as if in agreement.

"You should come and watch. We've got a five-goal player in the team in Archie Mayors. Bring a picnic lunch. You see where the ground rises over there?" Jack pointed further up the valley. "Spectators usually camp out there on rugs and deck chairs. Your friends might like to come too."

"What an excellent idea! I'm sure they will love it."

"It's a good way to meet people. A lot of business is done at polo matches you know."

"And you will be looking after the horses?"

"Oh, I usually end up doing all sorts of things when Old Andrew is at home."

Caroline nodded her understanding. "Where does this path lead to?"

"Through the valley for about six miles in all. I wouldn't go too much further today though; the stream is across the path in a couple of places."

"I don't think I will go any further today; I walked up from the station earlier."

"Well, I'd better get this one rubbed down. You can help if you want?" Jack grinned at Caroline confident she would decline. He was correct.

"Actually, I think I will be getting along. It's rather chilly here in the shade still. It's been nice to talk to you Jack."

"I'll see you in church if not before."

Caroline spent the next few days exploring in more detail the rest of the village. She took her sketch book and drew the watermill, the Yarn Market, some of the houses and cottages and the church. The walk up to the folly was along a narrow footpath, but the view when she reached the tower was worth the climb. She took tea with two ladies from the Women's Institute, through invitations passed to Mrs Harding. Daisy Clare invited Caroline to lunch after church the following Sunday which Caroline accepted. Caroline then had to apologise to Mrs Harding as she would be missing the crowning glory of that woman's culinary repertoire for a second weekend. She promised that she would be at home for Sunday lunch the weekend afterwards, no matter what.

St George's church was larger than, though not dissimilar to, St Mark's in Cheltenham that Caroline's friends Reverend Philip Rose and his wife Mary were now responsible for. It had been built on the site of a much older structure, the village of Dunster being an excellent example of a medieval community which in turn sat on a pre-Christian meeting place. A spring, known locally as St Leonard's Well, had drawn people to the area for centuries. Caroline learned from the vicar that the bells of the church had been paid for by Sir Andrew Fines' father the century before. He had also chosen the peals that were rung each day.

The inside of the church was adorned with heavily carved oak screens and ceiling bosses. Underfoot, small, coloured clay tiles were laid in geometric patterns, and the windows at the altar flooded the space with a golden light on sunny days. A memorial to the village men who had fallen in the Great War was on the northern wall, accompanied by a regimental flag fixed to the white-washed lime plaster. After spending an hour with the vicar, Caroline understood how Mr Cartwright had become engrossed in the history of the church.

Mrs Harding knocked on Caroline's bedroom door. "Are you ready Miss Munhead? I shall wait for you downstairs in the hall."

Caroline sat at the dressing table looking at her reflection in the mirror. Her hair was set, though she would of course cover it with her new straw hat. She was wearing her cotton blouse and her tweed skirt and would put on her overcoat at the front door. She was hesitating however, over whether to apply some lipstick. She had noted at the Women's Institute that hats were in order but not make-up. She sighed and stood up, leaving the lipstick on the dressing table. It was all very well being a modern woman, she thought to herself as she went down the stairs, but it brought with it decisions she would much rather not have to worry about.

It was only a few hundred yards to the church door. Dunster was alive as if it were market day, and Caroline was amazed to see so many people emerge from their homes in their best clothes, like bees returning to the hive from the surrounding meadows. The village had been so quiet when Caroline had been out sketching, it was hard to believe that so many people really lived there.

Naturally, everyone in the congregation knew everyone else. Caroline was the star attraction as Jack had suggested, with a constant procession of people bidding Celia Harding a good morning in anticipation of an introduction. The ladies Caroline had been to tea with were most insistent that she and Celia squeeze into their regular pew. Though neither of them was particularly large, there was only room enough for one more bottom and Caroline was relieved when Daisy Clare came up the aisle in her wellingtons and wax coat and suggested Caroline sit with her on the opposite pew instead.

"Thank you, Daisy, there really isn't enough space over there for me too."

"There wouldn't have been any room here either except the terrible winter carried off Mr and Mrs Munroe within a few days of each other. It was bitter, we were cut off for days and the storm in January brought down so many trees. You may have noticed the stumps around the estate? Of course, it created plenty of work for a while, and we all were grateful for the logs, but such violence of nature is frightening."

"There is a park opposite where I live, and several trees came down there in the storm. We weren't too affected by the snow, but then we have a centralised heating system in our apartment block."

"Really? How marvellous! You must tell me more about it over lunch. Look sharp, I believe the vicar is ready to start."

Caroline enjoyed the service. The congregation sung in good voice, with harmonies that Caroline found enchanting. The vicar's sermon focused on spring, new life, and planting seeds that they might grow and fruit later on. Caroline listened attentively and felt a connection between his words and what she was attempting to do in her own life. She was planting seeds, and she wondered if they might grow and bear fruit too.

After the service and the inevitable round of goodbyes at the churchyard gate, she walked with Daisy back to the bookshop. Daisy lived in the cottage next door and the smell of roasting meat came to the women as Daisy unlocked the front door to let them in. Gladstone trotted across the Yarn Market and followed them inside, keen to be situated in the kitchen while preparations were underway for lunch.

Daisy's kitchen was also her dining room and was at the rear of the cottage. A water pump stood in the narrow garden near to the back door; the privy had been built facing the back door for ease of use during the hours of darkness. It was primitive, but so many of the cottages and even larger houses still had these sanitary arrangements in the village and would do for years to come. There was no gas supply here, and electricity was often interrupted by damage to the cables from weather or enthusiastic tree growth. The inhabitants relied mostly on coal and wood fires, oil lamps and candles, and as a result many succumbed to bronchial infections and house fires were not uncommon.

Daisy retrieved her leg of lamb and exchanged it in the tray with potatoes and parsnips, returning them to the oven to cook. Then she took off her coat and hat, left them by the back door, and filled a pail and the kettle from the pump to make tea.

Caroline and Gladstone eyed each other across the scrubbed kitchen table. When Daisy had set the kettle on the stove to boil, she turned and realised her hostess skills were lacking.

"Goodness, I am so sorry, let me take your coat! Really, one gets out of practice having visitors. I usually go to other people's homes, they rarely come here. I've no idea why, it's not as if I don't invite people but somehow, we always seem to meet elsewhere." She bustled around the room, hanging up Caroline's coat and hat on a peg, fetching the milk jug from the cold shelf in the larder, and arranging the tea things on the table.

Caroline was content to stay in her chair and not interrupt Daisy's flow but offered to help so as not to appear rude.

"Oh that's quite alright, everything is where it needs to be, we have time for a cup of tea before I'll turn the veg over and then I can carve the joint. You were going to tell me about your gas centralised heating system."

The small kitchen windows became opaque with condensation as the two women talked and then ate together that afternoon. Daisy was keen to hear more about the apartment block and Cheltenham, and in turn explained that the bookshop had belonged to an aunt and uncle before Daisy had taken it over five years before. Daisy's parents were tenant farmers along the coast at Porlock but with no sons to take on the farm they had been keen for their only child Daisy to spend as much of her time with her childless aunt and uncle as possible and become proficient in a trade. She had learned how to operate the old printing press in the upstairs room of the shop, how to make ink if none were available locally, and how to set the blocks of type. Her aunt had instructed Daisy in the arts of bookkeeping and stock control.

When Daisy's uncle died of a heart attack in 1920, her aunt had carried on the business for almost two years before deciding to move to Honiton and live with her cousin there. Daisy was made legal owner of the business and cottage and paid a small rent for the shop yearly to her aunt. She was aware of her good fortune, particularly of not having been married off to some farmer's son by less outward-looking parents. There was something about her obvious distaste at that prospect that intrigued Caroline. Daisy enjoyed her work, enjoyed her life in the village, and had no desire to seek foreign climes beyond a week's holiday each year with her aunt in Honiton.

"Forgive me for saying, Daisy, but there don't seem to be many people of our age in the village. Don't you get lonely?"

"Only very occasionally. I have my correspondence to keep me entertained, and one can never be truly alone with a book in one's hand. You might be surprised at how many visitors we get in the summer and how many of them remember my little shop when they go home and write to ask for a particular book. Gladstone here listens to any woes I might have. I inherited him; he was my uncle's cat. I have no idea how old he is, he has been here forever. I suspect he has family all around the village, there are several other tabby cats if you look for them. And he's not the only one to sow his wild oats around here are you, old man?" She fed the cat a morsel of lamb from her plate.

"What do you mean?"

Daisy got up and began to clear the table. "I noticed Jack Herridge looking at you in church. You need to be careful of him."

"I don't understand."

"I don't like to gossip of course, but as one of the few eligible bachelors in the area, he has been responsible for a few broken hearts. Gloria Smith was the most recent. Fell head over heels for him last summer, quite made a spectacle of herself mooning around the village following him everywhere, convinced herself that they were engaged to be married. Now, who's to say he didn't lead her on at first? But in the end, he got tired of her and went to speak to her father about it all. Next thing we know, Gloria is packed off to secretarial college somewhere up the line."

"I see. Though it doesn't sound like Jack did very much wrong there."

"Perhaps not, no. But his father was just the same. Cut from the same cloth those two. And there's several people in the village who bare a resemblance to Jack if you understand what I mean, not least Abigail Fines." Daisy snapped her mouth shut, aware she had most definitely strayed into the realms of gossip.

Caroline chuckled. "Who would have thought Dunster would be such a hot bed of misdeeds! Oh Daisy, don't worry, I shan't repeat any of this to anyone. They probably already know it all anyway. Jack has been nothing but courteous to me so far, and I am old enough to tell him no if I have to."

As she spoke the words, Caroline's brain flashed an image of Harry Gregory, the young man who had tried to take advantage of her in Devon two years before and who had not paid much attention to her saying no. It had taken a scratch to his face by Caroline to stop his assault on her.

"Are you alright dear? You look like you've seen a ghost."

"Yes, yes thank you, I was just reminded of something, but I'm quite alright. Please let me help you wash up the dishes, it's the least I can do to thank you for lunch."

Tommy pulled up outside Celia Harding's house in the sunshine the following Tuesday morning. His car was, for once, running well and he was looking forward to spending a day on Exmoor with Caroline and their art materials. The weather was set fair, and he had considered the possibility of letting her have a go at driving if she felt like trying. As he got out of the car, the front door of the house opened and Caroline appeared beaming a broad smile.

Caroline was also excited to be exploring further than the village. Tommy drove them south along extremely narrow roads until they stopped at the small village of Wootton Courtenay. Tommy had discovered it a few weeks before, being forced to take shelter as the rain clouds descended across the hills. He had heard enough stories of people being lost on the moorland bogs and never seen again to not risk the same fate for himself. Having availed himself of a pint in The Boar Inn, he had got talking to another patron who directed him to the far end of the village where the view opened out and on a fine day Dunkery Hill could be seen. That was their objective today, he told Caroline over the rumble of the car's engine.

They pulled into a field entrance and carried their things from the car through the field gate and a little way along the hedgerow. The field had been recently ploughed and the earth lay in long rows of crumbling chocolate folds.

"Are you sure we should be here?" Caroline was a little nervous of trespassing.

"Of course! We're not doing any harm. We're not ramblers, after all! Now, isn't that view glorious?"

Dunkery Hill loomed in the distance, embroidered with the golds and purples of gorse and heather. The farmland closer to them layered itself in greens and browns with borders of dark hedges. It reminded Caroline of how she had drawn landscapes as a child. They set up their easels and shared Tommy's well-used travel painting case. Caroline had a small set of watercolours but borrowed the mixing pallet and water pot. Tommy preferred to work in oils with a pallet knife and thick stubby brushes. They painted in silence for over an hour before stopping to view each other's efforts.

"Your eye for perspective is excellent." Tommy said, wiping his hands on a rag.

"The way the fields roll into each other certainly helps. Do you think the shadow works? It's so dramatic as it moves across the view, I tried to capture it as best I could."

"Oh yes, you've done it very well. I've been more focused on distilling the shapes in it all, see?" They moved to Tommy's easel. His canvas was a collection of triangles and bold lines.

"It's so different Tommy. I mean, I can see that it is a landscape because I've been looking at the same one all morning, but the way you have used completely different colours is extraordinary."

"It was the gold of the gorse that inspired me. I thought, why not use the opposite colours, a negative if you like, just to see how the thing might turn out. I rather like the effect."

"It reminds me of a stained-glass window."

"If you're finished here, let's get some lunch in the village and then I want to take you over to Porlock Wier. It's a totally different scene and will make a nice contrast to all these bleak hills."

Over lunch in The Boar, mutton stew with fresh bread and butter, Caroline decided to gently probe Tommy to see if he had indeed made a new 'friend'. They were sitting alone in the dining room of the inn, away from the door, and would not be overheard.

Tommy pulled a piece of bread from his roll and slowly applied butter to it.

"No, Caro, there is no new friend. I know it is what Helen hopes for. She has told you of the letters, no doubt?"

"She did. She worries for you Tommy. She burns the torn pieces each morning before Mrs Rich arrives so that she won't find them. Does it help to write them?"

"At first it hurt. And they were hurtful, and I am so relieved that I did not send any to him. Then after a while I found them cathartic. I was less angry. And then last month I did send one to Christopher. Helen doesn't know of course. I'm sorry to put you in this position Caro, but I feel I can tell you."

"But how did you know where to send it? He moved back to Exeter, didn't he?"

"I was foolish, I sent it to the college. I know, I know, it could have caused even more damage, I do know that, but I had to do something Caro."

Caroline could see the animation and emotion on her friend's face. "Did Christopher respond?"

"I told him not to in writing. I suggested that if he still felt the same, we could meet at Barnstaple and I would drive us somewhere out on the moor. I gave him a date and time. Of course, I told Helen I was going out early to paint and would be home after dinner. I do so hate all of the subterfuge! Christopher met me at Barnstaple station. We spent the day walking around a place called Shallowford. It was bitterly cold, but dry. Then I drove him back to Barnstaple. He is going to save up for a car."

"So, he still feels the same way about you. But Tommy that was a terrible risk."

"I know. But I have his address now, so I don't need to write to him at the college. He has taken rooms at an inn on the edge of the city so there is no housekeeper to nose around his belongings or correspondence." He took a drink. "Do you think me foolish?"

Caroline said very quietly, "I think you love him. I cannot imagine what that is like, but I believe you do. It is much more dangerous for Christopher. You both risk imprisonment, but he would lose his job, his home, everything if you were discovered together. Is that fair on him Tommy?"

"We have discussed it. He says he is willing to take the risk, as long as we can be discrete. That will always be the difficulty of course, but one has always been aware of that."

"You must tell Helen."

"I will. Now that I have said it all out loud to you, I feel I can. Thank you, Caroline, thank you for being such a brick and listening to an old waster like me."

Porlock Weir was indeed a contrast to the inland moor. Tucked into the coast with the land rising steeply on both sides of the valley, the small shingle beach and harbour were picturesque. The tide was high, and boats were tied up along the harbour wall unloading fish, crabs, lobster and oysters. There was shouting and good-natured chatter between the fishermen and those waiting on the quayside for the catch. Tommy set up his easel and Caroline chose to sketch this time, sitting on a stool by Tommy's side. They were soon joined by a middle-aged man in rough dark clothes. He smoked a pipe of pungent tobacco, but the crest badge on his navy-blue cap gave away his profession. He was the harbour master.

"Timed it right then." He said to Tommy, keeping his pipe between his teeth.

"Unexpected good fortune, but a good scene to capture."

"If you want a harbour, you could do worse than down at Watchet."

"Is that to the east? I haven't been that far yet."

"It's quite near to Dunster isn't it? I remember noticing a sign for it."

"That's right, Miss. Cousin of mine is coastguard there. Lots more boats than we have here."

"We shall add it to our list of places to explore, eh Caroline? I'm told the Valley of the Rocks is spectacular too."

"If you like goats, I dare say it is." He chuckled to himself and walked back towards the boats.

"Did he say goats?" Caroline looked up at Tommy.

"I believe so. How interesting. We must do this again before you go home."

"Gosh, I almost forgot to tell you, there is a polo match happening at the castle at the end of this month. I was rather hoping you and Helen would come. We can picnic on the grass and watch them play. Tuesday the twenty-ninth if you're both free then."

"Now that sounds just the ticket! I'm sure the old girl would love that, just her kind of people. Yes, we'll come. So, let's say next Tuesday for the Valley of the Rocks and its goats, if that's what the chap really said."

"I can hardly believe I am halfway through my stay here already!"

4

GLINTING IN THE SUN

They had been lucky with the weather. A few spots of rain had started to fall as Caroline said goodbye to Tommy, and for two days afterwards it poured. Celia Harding ventured out to the Yarn Market on the Thursday for provisions and reported on her return that the river had flooded the road at the watermill. Luckily, they did not have to go that way to get to the schoolhouse for the Women's Institute meeting that afternoon. There was no guest speaker this time, and more parish business was decided along with a detailed itinerary for Easter celebrations in the village. Caroline felt she had been accepted as a temporary member there, and regretfully had to remind the ladies that she would not be staying long enough to help with their Easter activities.

Daisy Clare chattered on to Caroline whenever Celia Harding gave her an opportunity. Caroline mentioned again to Daisy that she would be interested in the details of any property that might be available to rent in the area.

"Rooms do come up occasionally, though I don't know

of any at the moment. Perhaps you could put a card in the tobacconists' window?"

"I would prefer a small cottage really."

"By yourself?"

"Why not? You live by yourself, Daisy."

"Yes, but my aunt made the house over to me. You'd have to find a man to sign a rental contract for you."

"My father would take care of that. I'm sure he will take care of my bank account as well and have it transferred to Minehead."

"Yes, it is a bit of a nuisance not having a bank in the village. I keep some of my savings in the Post Office for daily expenses, you might want to consider that."

"I hadn't thought about it, but it's a very good idea. If I open an account when I go home, I'll be able to draw on it anywhere, won't I?"

"That's right, it's so convenient. And it would certainly be delightful to have you take up residence here, or somewhere nearby. I've never really had a good friend of my own age in the village. The ladies here are lovely of course in their own way, but one would like to have someone to discuss current topics with and they really have no interest in anything other than how much half a pound of butter costs."

"Where are all the young women? One expects to see more of us than young men of course, but you're right, it is almost all older people here."

"They go away to work, find husbands, and don't come back. Farm work is hard, particularly in the winter. There aren't as many big houses needing domestic staff these days. The castle used to employ dozens of people of course, but Lord Fines rarely visits now. You're a bit of an oddity, you know, a town woman wanting to move to a quiet little village. It usually works the other way round."

"It's the sea. I never imagined I would find it so irresistible."

Daisy screwed up her nose. "You might not think so when the winter storms roll in."

Friday dawned as if it were already summer. The change was dramatic, almost dream-like after the heavy rain. Caroline lay in bed listening to the birds competing in song for their mates. She felt as if she must not waste the good weather; the simple act of talking to Daisy about the sea the day before had stirred her attraction again. It would still be too cold to bathe, but she needed to see it at the very least.

At breakfast she asked Mrs Harding if she would make up a packed lunch. The older woman duly produced a small canvas rucksack that a previous visitor had left behind having purchased a newer one. She filled it with sandwiches, an apple and a thick slice of fruit cake.

"Will you be wanting a hot drink or cold?"

"Cold I think, please. Do you have anything to carry it in?"

"I'm sure there's a Thermos flask in the cupboard. You'd be surprised what people leave behind. Why, I had a single shoe left under the bed not that long ago. A single shoe! You'd think a body would miss something like that."

Armed with her provisions, her straw hat and her sketch book and pencils, Caroline set off once again to the railway station. This time, she caught the train eastwards just a single stop. Blue Anchor Bay had been recommended by one of the Women's Institute ladies as a nice place to stroll along the sand. The station master here was a round jolly fellow with a white curling moustache. He clipped Caroline's ticket as she walked towards the exit and wished her a 'beautiful day'.

The beach was indeed a long stretch of sand, although the tide was much further in than when she had visited

Dunster beach. It rolled lazily back and forth, and Caroline could not imagine how it might rise up with the anger of a storm. Everything seemed so peaceful here, the people were, on the whole, friendly and she would have everything she could need if she found a place to live. A thought occurred to her as she walked westwards following the line of the railway track; did she really want to live here, or did she simply want it as her holiday destination? Somewhere to escape to, rather than escape from as so many of the young women in the area seemed to have felt. Perhaps the grass was always greener on the other side.

Caroline stopped and turned to face east again. The signal box and station platform would make a good sketch. She shrugged off her rucksack and sat on the dunes with her sketch book. Occasionally women, by themselves, with friends or with young children, would pass by and say good morning, but Caroline was largely left alone to work. After a while, a train appeared and stopped at the station facing her. She took advantage and hurriedly sketched it into her drawing. There would be another in thirty minutes or so, and she would be able to fill in more detail then.

It was warm in the sun. Caroline was glad of her hat and had soon shed her light coat. After the second train had stopped and then carried on its journey to Minehead, Caroline felt she had sufficiently captured that particular scene and looked around for another subject. As she gazed up along the horizon where the hills rose and were covered with green, she noticed a glint again. Something was reflecting the sun, just as when she had looked in that direction from Dunster beach. She gathered up her belongings and went back to the station.

The station master was sat in the sun on a bench outside the ticket office smoking his pipe.

"Excuse me, could you tell me please if there is a way to walk up that hill?" Caroline pointed in the direction of the headland.

"Well yes, that's Cleeve Hill. You can take the road that runs to Watchet, though it's steep and might ruin your shoes if you walk all the way there and back again. That's a good six miles in all."

Caroline looked down. First the hat, she thought, then wellingtons, and now it looks as though I might need to buy some walking boots as well!

The station master drew on his pipe, and seeing Caroline's indecision said, "You could take the bus. I'm sure the driver would stop at the top for you, and you could flag him down on the way back again. Or you could take the next train to Watchet and then just walk back again if you're not worried about your shoes."

"Is there a bus due?"

He looked at his pocket watch, "In twenty minutes, from outside the Station Inn. Go out of the ticket office and turn left, over the crossing and then up on your right a little way. They run every hour in both directions."

Caroline thanked him and followed his directions. She waved down the bus in its burgundy and cream livery and negotiated a fare to the top of the hill. The driver was slow and considered of speech and took a moment to understand Caroline's request.

"There's no stop there, Miss."

"But the station master said you would drop me off, and I could flag you down to come back again."

"So, you'll be wanting a ticket for both ways? A return?"

"Yes please."

Two older ladies gave disapproving looks from the comfort of their seat just behind the driver, arms crossed over their shopping baskets and hats firmly pulled down on to their heads. Caroline started to blush when she realised she was holding everyone up with her extraordinary request. Clutching her ticket and change, she sat in the first available seat as the bus moved away from the stop.

It took no time at all to reach the top of Cleeve Hill. Caroline's stomach had given a funny turn when she had heard the station master say its name; the hill that loomed over the northern reaches of Cheltenham was also called Cleeve Hill. A coincidence? A sign of some kind? The bus pulled to a stop.

"Will this do you, Miss? There's a footpath starts there by the style, if you can see?"

"Yes, thank you so much, you've been most kind!" Caroline waited for the door to swing open and then climbed down the steps and on to the road. The bus door swung smoothly closed again and the brakes gave just a slight squeal as it moved off towards Watchet. Caroline set off for the footpath.

She soon put her coat back on as the breeze was much stronger up on the crest of the hill. Caroline followed the path for a little way, and then decided to strike out in the direction of where she thought the glint had come from. The ground was uneven; she had to take care not to go over on her ankle in a sudden dip or on a tuft of grass. After a few hundred yards, she stopped for a moment to take in the view. The sea glistened below, today an expanse of blue-green like tumbled glass with tiny white crests here and there. Seagulls wheeled and swooped, calling to each other for the fun of it all. She could see all the way to Minehead on the other side of Bridgewater Bay, the sun glinting off the many windows in that town's composition.

In the same way that I saw the glint up here, she thought suddenly. But there was no building here, how could it have

been glass? She walked thoughtfully on towards the cliff edge
and almost stumbled over a pair of boots sticking up from
the ground on the end of two long legs. Caroline gasped.

"Oh my goodness, I'm so sorry, I wasn't looking where
I was going."

In front of her on the grass, stretched out with his hands
behind his head and a cap over his face, was a man. Dressed
in dark blue rough trousers, a shirt with no collar or tie;
his sweater also in dark blue was rolled up as a pillow. He
removed the cap and squinted up at Caroline.

"This is the last place I expected to be caught napping!"
He said with a half-smile.

Caroline realised that he was looking into the sun, so
she moved around a little to the east. Then she spotted his
binoculars, a fine large pair with an adjustable strap so that
they could be worn around the neck or over the shoulder.

"So that's what I could see!"

The man sat up and followed her gaze. "These? Would
you like to try them out?"

"Well, I really didn't mean to disturb you."

"And I shouldn't really have been sleeping on the job,
but it's such a nice morning. Here."

He handed the binoculars to Caroline, who took them
carefully so as not to tangle herself in the strap. They were
much heavier than she expected.

The man stood up, with a quick grimace of discomfort
that was gone in a moment, took hold of the strap and
navigated it over Caroline's hat. "There now, you won't drop
them." He moved around and stood just behind her. "Hold
them to your eyes and turn the dial in the centre there with
your finger to make the view clearer."

"I can only see the sky, let me look down a little. Oh! I
see something but it's rather a blur."

"Turn the dial a little more."

"Gosh it's hard to hold them in place. Ahh, that's it, I understand now, I can see the signal box at the station!"

The man put one hand on the side of the binoculars over Caroline's and gently moved them to the left. "Now turn the dial some more and you'll see Minehead in all its glory." He took his hand away again.

"Oh yes! My word, these are very powerful aren't they! I wonder, ah, no."

"What?"

"I thought I might be able to see my friend's house, but it's set further back in the town." She took the binocular strap off over her hat and handed them back to the man. "Thank you. I've only used binoculars once before and they were much smaller than these. That was rather exciting, and unexpected for today!"

She looked at him properly now that he was standing next to her. He was a little taller than she was, with sandy short hair that would probably become white-blonde by the end of the summer. His face was freckled; bright blue eyes looked out from under sandy eyebrows and very pale lashes. A day's stubble showed on his chin and upper lip.

Caroline realised she was staring at almost the same moment as the man did. He had been taking in the grey of her eyes, the small mole on the side of her neck, and the way her hat cast a pattern of dappled light across her face. She was modern but not made up. She wore her hair slightly longer than the fashionable cropped bobs, and her clothes were of good quality yet not impractical.

They both looked away, and out towards the sea.

"Did you come …"

"What were you…"

They both spoke at once.

The man smiled, looked down and then again at Caroline. "You go first." It was almost a cheeky grin, she thought.

"I wondered what you were looking at with your binoculars."

"Ships. We're expecting a couple in this evening. Well, we're expecting the harbour to be full, but these two are large vessels and I need to make sure they are on the right path so to speak."

"You work at a harbour then?" Caroline glanced out to see but couldn't see anything on the horizon besides the feint outline of Wales.

The man put his cap back on his head. "I'm the coastguard. Based at Watchet, three miles or so that way." He pointed west of where they stood.

Caroline suddenly remembered. "We met your cousin at Porlock Weir! The harbour master!"

"Well now, that would be Jim. Jim Kingston, my father's eldest brother's eldest son."

"It sounds like the sea runs in your family."

"It did. I suppose it still does. But what brings you up here? Forgive me but you don't look like you are dressed for hiking."

"I hadn't intended to come up here, but I saw the sun catch your binoculars when I was down on the beach and was curious as to what it could be. I was doing some sketching. I'm staying at Dunster for a while. I say, I'm rather hungry, would you care to share a sandwich?"

"Now you mention it, it must be past lunchtime. Are you sure you have enough to share though, miss…?"

"Munhead, Caroline Munhead." She held out her hand for him to shake. "And yes, I have plenty, Mrs Harding is determined that I shall not starve under her watchful eye while I am here. Shall we sit, Mr…Kingston is it?"

"It is. Noah Kingston, at your service. Would you care to sit on my sweater to save your frock?"

"Thank you, but I shall spread out my coat." What an appropriate name for someone who works with the sea, she thought.

They settled down and Caroline unpacked the picnic that Mrs Harding had given her. She offered Noah some milk to drink, but he declined, producing a hip flask from his pocket. He saw her face and laughed.

"It's water! Here, sniff if you don't believe me. I take my job too seriously to be drunk in charge of the coast."

Caroline declined to sniff. "I'm sorry, one shouldn't assume. But what does a coastguard do exactly?"

Noah explained his duties, how he spent most of his time at the harbour in Watchet in the office he shared with the harbour master there and three boatmen. He described himself as principally a 'look-out'. He had to know the tides and the weather forecast intimately and would be responsible for co-ordinating rescues if a ship were in distress.

"The office is above the boat shed. I live in the rooms next door. It was my brother's before me."

It was as if a light had been switched off behind Noah's eyes. Caroline recognised the sign, heard the sadness in his voice despite the years now that lay between them and the war. She waited a moment before she asked, "Were you both in the navy?"

Noah sipped from his flask before answering. He looked out to sea so as not to meet Caroline's gaze.

"No. We were both in the Fourth Army, III Corps. He was killed fighting for Mouquet Farm. Did you know that coastguards are exempt from the call up? But only if they are over 25 years old. Peter was 22."

"I'm so sorry for your loss."

Noah shook his head slowly. "I was transferred to the 55th West Lancashires. Everyone was being posted left and right by that time, we'd lost so many men. I was there until the battle of Messines in '17. Got caught by a shell, trench collapsed on me. Had to be dug out by the lads. I was the only one they bothered to send back with the medics." His voice had dropped to a whisper.

"My brother, Freddie, was killed also. At a canal in France just as the war was ending. He almost made it home."

Noah nodded his head, not trusting his voice. He picked up his binoculars and scanned the horizon for any sign of the ships. There was none, but it gave him time to compose himself.

"Can I see your sketches?"

Caroline retrieved her sketch book and handed it to him. She broke the slab of fruit cake in half while he turned the pages. It occurred to her that being alone with a man, on top of a cliff, unchaperoned, was behaviour that many people would frown upon. She remembered the faces of the women on the bus and chuckled to herself.

"What's funny?"

"I was just thinking how some old women would be appalled to see how I am carrying on."

"Do you care?" He looked directly at her now with concern on his face.

Caroline looked back at him. "I would care if I thought it would upset my father."

"Uh ho. That sounds like trouble. Perhaps I should be getting back." He made no attempt to move.

"My father won't know unless I tell him. He knows that I am thinking of taking a property here."

"Oh? These are very good, by the way. Who is this?"

"My friend Tommy. We were out on the moor on Tuesday, and then we went to Porlock Weir, that's where we met your cousin. Tommy is an artist. He's married to my friend Helen, it was their house in Minehead I was looking for."

Noah closed the book and handed it back. He picked up the half slice of fruit cake and took a bite.

Caroline finished her milk and packed everything else back into the rucksack. "Perhaps I should be getting back now. It's been nice talking to you, Noah."

"How are you getting back to, Dunster did you say you're staying at?"

"Yes, I can wave down the next bus to Blue Anchor and then get the train."

Noah looked at his watch. "You'll have a bit of a wait. Why not walk along here with me a bit and then we can turn back to the road by that place where the hedge stops, see it?"

"Alright."

Without asking Noah picked up the rucksack. Caroline gathered up her coat and they set off, picking their way across the grass. They did not talk as they walked; each was thinking of the other, and of what they had learned over the past hour. They reached the end of the hedge that Noah had pointed out. He stopped and lifted the binoculars to his eyes once more, and this time Caroline saw him smile.

"Do you see your ships?"

"I do. Here." He took the strap off his neck again and handed the binoculars to Caroline. This time he stood behind her and put both his hands over hers to guide her.

Caroline looked. She allowed him to steer her to the right spot on the sea. "Yes! I see them!"

He released his hands. After a moment of watching, Caroline lowered the binoculars and turned to Noah.

"Are they on time? What will you do now?"

"There abouts. I need to get back down to the harbour and make sure no one has taken the space for them. Let's get back to the road."

He left her on the opposite side of the road to where she had got off the bus earlier, apologising that he couldn't wait with her but assuring her she would be perfectly safe until the bus arrived. She watched him march off down the road towards Watchet. She thought she detected a slight limp now that he was hurrying. What an interesting man. How terrible to be buried alive; she felt a wave of sympathy for him, and for the loss of his brother.

Noah tried not to limp as he went along the road, knowing that Caroline could be watching him. His leg felt weak; pain shot from his hip to his ankle each time he took a step, but he walked on. Damned shrapnel, they'd dug enough out of him, why hadn't they taken it all! He carried on until he was certain he was out of Caroline's sight and then he stopped for a moment to lean on a fence post. He must have sat awkwardly while they shared her lunch. He tentatively took another step and felt the pain, but it was less sharp. He couldn't wait, he would just have to walk it off.

What a curious girl. Rather attractive in a quiet way and not stuck up like some of the young women he had known since his return. He saw the bus approaching and felt strangely glad that Caroline would be safely on her way back to Dunster shortly. He wondered if he had made quite such an impression on her.

That evening, Caroline sat in Mrs Harding's sitting room in front of the fire while Mrs Harding clicked her knitting needles from the chair opposite. Caroline had just written a letter to her father. As she screwed the cap back on to her pen, Mrs Harding asked what her plans were for the next day.

"I have none, Mrs Harding. My next planned excursion is on Tuesday with my friend Tommy again. We hope to paint the Valley of the Rocks if the weather is fair. Do you have any suggestions on what I might do for entertainment?"

"You would be most welcome to come with me to Taunton. It's a town much like any other, but you might find it a little more stimulating than Dunster. I shall be meeting a friend for lunch, I'm sure she wouldn't mind if you joined us."

"That's very kind of you, Mrs Harding. I might travel with you and then explore on my own. Is there a cinema in Taunton?"

"I believe they show moving pictures at the Lyceum Theatre on occasion. Then there's the Palace, that's in the centre of the town. They run a *matinée* that you might catch."

Caroline spent a thoroughly enjoyable day wandering the streets of Taunton. She browsed the shops and bought one or two small things that caught her eye including a quarter of barley sugar and some sugar mice. She wandered along the river Tone for a short way and around a small municipal garden where she admired an ornate fountain and a monument to Prince Albert. She took an early luncheon in a coffee house and then giggled through the *matinée* showing of *Safety First* starring Queenie Thomas. It had been some weeks since she had been to the cinema and she had missed it. At three-thirty she met up with Mrs Harding again, exchanged pleasantries with Mrs Harding's friend, and then went on to catch the train back to Dunster.

5

SOCIAL CIRCLES

Tommy was late. Caroline stood at the sitting room window at five minutes to ten and tapped gently on the windowsill. They had agreed to start out early, Tommy had said he would be there to collect her at nine that morning. Caroline hoped nothing untoward had happened in the intervening week. It couldn't be anything terribly serious otherwise Helen would have telephoned Mrs Harding's number. It was probably his car.

At a quarter past ten Tommy pulled up outside the small garage near the Yarn Market with steam or smoke (he hoped it was steam) coming from under the bonnet of his cantankerous vehicle. He had stopped twice and begged buckets of water from houses along the way, suspecting that the radiator had somehow sprung a leak. After negotiating with the garage owner, and paying a small sum up front, he took as much of his painting equipment as he could comfortably carry out of the car and started off in the direction of West Street.

"Tommy, I was starting to worry that you'd had an accident!"

"Much further and I might have. The car is at the garage just as you come into the village. I might have to leave her there, so I'm afraid Valley of the Rocks is off old thing."

"That's a pity. It sounds so curious, and I did want to see the goats, but we'll just have to go on another day."

"We could paint that castle. I thought it looked impressive as I walked up."

"I already have several sketches of it."

"How about we catch the train to Watchet like the chap at Porlock Weir suggested?"

Caroline couldn't think of a reason to protest.

From the railway station at Watchet, they carried their equipment through the narrow streets down to the harbour. Clouds had steadily accumulated over the weekend and the day was overcast with a brisk wind off the sea. The harbour was an open expanse of water in a natural curve in the coastline. At one end, a slipway had been built, with a wall constructed and rising from the water. It supported a roadway known as the Esplanade and small gauge rail tracks for ore and coal to be brought to the waiting ships. Great stacks of lumber, flour and cloth, sat waiting to be collected or contributed to, and horses pulled carts to and from the sidings next to the railway station. There was general activity, but no sense of urgency about the place.

From the other side of the slipway, another wall had been built in a gentle curve with a small light beacon situated at the end. This was the breakwater, designed to protect the small boats inside the harbour from the worst of the sea swell. Between the beacon and the other end of the harbour wall was a gap of just under 100 feet where the vessels passed in and out. Larger ships could be moored on the outside of the breakwater, and that day there were two. Their funnels stood stark and black against the grey-green of the sea and the sky.

Caroline and Tommy chose a spot where they would not be in the way of the industry, just by the slipway at the start of the breakwater. As usual, their artistic styles were very different. Caroline would have liked to work on larger canvases with charcoal or oils but having to carry her equipment was prohibitive. As she sketched, she wondered if one day she would be able to convert her sketches into larger works, perhaps to have space for a studio. Her gaze frequently landed on the row of whitewashed cottages on the Esplanade. There were three doors painted in a bright blue to match the window frames, indicating three dwellings. The end closest to the slipway had large double doors, Caroline assumed to allow a boat to be stored inside, and stone steps leading up to a door on the first floor. Above the double doors, a large oriel window looked out on the water. There was a steady procession of men entering and exiting through the first-floor door. Many wore smocks with wide collars, others had sweaters of cream or navy-blue wool.

Caroline had not mentioned Noah to Tommy. On the train from Dunster, Tommy had informed her that he had told Helen of his meeting with Christopher. Helen had been concerned and exasperated in equal measure. Tommy said it was the closest they had ever come to a full-blown row, but eventually Helen accepted that Tommy intended to continue to see Christopher. They had been able to talk freely in the carriage as there were no other passengers until they reached Washford. Caroline had many questions, but some were simply too intimate for her to ask even a good friend such as Tommy. What was clear to her was that Tommy loved Christopher deeply. She hoped that Christopher felt the same.

Once they had been joined by other passengers, their conversation had turned to the polo match. Tommy said that

Helen was very keen to attend, as several of the Minehead political class would be there. It was the place to be seen. Even if the car could not be repaired, Tommy and Helen would meet Caroline at Mrs Harding's. Caroline had also invited Daisy Clare to join them, who had accepted enthusiastically.

They caused a ripple of interest from passers-by as they painted. The local police constable stopped to chat and informed them that two weeks before a young man with a camera had visited the town and caused a lot more excitement. He had been there to document the town and had been rather rude to several of the children who had wanted to be in his photographs. Two mothers had descended on him, causing him to pack up and leave on the very next train. Caroline offered to include the constable in one of her sketches. He was suitably flattered and posed for her looking official and staring out across the harbour with the beacon in the background. When she had finished, she carefully tore the page out of her book and handed it to him.

"Thank you miss, very much. I shall give it to my wife, I think she would like it."

"When Caro is a famous artist, it will be a valuable piece!"

"Tommy, don't be absurd."

"I'm not. You have a knack for capturing your subjects. I say, make sure you sign it."

When the constable had moved on, Caroline and Tommy gathered their things and walked to the opposite end of the harbour so that they could work on a different view. As they were setting up again near to a small, covered seating area where fish could be laid out for auction, Caroline asked Tommy if he had been able to sell any of his paintings.

"One or two. I have a friend in London who takes them."

"I also have a friend who has taken up with a gallery owner. She has asked several times that I send more pieces like the ones I did in Cornwall. She says they would make a great deal more money than the watercolours I have produced."

"What's stopping you? If there is a ready market for them, you must take advantage of that."

"It's the paintings I made of the owners of the retreat." She lowered her voice. "The nudes."

Tommy chuckled at Caroline's embarrassment; she had turned bright pink under her hat. "Oh Caro! Those kinds of art always sell. But honestly, what's stopping you?"

"I have no model. I don't think I could draw from memory, and I certainly don't want to create any self-portraits."

"I could model for you."

Tommy's words hung in the air between them. Caroline was surprised. She had never considered that anyone would simply offer. The silence stretched on until Tommy said again, "I said I could model for you, Caro."

"I heard you. I don't know what to say."

"You could say yes. Unless the idea is offensive to you?"

"Goodness no, that's not it at all. But how could we arrange it? I will be going back to Cheltenham after the polo match, and there is certainly nowhere there that we could use. You see, this is why I told Elsa that I didn't think it would be possible." Caroline had put down her pencil and was looking up at Tommy though the sun was in her eyes.

Tommy took up his rag and wiped the brush he was using.

"We could arrange something for the summer perhaps. I rather like the idea of being wild and free in nature and there are simply miles of empty moorland that no one would ever disturb us on. If you haven't found your own place here by then, you could always holiday with us and work on your canvases. No one in Cheltenham need ever know. Look here, I'm hungry. I'll go and get us something to eat for luncheon and you can think about it while I'm gone."

Tommy headed off to the Ring of Bells pub which was set back from the harbourside on Church Lane. Caroline took up her pencil again but found she couldn't concentrate on her drawing now that Tommy's proposal was in her head. As she sat staring at the fishermen on the quayside a shadow fell across her.

"Hello again."

She had hoped she might see Noah again once Tommy had suggested going to Watchet, but she had not expected to feel quite so happy to hear his voice.

"Good morning, or is it afternoon now?"

"A little after twelve. Can I see?" He gestured towards her sketchbook, and she held it out for him. "The tourists would love these, you know."

"Do you think so? I feel I am still learning."

"I do. Do you colour them later?"

"Yes, these are really only sketches. When I go home, I hope to rework them onto canvases with my watercolours."

"Ah yes, remind me, where is home again?"

"Cheltenham. For now."

Noah handed the sketch book back. "Are you hungry? I was thinking of lunch and I owe you a meal."

"My friend has just gone to get us some, but some other time perhaps?"

"Is this your friend now?"

Tommy was approaching, his arms full of small, wrapped packets and gingerly carrying a brown earthenware quart jug in front of him. Caroline got up and took control of the jug, allowing Tommy to deposit the food.

"I say, well done for catching the beer, I thought I was about to spill it all over the harbour!"

"Yes, it rather looked as if you might! Tommy this is Noah, he is the coastguard here. Noah, this is my good friend Tommy Gersen-Fisch."

The two men shook hands.

"I'll let you get on with your lunch then. But if I can make up for last week, I'd be happy to. Good-bye for now." His smile was warm and sincere, and Caroline felt a little light-headed.

When Noah was out of earshot, Tommy handed Caroline a parcel with two pickled eggs inside and whispered "He's a jolly handsome fellow. A coastguard, eh?" He gave a wink as he spoke.

"Tommy! I don't know what you mean, I'm sure." Caroline played coy.

"I think you do. What did he mean by making it up for last week?"

Caroline explained how they had met.

"Should I chase after him, call him back? I can make myself scarce rather than play gooseberry."

"Tommy, don't be absurd."

He looked at her, no longer teasing. "But you like him, don't you?"

Caroline took a bite of one of the eggs as Tommy spoke and he had to wait for her answer. "I like him, but I have only just met him. He seems a steady, respectable sort." She stopped herself from saying out loud that Noah was not like Max. It was true, she felt an attraction, but there was no powerful force to it. At least, not yet.

"Caro, I know you felt James wasn't right for you, I understand his passion for his work put you off. But you must understand that most men have a passion of some kind. If you are waiting to find one that wants the same things as you, you may never find him."

He unwrapped a parcel and inspected the contents of a roast beef and mustard sandwich, then took a bite.

Caroline picked up the jug. "Are we sharing this?"

Tommy nodded and she took a sip. It tasted much like the beer she had drunk at Midge's parents' house in Berkshire and she smiled at the memory.

"I'm sure you are right that most men have a passion, but I don't want to be subordinate to someone else's. I want to at least be on equal terms. If that means I remain a spinster, then so be it."

"Mankind's loss if you do, dear heart. Now, to change the subject, have you discovered any likely abodes that you might want to call home around here?"

They chatted while they ate and drank, attracting looks from some of the town's folk. When they had finished, Tommy took the jug back to the pub and Caroline cleaned off some of his brushes. Then they carried their equipment back towards the railway station, and caught the next train to Blue Anchor Bay. Caroline wanted to show Tommy the expanse of sand and how Minehead could be seen in the distance. The station master there remembered Caroline and they exchanged pleasantries while waiting for another train to carry them back to Dunster. Caroline spotted a notice board with several small cards attached and went to read them.

When she re-joined the men, she asked, "Is there a charge for placing a notice on the board?"

"Ha'penny a week, Miss, paid in advance."

"I shall make sure I bring a card for it before I go home."

The mechanic had done his best to locate the hole in Tommy's car's radiator but warned that it would probably only hold for long enough to get Tommy home to Minehead.

"Looks like Helen and I will be arriving by train for the polo match." He told Caroline as they put his art materials onto the rear seat.

"Will it be terribly expensive to fix?"

"Not so much that, as having to wait for the garage to find a new radiator. Could take a week or so, and I had hoped to give you at least one driving lesson while you were down here."

"That's quite alright, I'm sure there will be other opportunities and I think I could manage with the trains and buses if I do find a place here. It's not looking very likely at the moment though. There are several short-term options but nothing on a more permanent basis that anyone can point me at."

She waved him off having agreed that he and Helen would get a taxi from the railway station to Mrs Harding's on the following Tuesday. Then she picked up the rucksack that she now thought of as hers and set off for the Post Office to purchase some blank postcards and a copy of the *Minehead and District Courier.* Perhaps there would be a small cottage to rent in this week's edition, she thought as Gladstone crossed her path on patrol of his domain.

Caroline's final full week at Dunster consisted mainly of walks around the village in the mornings, and tea with various ladies in the afternoons. There was a choral recital in St George's church on the Friday evening, and a Bridge night arranged by Daisy Clare on Saturday evening with the Tobacconist and his wife. Caroline enjoyed all of these activities and found the Tobacconist to be a most entertaining man, full of anecdotes and tall tales. His wife was a tiny woman, who clearly adored her husband. Caroline found herself wondering how they had met and fallen in love, and as if she had read Caroline's mind, the Tobacconist's wife explained that she had first seen her husband across the school yard on her first day of attendance. He had been charged with looking after her because she was so small, and he had done so ever since. It was an enchanting story, Daisy and Caroline agreed.

Horses began to arrive at the castle on the Saturday, ahead of the polo match. They had travelled with their grooms by train and were led up to the village from the station and settled into the stables and the paddock. Jack Herridge was kept busy directing the grooms to their quarters – large canvas tents pitched in the castle grounds. They would be fed and bathed in the castle servant's quarters. Jack's attention was then focused on making sure the polo ground was in good condition, with areas roped off for various parties and spectators. There was room for motor vehicles including two buses that had been hired for the occasion to bring in enthusiasts from Minehead.

Caroline walked along to the stables on Sunday afternoon after another plentiful lunch supplied by Mrs Harding. She put her head around the entrance but couldn't see or hear Jack amongst the industry inside. She continued down the footpath to the polo ground and found him writing with a stub of pencil into a small notebook at the side of the field.

"Hello Jack."

He looked up with a smile. "Well, you're a sight for sore eyes!" He closed the notebook and dropped it into the pocket of his jacket. "Would you like to see the trophy?"

Caroline was surprised by his offer. "A trophy? Goodness, that would be exciting. Yes please."

"Old Andrew will be here tomorrow, so we can have a look now without getting in anyone's way."

They walked back towards the village and then took a pathway that wound up through the landscaped gardens of the castle and a gated entrance. Jack led the way in through a plain wooden door, up a staircase and across a landing with windows that looked out onto the driveway where several dark-skinned men were gathered around a white man holding the reins of a glistening black horse. Caroline felt as if she were a burglar, creeping along behind Jack and hoping no one would challenge their presence inside the castle. Eventually they came to a room that was panelled with dark wood, and where, in a glass fronted case, stood a silver trophy. The lid was topped with a rearing horse on its hind legs. The whole thing was almost two feet in height.

"It's enormous!" breathed Caroline.

"Heavy too. It's been won by the Indians the past two years, but our riders are at their peak, so we stand a good chance this year."

"Jack, should we really be in here?"

He looked at her with a glint in his eye and she felt a prickle of fear. Daisy's words came back to her, how Jack was to be kept an eye on.

"I've spent more time in this castle than Old Andrew; if anyone has a right to be here, it's me. But if you want to leave, we can. After you." He held out his hand towards the door.

Caroline felt the fear subside. She knew in that moment that she did not trust Jack, and although she found him friendly on one level, there was something about him that spoke of entitlement with an undercurrent of anger. He followed her through the doorway and closed the door behind them, then led her back the way they had come. A maid emerged from a side room and almost collided with Jack. He grabbed her with both hands and spun the maid around before giving her a kiss on the cheek. The maid squealed but didn't appear to seriously protest. Then she noticed Caroline and blushed profusely, her eyes

lowering as she bobbed a small curtsey and scurried off
along the landing.

Back down on the castle drive with others milling about,
Jack seemed to stand taller and adopt a more aloof air. "You're
still planning to watch the match I hope?"

"Yes, my friends are coming, and Daisy Clare will make
up our party."

"I'll look out for you, but should I be engaged elsewhere,
tell the stewards you are my guests, and they'll direct you to
the best location for a good view of the match. There will
be refreshments afterwards and then the presentation of the
trophy and awards."

"I'm very much looking forward to it. Thank you, Jack,
I'll see you on Tuesday."

It was a relief to all that Tuesday dawned as if summer
was already well into its stride. Helen dressed with care.
She had asked some acquaintances at the Primrose League
discretely about the form expected at a provincial polo match
and was confident that her silk dress was both practical yet
sufficiently striking to make an impression. It would be
a small inconvenience to have to arrive by train, she had
become accustomed to Tommy's car being available to her.
The seats on the motor coach hired by the Primrose League
were already all allocated by the time Helen had inquired.

Daisy Clare sat on the edge of a chair in Mrs Harding's
sitting room waiting for Caroline to come down. She had
been to the polo matches before, but this time she felt a
little nervous. She was not used to meeting new people,
and she had the impression that Caroline's friends were of a
higher social class than Daisy was herself. She had worn her
best frock and polished her shoes vigorously that morning
to hide the scuff marks. She would have preferred to wear

her wellingtons and they would certainly have been more practical. After a light lunch, mainly due to her nerves, she had checked three times that Gladstone was safely outside the shop before locking the door and walking along to West Street.

Dunster was alive with strange faces. Like soldier ants, people streamed up from the railway station and jostled with the motor vehicles making their way to the polo ground. Carters made a few extra shillings by providing transport from the station to the castle drive, and young boys with shovels and buckets tried valiantly to keep the high street clear of dung. Helen and Tommy shared a ride on the back of a cart with several other acquaintances from Minehead; they had caught the train as a group and intended to return together later after the match for dinner at the Plume of Feathers. Tommy helped Helen down from the cart and then showed the way to Mrs Harding's. Helen was careful not to dismiss the village as a dingey little hamlet, though that was her first impression of it. A very odd place to hold a polo match, she thought, picking straw from her coat.

After introducing Helen to Mrs Harding and Daisy Clare, the quartet gathered up picnic blankets and the large basket of food and bottles of beer that the landlady had provided and set off to the polo ground. Daisy chattered continuously, pointing out the houses of certain people and then providing a brief history of the castle and its inhabitants. Tommy was interested in the watermill and suggested they take a look after the match. Helen listened without saying very much; she was looking out for people she knew and people she ought to know.

At the entrance to the polo ground, Caroline did as Jack had suggested and told the young man on the gate that they were Jack's friends. He pointed to an area on the right of the slope on the far side of the field and gave them each a bright pink ticket. The tickets would enable them to enter the refreshments marquee and team enclosures should they wish to inspect the horses. Daisy was very excited at this elevation in status. She had only ever watched from the unreserved area before. As they crossed the grass, Daisy waved to people she recognised, and with satisfaction noted the surprised looks she received in return.

The sun shone. Spectators filled their allotted spaces on the grass. The horses gleamed in the bright light and their exotic riders smiled broadly at the polite applause as they rode around the perimeter of the ground before the match. A group of local young maidens in their best frocks gathered near to the enclosure to perhaps catch the eye of a visiting officer. Tommy said repeatedly how he wished he had brought his sketchbook; it was so rare to see such colourful figures. A large motorcar drove onto the field and followed behind the Indian team. Daisy explained that the man inside, waving like royalty, was Lord Fines.

"You say he doesn't live here, despite owning the castle?" Helen asked, her eyes on the car.

"No, he hasn't lived here permanently for years. Since Lady Fines died. It was rather a blow to the village, some of the staff went with him to Tiverton but many had to seek positions elsewhere. That's his daughter, Abigail, with him."

Helen had noticed the young woman step out of the car behind Lord Fines now that it had come to a stop by the marquee. She was tall, slender, with sleek, dark hair. While her father took her arm, Abigail looked out across the spectators just as Helen had done when they arrived. Daisy shaded her eyes from the sun with her hand and commented that she could probably make introductions as they all had tickets to the teams' area.

"That would be exciting, Daisy! Shall we all go to meet Lady Fines, Helen?" Caroline was conscious that Helen was quieter than usual. "Are you feeling alright?" she asked in a lower voice.

"Yes, I am quite alright, thank you. It would be interesting to meet Lord Fines' daughter. She won't be Lady Fines though darling, that title would only be held by Lord Fines' next wife, should he marry again."

"That's correct," said Daisy, "Andrew is the Earl of Bridg-water, and the title only descends through the male line. If Abigail were to marry, her husband would inherit the title on Andrew's death."

Helen turned to Daisy. "It is refreshing to meet someone with an understanding of the titular system."

"I have an interest in our nations' history. I read a lot. It comes with owning a book shop I suppose."

"And a printing press." Added Caroline.

"Printing? That is interesting." Helen smiled warmly at Daisy, who blushed a little but smiled in return. "I should like to see that some time, if I may?"

"Of course. Any time you are available. In fact, if Caroline would show Tommy the watermill later on, I could show you my shop after the match? Before you meet up with your friends again?"

"That is an excellent idea, Daisy." Tommy raised a bottle of beer in toast.

The polo match lasted just under two hours. At half time, the spectators descended onto the pitch to stomp down on the divots that the horses had caused. This was a source of much merriment, as many of the stompers had already consumed considerable amounts of alcohol. Even Helen joined in enthusiastically, holding Daisy's hand to steady herself as they both stomped and jumped together.

Caroline and Tommy had been content to drink the beer Mrs Harding had provided, but after significant stomping, Helen declared she would simply die for a glass of champagne and Daisy led her off to the marquee.

As Tommy and Caroline returned to their picnic, Tommy asked how well Caroline knew Daisy.

"I've only known her since being here in Dunster, but she seems a good egg. I think she chatters so when she feels nervous. She is intelligent, though hasn't really had the opportunities that we have had."

"Yet she owns a book shop and a printing press?"

"She inherited from her aunt and uncle a few years ago. Daisy never went to school beyond the village as far as I know."

"It would be good for Helen to have a friend, rather than simply socialising with people to advance her aim of becoming a councillor."

It took a moment for Caroline to understand what Tommy meant. "A friend like Vic?"

"Yes. I think that was why she was so upset about Christopher and I."

"You think she was jealous of you? Surely not, Tommy. I think she was probably more worried for you. You do have to be so careful."

"Isn't that the most ridiculous thing? I have to be so careful. She can do whatever she likes."

Caroline didn't know how to respond. She understood how the law applied to homosexual men, yet there was no such corresponding law prohibiting women being intimately involved with other women. She didn't know why.

Daisy and Helen returned as the second half of the match was starting. They had been introduced to the Fines through Daisy's seeking out an older member of the Women's Institute.

It had been an opportune moment for a photographer from the *Courier* to appear and Helen nudged her way to stand next to Abigail. Helen had consumed three glasses of champagne in the refreshments tent and was a little unsteady on her feet returning to Tommy and Caroline, which she blamed rather too loudly on the uneven surface of the field. By the end of the match, Helen was asleep on the picnic blanket. The others packed away their belongings around her, before Tommy gently woke her and helped her up onto her feet. They all agreed that attending the trophy presentation would be hot and uncomfortable in the marquee, so they made their way carefully out of the field and back towards the village. Helen held on to Daisy's arm as they continued along the High Street to the bookshop, while Caroline and Tommy carried the picnic basket between them back to Mrs Harding's and then went to look at the watermill.

It was almost time for Tommy and Helen to re-join their fellow residents of Minehead on the train journey home. Caroline pushed open the door of the bookshop, causing the bell above the door to jangle wildly. Gladstone sat on the desk at the far end of the shop washing his outstretched leg. He paused to inspect his visitors without moving and then, satisfied they had nothing for him, continued with his ablutions. Caroline called out to Daisy up the stairs to the print room, and hearing movement above, stepped back into the shop to wait with Tommy.

A few moments later Daisy and Helen emerged from the stairway. In the dim light of the bookshop, no one noticed their flushed faces.

6

INDEPENDENCE LOST

Cheltenham was a riot of yellow. Daffodils and narcissus had been planted in hundreds around the town's flower beds and grassy verges the previous autumn and several autumns before that and were now repaying the investment in gold. After a month away, it was the smell that Caroline noticed first when she stepped out of the taxi at Norwood Court. No longer could she smell horses and beer from the inn next door to Mrs Harding's home. Cheltenham smelled faintly of cooked cabbage and the internal combustion engine. Ferris came out to take her cases and greeted her warmly. Miss Kettle waved from her sitting room window. Caroline was home.

In the apartment, Caroline's father George had piled letters addressed to her on the dining table. After making herself a cup of tea and cutting a slice of cold pork pie, Caroline went through her correspondence, picking out letters from Midge, James and Lina as ones to be read first. However, she did not open them immediately. She wanted time to be completely alone and peaceful after a morning's travelling and a month living in someone else's home.

Tiredness crept over her, and she took her tea and letters into her bedroom and lay on her bed thinking she would rest her eyes for a few minutes. The next thing she knew, George was gently nudging her shoulder.

"I'm glad to have you back again." He said with a smile. "I have brought you some more tea, you had let the other get cold."

Caroline looked at her watch. It was ten minutes past five. "Thank you, I only meant to rest for a while."

"Are you quite well? I can bring your dinner here for you on a tray."

"Yes, I was just more tired than I thought. I will take a bath and then eat with you at the dining table. It is good to be home again."

They talked long into the night. Caroline found herself reliving every detail of her month away, she recalled everything vividly for her father who listened intently despite having received weekly written updates from her. Occasionally he would ask a question or for clarification when Caroline's story strayed out of sequence. They moved from the dining table to the sitting room chairs. They had small glasses of sherry as the story wound on. George was interested in the different characters and showed no preference for male or female. By the time Caroline went to bed, her mind was clear again.

Naturally, Caroline found herself repeating the story several times over the following week as she caught up with her friends around Cheltenham. Each one seemed interested in different aspects of her tale. Annie was curious about the castle, having never seen one in person before.

"Were there lots of towers? And a drawbridge? And the spikey gate thing?" Annie was kneading dough, her apron smudged with flour.

"Towers yes. I don't think there was a drawbridge though, the drive runs from the street right up to the main door. I think you need to have a drawbridge and a moat to have the gate, it's called a portcullis."

"They always have them in books."

"And do you have any news for me?" Caroline was sat at the dining table with a pot of tea.

Annie put the dough back in the mixing bowl and covered it with a tea towel. Caroline waited while she washed her hands and dried them, folding the hand towel neatly over the handle of the oven. When she looked at Caroline at last, a wide smile spread across her face.

"Yes, I think so. I haven't told your father yet, but I really should soon I know." Her hand went to her stomach which had started to gently fill out.

"Annie that is marvellous news! I am so thrilled for you. Have you thought of any names?"

"We can't agree on one, or even two or three at the moment. Jacob likes George, Matthew − after his father − Lewis and Victor."

"And what do you prefer?"

"Samuel, and Alfred. I don't dislike George, it's a good name and of course it's your father's name too, but I don't think I like it as a Christian name."

"But those are all boy's names. You might have a girl, have you thought of any of those?"

"Jacob is convinced it will be a boy. I've always like Vera and Katherine for a girl, but that would be shortened to Kitty in no time."

"How is the yard getting along?"

"Very well, thank you. Jacob has put so much time into it. And he's started an evening class at the college to learn proper bookkeeping. He says his father only has a rough set of accounts and Jacob wants to be sure of every penny."

"What an excellent idea! I had heard that the college had begun to offer night classes. You'll certainly need to watch the pennies when the little one arrives!"

When Caroline called on Mary Rose, she found her in the vicarage sitting room with her feet up on a stool with a cushion on top. Angelica gave a yell when she saw Caroline behind Philip and got to her feet for a few wobbly steps before collapsing to the floor and making the rest of the way on her hands and knees. Caroline picked her up and breathed in deeply the aroma of baby powder and ammonia.

"Darling girl, Angelica, have you missed me?" Caroline chuckled.

"We all have. Sit down, won't you? No, don't get up my dear, I will make us some tea and Caroline can tell us all about her adventures." Philip went out to the kitchen.

"Are you well?" Caroline asked Mary as she sat on a chair and let Angelica slide to the floor and back to her building blocks.

"I am well, Miss Caroline. In a few weeks Angelica will have a brother or sister and I shall have twice as much washing to see to." Mary smiled as she spoke, showing that she did not think it quite as much a hardship as she suggested. Her Caribbean–Bristol accent was strong, and she explained that her mother Celestine had been to visit the week before.

"Oh, I'm sorry I missed her." Caroline was rather fond of the large black woman and her rolling, scolding, laughing speech.

"Celestine said the same of you. She told me to tell you, you must not stay away too long even if you move to the far end of Cornwall."

"I shall always come back to visit you know, no matter where I end up."

"Did you find anywhere in Somerset to live?"

So began the story again.

It occurred to Caroline later that evening, as she wrote a less detailed version of her travels to James in reply to his letter, that while she had hardly thought of Bob she had certainly missed him while she had been away. This puzzled her, given that she was writing to James at the time. She supposed that she had drawn a definite firm line under her potential engagement with James; it had put them back on a friendly footing and she was more comfortable with that. With Bob, however, the line was not as clear. More of a sketch, she mused.

Caroline turned to her father, who was reading the newspaper and smoking his pipe. "Have you heard anything from Bob while I've been away? Has he finished the repairs to the chimney and roof?"

"I saw him last week as a matter of fact. I was in the office when he came to pay his mortgage. I believe the repairs are completed and he intends to begin moving the furniture back in very soon."

"So he is still living with his parents? I wonder, should I call on them, I'd like to know how Lottie and Eric are getting along."

"Bob did mention that his brother-in-law had received some good news. He was in good spirits himself."

"I shall wait for Lottie tomorrow at the end of her shift and walk along with her. I don't miss the actual work so much, but I do miss the girls there."

True to her word, Caroline leaned her bicycle against the railings outside the Sunningend Engineering Works at a few minutes to six the next evening. It was a bright day, but a keen wind tugged at her skirt and she was glad of her light coat. The smell of the works, mixed with the railway across the road and the general smells of Cheltenham were strangely comforting. The works' bell rang and doors began to open; men and women, young and old, walked into the light and screwed up their eyes for a moment before their shoulders relaxed and their faces turned slightly up towards the sun, caps and hats held on with a hand to stop the wind stealing them away.

Lottie saw Caroline and waved to her as she walked across the yard.

"Caroline! So good to see you! Have you just come back from your trip?"

"I have. You are looking very well, dear. I thought I would walk along with you and perhaps wait to see Bob, is that alright?"

"Of course it is. He'll be pleased to see you. Tell me all about your trip!"

"That can wait a moment, my father seemed to think that Eric had had some good news last week. Tell me about that first, please."

Lottie's face beamed from under her hat. "Yes! He passed his cadet probation and he's been put forward for a Constable's job in Stroud. And the very best thing about it, is we should have a house if he is accepted!"

"Lottie that's such good news! I'm thrilled for you both. But in Stroud, that would mean you'd leave the works?"

"Yes. It will be strange not to work, but I'll have the house to look after, and hopefully children after not too long. We'll manage well on Eric's wages, and we have a bit saved now too. So come on, tell me all about your trip. Did you meet anyone interesting?"

Caroline talked for almost the rest of the way along Gloucester Road until they reached the side street near to the Gas Works where Lottie and Eric lived with her parents and Bob. She started to feel a little nervous about seeing Bob again but didn't have a chance to change her mind as he was sitting on the doorstep in the sun as the girls approached the house.

"Buck up! I need to get inside and wash my hands!" Lottie nudged past her brother as he stood up.

"It's good to see you, Caroline. You look well." He was surprised to see her, unprepared, but happy all the same.

Caroline studied his face. Dependable Bob. She knew the time away had drawn a line under the possibility of a relationship with him for her now. She liked him very much, but as a friend only.

"Thank you. Father said he had seen you last week, and as I wanted to see Lottie, I thought I might catch you too. How is the house coming along?"

Lottie came back to the front door. "Would you like some tea, Caroline?"

"No thank you, I won't stay long. Perhaps a glass of water if that's possible?"

Lottie disappeared again.

"She's missed you. Has she told you she's off to Stroud with Eric? Mother can't make up her mind if she's happy or sad about it."

"It's an excellent opportunity for them. Stroud isn't so far though."

"True. The house is almost done. That storm did more damage than I first thought, but the roof and chimney are sound now and we took down the rest of the tree that came through so I've plenty of wood for the fire at least. Would you like to see it, perhaps at the weekend? Sunday, after church?"

Caroline bit her bottom lip. She really mustn't encourage him, but as a friend she did want him to be happy in his new home.

"As a friend." She said out loud.

"As you say."

Lottie reappeared with a glass and a mug of water and handed the glass to Caroline. "I thought you might get your own," she said to Bob with a grin.

"Yes, well, I can't sit here all evening. If you'll meet me at Pittville Gates at three on Sunday, we'll take the tram out to Prestbury." He went indoors after Caroline had nodded her agreement over the edge of the glass.

"The house will be so quiet for Mother and Father when Bob's gone too."

"Will they stay here, do you think?"

"Oh yes, I don't think they will move anywhere else now. And Charlie will be able to stay when he comes back to visit." Lottie looked up at Caroline. "There's no hope for you and Bob now, is there." She said it quietly so that her brother wouldn't overhear.

"No. No, I'm sure of that now. I hope we can still be friends, but I simply don't feel for Bob as he does for me."

"I'll make sure I come with you on Sunday to the house," said Lottie as she took Caroline's empty glass.

On her way back to Norwood Court in the fading evening light, Caroline's mind was not fully on her cycling. She felt bad about Bob, but what could she do? She hadn't felt like this when she declined James' offer of marriage. She was still perplexed by the time she arrived home. As she wheeled her bicycle across the gravel driveway, Agatha Kettle rapped on her sitting room window to attract her attention. Caroline waved, and nodded when Miss Kettle beckoned her in. She locked her bicycle in the small garage at the side of the drive and went into the apartment building through the glass door. Miss Kettle had opened her own front door and Caroline went inside and into the sitting room.

"I'm so relieved to see you, Miss Munhead. I was hoping Ferris would have returned by now, he has gone to feed a friend's pet cat."

"Is something wrong? Are you alright?"

"Yes, dear, I am quite alright. However, a few minutes ago I heard a terrible crash from Captain McTimony's apartment, and I am concerned that he may be unwell."

"You stay here. I'll go and get Father. Perhaps the Captain simply dropped something."

George was about to sit down to his dinner but placed his plate over a saucepan of water as he had with Caroline's a few minutes before and went with his daughter to knock on the Captain's door. They stood for a moment and then heard a groan.

"Do you think he is drunk?" Caroline asked.

"It is possible, though it would be out of character." He raised his voice to call out, "Captain McTimony, are you alright?"

They were answered with another groan. George tried the door, but it would not open. Ferris would have a key, but if something were wrong then it could be dangerous to wait. He sent Caroline back downstairs to see if Matthew Monk was at home. She returned a few moments later with Matthew and his wife Rebecca. The women were instructed to stand back, and the men proceeded to charge against the door with their shoulders until the frame splintered and they gained entry.

Captain McTimony was on the floor between his sitting room and the hallway, with a side table on top of his legs and a number of his statues and African trophies scattered around him. His face was purple with one side dropped, his eyes bulging and panicked, one hand reaching out to his neighbours. Rebecca stepped forward and took charge. She sent Caroline to telephone for a doctor, while she instructed George and Matthew to help lift the Captain and move him into the bedroom. She felt his pulse which was erratic but was more concerned at his paralysis which seemed to affect the whole of one side of the Captain's body. He tried to speak but could only make guttural noises. Rebecca answered in soothing tones and tried to reassure him that a doctor would be there soon. She sent the men out of the room so that she could help the Captain out of his soiled trousers and underwear, all the while explaining what she was doing and why.

By the time the doctor arrived, Captain McTimony had calmed down a little, his face was a little less purple, and Rebecca had pulled a chair to the side of his bed so that she could sit with him. George and Matthew had straightened the fallen items in the sitting room, and Caroline had returned to update Agatha Kettle.

"Poor man. We are all so vulnerable living alone, don't you think?" Agatha had made some weak tea while waiting for Caroline to return, and they sat at her small table in her sitting room sipping from bone china cups.

"It was unfortunate that Ferris wasn't here. I'm sure he will be very sorry when he returns to find that he missed the excitement."

"Indeed, it is a comfort to generally have him on the spot as it were. One could fall, and no one be aware of one's predicament for hours. Captain McTimony was certainly fortunate that I heard his fall."

"He was. I wonder if he will be able to remain in his apartment, or whether he will need to stay in hospital to recover."

"You say he seemed unable to move his arm or legs?"

"Yes, and he couldn't speak coherently."

"It sounds very much like an attack of apoplexy. I remember another neighbour of mine in London some years ago, he was not much older than the Captain, who suffered a similar attack."

"Did he recover?"

"Sadly not. Medicine has advanced since then, however. I am sure Captain McTimony is in good hands."

Captain McTimony was under the care of Doctor Eastman. He was a Scot in his mid-forties and had served in the army for much of his career before setting up a civilian practice. He looked after a number of old soldiers in the area, who respected his military credentials. After a thorough examination, he decided against moving the Captain to hospital. He took some blood and urine for analysis, and after making sure the Captain was as comfortable as he could be, spoke to Rebecca and Matthew in the Captain's sitting room.

"He is going to need a lot of assistance, but I think with some regular manipulation and a healthy diet, he should survive and may even regain some use of his limbs."

"Are you sure he shouldn't be in hospital?" Matthew asked.

"I see no benefit at this moment, although of course should his condition deteriorate then that would be the next step. Does he have any relatives nearby?"

"No, none that we're aware of. He has certainly never spoken of any relations."

"That presents a problem. Mrs Monk, it was you who helped him to clean himself?"

"Yes. I was a nurse in the war. I had been a volunteer at the hospital until they withdrew the befriending service."

"Would you be willing to help the Captain until we can engage a more permanent nurse for him? He will need someone to stay with him constantly for the next few days. He may become resistant, men often do when their dignity is threatened by illness, but he will not be able to manage by himself."

Rebecca looked at Matthew. He nodded; he knew his wife was an excellent nurse and had only left the profession because of the horrors she had witness years before.

It was arranged that Rebecca would sleep on a camp bed in the Captain's bedroom and see him through the following few days. She was in her element; she bathed, fed and moved the Captain as Doctor Eastman had shown her. She quickly learned to understand the noises the Captain made and chattered away to him as she worked as if they were in conversation. Rebecca was sensitive to the Captain's dignity, and through trial and error they found a routine that appeared to suit them both. After a week, Rebecca told her husband that she wanted to become Captain McTimony's full-time nurse. She had found her purpose again, and though tired, she was renewed.

They spoke with Doctor Eastman when he next visited. He agreed to arrange the financial compensation with the hospital board, with a portion contributed from the Captain's pension. It was a satisfactory solution, as he had not had any luck in identifying a suitable nurse to engage through the usual agency channels. Rebecca moved from the camp bed to the spare room in the Captain's apartment. Ferris was instructed to change the front door which had been secured with a hastily applied hooked latch, to one that had a draw bolt on the inside and no lock on the outside. There was some discussion over fixing up a bell in Ferris' office attached to a cord that could be fed through to the

Captain's bedroom, similar to the bell systems used in large Victorian houses. Everyone agreed that the Captain would be perfectly safe if Rebecca needed to go out for an hour, and help could be summoned and enter without causing any further damage.

Matthew was unconcerned about his wife's absence from their apartment. He was also absent for much of the week as he stayed at the air force base. On Thursdays at six o'clock in the evening, his driver took him in to Oxford, to the Randall Hotel where he went up to the room reserved by Mrs G Bassett. On Saturday mornings after breakfast, he caught the train back to Cheltenham to spend the rest of his weekend in his own home. Galina Bassett returned to Cheltenham on the Sunday or sometimes the Monday. They had felt an instant attraction in Vaughan Rickard's sitting room, and it was only a few days afterwards that Matthew had slipped a note under her door asking her to meet him at the Queens Hotel the following Thursday evening for dinner. They had quickly agreed the current arrangements after Matthew made an excuse to Rebecca for his lateness that night. As they were all relative strangers in Cheltenham, Matthew and Galina did not fear gossip or discovery. Galina was amused by the danger of their liaisons and enjoyed Oxford far more than she did Cheltenham.

Easter day 1927 was the third Sunday in April. The wind was no longer from the north but blew from the west bringing squally showers with broken brilliant sunshine. As such, the attire of the parishioners at both Christ Church and St Mark's was a mixture of winter and summer clothing, umbrellas and mackintoshes.

Caroline was starting to wonder if she would ever receive a response to the postcards she had placed on various notice boards in north Somerset. She was more determined than ever to find a small cottage for herself and had started to purchase her own copy of *The Lady* magazine rather than borrow Miss Kettle's to pore over the advertisements. She had written to Elsa to request that she ask her acquaintances if anyone knew of somewhere suitable and had replied to Lina's letter informing Caroline of her pregnancy and Albert's confirmed nomination as Conservative candidate for the Parliamentary seat of Hereford East, to request the same.

Caroline had resumed her attendance at the Women's Section of the Royal British Legion, finding comfort in the activities the women organised. It occupied two afternoons of her time a week and gave her an opportunity to hear the gossip of the town as well as assisting the local veterans and their families. Caroline's other occupation was attempting to engage a young girl to replace Annie. They had been sent three by the employment agency so far, none of whom Caroline felt would be as reliable or efficient as Annie had been. George was happy to leave the arrangements to his daughter, as he had to his wife in the past. As long as someone was available for a few hours each day to prepare him a meal and see to the laundry and cleaning around the apartment, he would be content.

"I can stay until the end of June if you don't find anyone." Annie offered when Caroline told her of the most recent unsuitable interviewee.

"You'll be what, seven months pregnant? I don't think you should be riding your bicycle then. I actually don't think you should be riding it now."

"No, Miss."

Caroline recognised the familiar response when Annie disagreed with her but would not say so. "I understand that it is less expensive than the tram, but you could topple off and hurt yourself, or the baby. No, we really must engage someone to begin as soon as possible." Thinking quickly, she added, "Even someone who is not as good as you have been to us for all these years."

Annie was rubbing butter into flour to make a batch of scones. "Sara isn't happy at her current position. I could ask her if she would be willing to take less money for less hours. With Louisa at Sunningend and Julia at Cavendish House, I think Sara would prefer to be at home more to look after Mother."

Annie's mother had long suffered with arthritis that had slowly confined her to the house. Annie's three younger sisters had all taken turns to look after their mother, but Sara seemed the one most suited to the support Mrs Johnson required. Annie's father worked when he could as a general labourer at Arle Farm, and sometimes for the brewery near St James' in the town, but his daughters' wages provided for the family more reliably than he could.

"Where does Sara work at the moment?"

"She is at the solicitor's still, Mr Harris, over at Fairview. This would be a little closer for her, and she could use the bicycle."

"Would you ask her please? I think Father knows Mr Harris, but it shouldn't be too much of an inconvenience for him to find another full-time maid. That's the sort of position everyone appears to want, rather than the few hours every day that we are offering."

It did not take long to convince sixteen-year-old Sara that daily maid to the Munheads would be a more suitable position for her than live-in maid of all work at the Harris residence. George took Harris the solicitor out to lunch and explained the situation to him on behalf of the girl and suggested one of the women that the agency had sent

could become a replacement for Sara. It was agreed over
port and cigars, and Sara would be released on a Tuesday
afternoon each week to spend two hours with Annie at
Norwood Court until she took up the position permanently
on Monday 30 May.

1

NEW
NEIGHBOURS

The telephone on the hallway table rang. It was still an unusual event in the Munhead's apartment, and Annie was nervous of picking up the receiver.

"You should learn to answer the telephone, now's your chance," she said to Sara.

The younger girl had no such reservations. She went into the hallway, picked up the the telephone and cleared her throat before answering in a clear voice.

"Hello, Cheltenham 219, Munhead residence."

The operator spoke at the other end of the line.

"I will see if Miss Munhead is at home, if you will wait?" Sara paused, and then placed the earpiece and transmitter on the small table and went into the sitting room.

"Telephone call for you, Ma'am. Are you at home?"

Caroline smiled and stood up to take the call. She found Sara's ways, learned from a severe housekeeper who had been in the solicitor's employ for many years, endearing. Sara returned to the kitchen, pulling the door closed behind her. Caroline picked up the earpiece and spoke into the transmitter.

"Hello?" She waited. The line seamed dead. She replaced the earpiece in its cradle and was about to return to the watercolour she was working on from one of the sketches she had made in Somerset when the telephone rang again.

"Hello? Yes, it is. Yes... Hello? Daisy! How lovely to hear from you!"

"I'm sorry, Caroline, I pressed the wrong button just now and cut myself off. How are you dear?"

"I am very well, thank you. Still no luck finding a place of my own though."

"That's my reason for telephoning. Mrs Arnold, you might remember her from the Women's Institute, the lady with the red gloves? Never mind if you don't. She has, or rather had, a cousin over at Doniford, did you get that far in your explorations?"

"I remember seeing it on the map at the railway station, and I think we went through it when Mrs Harding and I went to Taunton."

"Yes, you would have, it's the stop after Watchet. Now then, Mrs Arnold's cousin sadly died a few weeks ago, and now that probate has been settled, Mrs Arnold finds herself with a house that she does not want to move in to. She mentioned it to me yesterday, having quite forgotten that you had been interested, and I took the liberty of suggesting she might want to consider letting you have it on a long lease. She was very enthusiastic, you made quite an impression on everyone here you know!"

"Daisy that does sound very interesting. Do you know what the property is like?"

"No, sorry, I didn't think to ask. But I could go and take a look if you'd like me to? Let me see, not Friday as Helen will be here, but I could take the train over on Saturday and have a nose around. Mrs Arnold won't place it with an agent until she has your decision, she is in no hurry as I understand it."

"Did you say Helen just then?"

Daisy was silent for a moment. "Yes, Helen. She has visited once or twice since we met at the polo match." Another pause. "For tea."

Caroline smiled to herself. Perhaps Tommy had been correct that Helen needed to find a friend of her own. "I'm so glad you two are getting along," she replied, and she meant it. "But back to the house, if it's not too much trouble for you Daisy, it would be very helpful if you could take a look for me. I would hate to agree to take a property only to find that it had no roof!" She was thinking of one or two buildings she had seen around the area that were uninhabitable and had been for some years.

Daisy agreed, happy to return to the subject of her call. They arranged that Daisy would telephone again on Sunday afternoon and give Caroline as detailed a description of the property as she could. She said she would speak to Mrs Arnold again and find out how much she would require for a year's rent, and as much other information as Daisy could obtain on Caroline's behalf.

George was interested in the proposition but withheld his questions until after Daisy's telephone call that Sunday. He would need to arrange the lease agreement and sign it on Caroline's behalf, and as such would be liable for any management of the property while she was resident there. They had already opened a Post Office savings account for Caroline and deposited some funds in case she took any more trips where she could not reach a branch of the Cheltenham and Gloucester Benefits Building Society.

The days between Daisy's phone calls dragged by for Caroline. She visited Mary Rose and Angelica again.

She went to the Women's Section meetings. She finished the watercolour she had been working on and sent it off to Elsa at the gallery in London. She went for walks in the sun and in the rain around The Park and fed the ducks and geese with ends of pastry and crusts of bread. She tried to remember what she had seen of Doniford from the train carriage but could only see the railway station in her mind's eye. She knew it was by the sea, and only a couple of miles from Watchet and the village of Williton further inland.

On Saturday afternoon Caroline and Lottie went to the cinema. It would be their last day out together for a while as Eric had been approved as the new Constable in Stroud and the couple would be taking up the cottage next to the police house where the Sergeant lived the following week. Caroline expressed her excitement, but also her one reservation that she knew no one in Doniford village.

"But if it's only a little way from the other places you know, you'll soon make friends there. The people sound friendly."

"They are. And I do know one or two people in Watchet. I met the local police constable and the coastguard while Tommy and I were painting there."

Lottie's ears pricked up at the change in Caroline's voice. "You didn't tell me that before. What's this coastguard like?"

"Perhaps not how one would imagine a coastguard to look. He is rather young for a start. His brother had just become the coastguard when they went off to the war and he didn't return home. Noah took on the position when the war ended. He is a little taller than me, has sandy-coloured hair, quite fair though being out in all weathers he rather resembles ..." she looked around as they walked towards Montpelier through Imperial Gardens, "... a park bench!"

Lottie giggled. "Is his paint peeling? He sounds a real catch I must say!"

"He has some damage to his leg from the war. So many men do now, don't they?"

"Yes. And his name is Noah? Honestly Caroline, he sounds like a cartoon character from a newspaper. Are you sure you didn't simply dream him up?"

"He is very real, Lottie." Caroline could see him as they had sat together on the cliff top sharing her picnic as she spoke. Her stomach gave a small flutter.

Daisy's report on Sunday afternoon was favourable. The cottage was a little way from the railway station and its garden backed on to the tracks. It was detached, standing a few hundred yards from another similar cottage, and on the road into the village. The whole area was in the parish of Saint Decumans, though there was only a small Methodist chapel in the village itself, the nearest church being in Watchet. Quantock Cottage, as it was known, was a picturesque, whitewashed building with a dark slate roof and small windows. The garden was neatly kept at the front with a crab apple tree and a privet hedge enclosing a lawn and flower borders on either side of a brick pathway to the front door. The pathway continued around one side of the building where a vehicle could be parked. To the rear there was a larger garden where a privy and a tool shed stood close to the house. Beyond them, a washing line was strung between two concrete posts on a small patch of lawn, then an allotment followed which ended in a chicken house (devoid of chickens) next to the hedge that separated the garden from the railway track.

The inside of Quantock Cottage sounded similar to Mrs Harding's house to Caroline. Small rooms with open fireplaces, a large kitchen and scullery, and two bedrooms on the first floor; one overlooking the front garden and out to sea, the other looking out over the railway and the farmland beyond. Mrs Arnold's cousin had lived in the cottage for some years by herself after her husband died, and it was still fully furnished. Mrs Arnold had asked Daisy if Caroline would be bringing furniture and Daisy had told her that it was unlikely. The lack of an inside bathroom was the only sticking point that Daisy had identified, and when speaking with Mrs Arnold, the older woman had suggested that if Caroline could wait one or two more months, a bathroom could be added, connecting the privy to the main house. Apparently, her cousin had been considering it and had already spoken to a local builder when she was taken ill.

"So really dear, the ball is in your court!" Daisy finished after speaking for almost 5 minutes.

"It sounds rather what I have been thinking of, and if Mrs Arnold is sure that adding a bathroom is possible, then I think I could certainly wait for that to be completed. How much did she say for the rent?"

"For a whole twelve months, the princely sum of twenty-five pounds. I thought that was a bit steep, but I suppose if she is willing to put the bathroom extension in place, she would want to recover some of that cost."

"I see. How long do I have to make a decision? Did you say she wasn't in a hurry to find a tenant?"

"I rather think she wants it to go to the right person, if you understand me. I can let her know you are considering it all and perhaps you could write to her and let her know in a week or so? If you have a pencil, I'll give you her address."

Once again Caroline and her father talked late into the evening. He had concerns that she would be on her own, some way from any other inhabitants. She shared his concern though she did not tell him so. The luxury of the bathroom in their apartment meant that Caroline did not want to forgo one in another property. She would be happy to wait for one to be installed if she knew the house would be hers. George agreed with Daisy that twenty-five pounds was a high rent for what sounded like a small house in the middle of nowhere, particularly as Helen and Tommy were paying a similar amount for their much more substantial town house. He offered to negotiate on Caroline's behalf, if she really wanted to move there.

She did.

After a flurry of letters and telephone calls between George and Mrs Arnold's solicitor, a twelve-month rental of eighteen pounds was agreed, on the condition that a bathroom be attached to the main house, the water rates included, and the existing furniture be retained. Caroline would begin her occupation on Friday 1 July.

This meant Caroline was still in Cheltenham when Mary Rose gave birth to a son at the end of May. She had declined the midwife in favour of their old next door neighbour Mrs Brooks who now kept an eye on the retired Reverend Lloyd. Mrs Brooks having delivered two sons of her own, was happy to assist as she had when Mary had miscarried her previous pregnancy. Two weeks later, baby Mark Philip Rose was christened by his father in the church of St Mark, with Caroline, and two young men of the congregation as Godparents. Caroline supervised Angelica while the main ceremony was conducted, then handed her over to Celestine when the time came for her to step up to the font.

Though Philip was as overjoyed as he had been at Angelica's birth, this time he did not proclaim the child's weight to everyone he met. Mark had weighed four pounds and one ounce when he was born, and Mrs Brooks had expressed her concern at his size. His christening was the first time the little boy had left the vicarage, and unlike his sister, his cries were like those of a new-born kitten.

Annie ended her employment with the Munheads and was presented with a set of linen for her expected baby that Caroline had picked out at Cavendish House, after recommendations from Annie's sister Julia. There were tears from both women, and Caroline promised several times that she would return from Somerset for Annie's baby's christening. Sara had many of Annie's ways but being so much younger she would never achieve the same level of friendship that Annie had with Caroline. Caroline was happy that her father would be looked after.

It was with some relief that Caroline readily agreed to George's suggestion that he might accompany her to Quantock Cottage at the start of her lease, for a few days holiday. He had not taken any days off work since they had moved into the apartment and George had only once seen the sea before on a trip to Weston-Super-Mare. He wanted to be sure that his only daughter was settled somewhere comfortable. Caroline had been increasingly worried that she might have bitten off more than she could chew in setting herself up as an independent woman. George's offer was the solution to both issues. It did, however, mean that Caroline had to dissuade Helen from descending on Quantock Cottage immediately. Helen understood and promised to drive over with Daisy once George had returned to Cheltenham.

George had the foresight to telephone the station master at Doniford and arrange for transport for Caroline's belongings to meet them there. He could of course have managed his own suitcase, and one of his daughters as well, but Caroline had packed several of her favourite books, her art equipment, the keepsake box that she had been keeping interesting and memorable items in, all of her clothes, and would also be taking her bicycle. With the apartment locked, father and daughter set off on their adventure.

Daisy had obtained a key to Quantock Cottage from Mrs Arnold and had been over to inspect the progress of the builders once or twice. She had felt very important, being the messenger between Caroline and her new landlady, and found she thoroughly enjoyed the short train journey there and back again in an afternoon. On the last day of June, Daisy took some provisions and opened as many of the windows as she could to air the place. The builders had left some debris to the side of the house, and Daisy made a mental note to ask Mrs Arnold to have it removed. She surveyed the garden from the rear bedroom after having put clean sheets on the bed. It had been a wet and warm summer so far; the garden was becoming overgrown. There was a mechanical lawn mower in the shed that smelled suspiciously like petrol and Daisy was tempted to go and see if she could get it started. However, she was wearing her second-best shop dress and good shoes, and it would be a pity to get them covered in engine oil.

Instead, she walked the few hundred yards along the road to the second cottage and knocked purposely on the red-painted front door. A woman a few years older than Daisy opened the door, wiping her hands on her apron as she did so.

"Yes? Can I help you?"

"Good afternoon. This may sound like a strange request, so forgive me, but my friend is moving into the cottage along the way tomorrow and I was just thinking how she will be in need of a gardener. Would you happen to know of anyone in this area who might be interested in a few hours work each week? The usual things I should imagine, clipping the hedges, cutting the grass, planting a few vegetables."

After half an hour in Violet Saddington's kitchen, Daisy had struck a tentative agreement. Violet would ask her husband Ronald when he returned home from work later that evening if he would be willing to take on the garden at Quantock Cottage for a few hours a week, depending on what needed attention and the weather. Daisy felt it was the most she could expect from the woman and asked that Mr Saddington call on Caroline at his earliest convenience. The women did not discuss wages.

Daisy had left the keys to Quantock Cottage under an upturned flowerpot by the front door. As George supervised the unloading of their belongings from under the tarpaulin stretched across the back of the cart that had brought them from the railway station, Caroline pushed the key into the lock and opened the door. It had started to rain as they pulled into Taunton station and the sky was a menacing deep grey. From Daisy's description, Caroline knew the hallway led to the sitting room on the right, and further into the cottage, the kitchen was at the rear. She went straight to the kitchen and saw the note that Daisy had left for her on the scrubbed table. The handwriting was deliberate, neat and very small; the complete opposite to Daisy herself thought Caroline with a smile.

Dear Caroline
Welcome to your new home!
    You will find bread, milk, cheese, eggs and bacon in the pantry – the Post Office in the village sells most things but will only be open from 9 – midday on Saturday. There is a small amount of coal in the shed, you will need to arrange

a delivery as the range powers the hot water. Heaven knows how the builders have arranged it, but they have attached it to a boiler in the large cupboard by the door to the bathroom.

Your neighbour Mr Saddington will call on you to discuss the upkeep of your garden. His wife is a most agreeable woman and might be willing to clean for you too if you choose to ask her. The laundry van comes on Mondays and Thursdays and has been instructed to call.

Do write me a note when you have settled in, and I shall visit. I may even bake a cake!

Good luck!

D Clare

George joined his daughter in the kitchen.

"All of our belongings are safely in the hallway, my dear, and your bicycle is propped for now by the front door. I cannot say if our man was happy or sad with his compensation, I understood less than half of the words he spoke to me, but we shook hands at the end of it all." He looked around at the kitchen with its large black range and row of cupboards. "Would you like me to light the range? I imagine we shall need to cook our supper on it this evening."

"According to Daisy's note there is coal in the shed, and she has left us some groceries. I rather think we shall need to visit the village in the morning for more. I wonder…" She reached up for a tin that sat on the mantlepiece above the range. When Caroline removed the lid, they both broke into grins. It was the tea caddy, and it was full.

That evening, with the rain beating down outside, Caroline and her father sat in companionable silence at the kitchen table. They had had electricity for a while, but the supply had become intermittent as the weather worsened and eventually failed completely. There were lanterns dotted around the cottage, they assumed for such occasions. Caroline realised it was the first time in a very long while since she had seen her father without his jacket and with his shirt sleeves rolled up. He was reading a local newspaper printed several weeks before that had been saved for the fire. After a moment he looked up as if he had felt her eyes on him.

"This is a most interesting publication. So different from our own *Chronicle*, the main news here appears to be the arrivals at Watchet harbour and the price of sheep at the various markets."

"The markets are very important to the people here. Families use them as reunions."

"It is heartening to know you are not quite as remote as I had first thought. The station master was jovial, and you have your neighbours the Sandtons."

"I think their name is Saddington. Yes, I am glad to have someone to call on if there are any emergencies. I'm sure there won't be any though. Would you mind terribly if I went up to bed now? I'd like to hang up my clothes and read for a while. I'll take up the lantern from the sitting room, this rain is making it so dark, it's as if it were autumn!"

As Caroline lay in the dark later that evening, she listened to the rain and wind swirl around the cottage. There was another noise, one she had difficulty placing for some time and then suddenly she realised; it was the sea. She hadn't thought to enjoy the view from the front of the house when they had arrived, but now she understood that the sea was across a field and a stretch of pebbly beach, almost within touching distance. When the weather clears, she thought as she drifted off to sleep, I shall go swimming again.

On their first full day at Quantock Cottage, Caroline and George carried out a thorough inspection of the furniture and kitchen equipment, the contents of the garden shed, and the pantry. George was reassured that Caroline would have everything to meet her immediate needs. They walked into the village, which was really no more than a hamlet as it had no church and introduced themselves to the post master, Arthur Bright. The Post Office was also a small shop, newsagent, coal and paraffin merchant and ironmonger. George had instructed Caroline on what to say, and she had rehearsed a few times as they had walked, so that she could order her own coal and arrange for a delivery of milk and a weekly newspaper, as well as groceries which would arrive in the basket of the delivery boy.

George inquired where a radio set could be purchased.

"Well, I could probably get you one, but it would come from Minehead or Taunton. You might want to go and select it yourself, if you're in a hurry for it."

"Shall we take the train to Taunton on Monday?" Caroline asked. She suddenly felt she did not want to bump into Tommy or Helen while her father was there. She wanted this to be just their holiday, by themselves.

That evening, as they were sitting down to a simple dinner of sausages and mashed potatoes with sliced tomatoes, there was a knock at the front door. George started to get up to answer it, and then stopped.

"It is your home, my dear, your front door to answer."

Caroline stood up and went to investigate. She opened the door to a man who was perhaps a few years younger than her father, and who was short and sturdy where George was tall and straight. Ronald Saddington held out his hand.

"Good evening, Miss. My wife says you need someone to take the garden here in hand?"

"Oh yes! Do come in."

"Just a little way, I don't want to muddy your floors." He stepped over the threshold but went no further.

"You must be Mr Saddington? Yes, I would very much like some help to manage the garden, though I would also like to learn how to grow some vegetables, and is that an apple tree by the front gate?"

"Call me Ron, everyone does. It's a crab apple, Miss, good for jam but not eating. You might be a bit late for vegetables this summer, but we can get some winter greens in later on and there's always lettuce. There's a rhubarb crown already towards the back."

"I shall be in your capable hands, Ron. Do you know the garden well?"

"I used to help Mrs Elphick with the digging and mowing the lawns. We were sorry to hear she'd passed on. Vi, my wife Violet, she misses her terrible."

They were both silent for a moment.

"Still, it's good to see the house lived in again. Is it just you on your own?" He looked at George's coat hanging in the hallway.

"My father is staying for a few days, and then it will be just me. I have friends in the area, so I shan't be completely alone."

"No, that you won't, Miss. You'd have to work very hard to be alone around here." He chuckled.

They agreed that Ron would cut the grass at the first opportunity once the rain abated and would then make a start on the allotment plot. Caroline impressed upon him that any food they could produce she would happily share, and they shook hands over the small financial remuneration for his time.

When Caroline had closed the door, she returned to her dinner (which George had placed on the range).

"He seemed a jolly nice fellow. I think I will be able to learn a lot from Ron about how to grow my own food. It's rather exciting, don't you think?"

"I think this new chapter in your life will be a productive one indeed. What will you make with the yarn you purchased today?"

"I hope to make a jacket for baby Mark, similar to the one I made for Angelica. And then I should like to make one for Annie's baby too."

George was quiet for a moment. He had never once been critical of Philip Rose's choice of wife, had never said out loud anything that could be taken as disparaging towards Mary. He knew how fond Caroline had become of the family. Yet he could not help but feel just a small amount of concern about her association, and an equal amount of concern for the future of both children. He found himself wondering what he would do or say if Caroline herself were to fall in love with a black man.

Caroline broke into his thoughts. "Father? I said, you will let me know as soon as Annie's baby is born, won't you?"

"Yes of course, I am sure Sara will have news within a day of it."

The rest of George's holiday was spent in companionable and contented exploration of Doniford and the surrounding area. Father and daughter travelled to Taunton and inspected the town's shops and cinema. They had their photograph taken together in a small studio by a man who kept a cockatoo in a large cage, and returned with the receipt for a small wireless set that would be dispatched to Quantock Cottage within a few days. The rain cleared temporarily and allowed for long walks along the pebble beach skirting around Helwell Bay. Ron returned and with George's help managed to start the mechanical mower. His wife Vi came with him, carrying jars of jam and lemon curd, some carrots and radishes from their own garden, and a Dundee cake in a tin that Vi said Caroline could keep.

As Caroline waved George off from the station platform at the end of his stay, she felt a wave of worry. Would she be alright by herself? She would soon find out, she supposed. For his part, George tucked his head back in through the carriage window and sat down on the sprung seat with a sigh. He had known this day would come of course, the day his little girl struck out by herself into the world. He had done all he could to ensure she would have the provisions she would need; coal, electricity (as erratic as it appeared to be in Doniford), groceries and whatever assistance the Saddingtons could offer.

George settled into his seat. The carriage felt damp. What if Caroline became ill, would she be able to summon a doctor? Despite only having a telephone for a short while at the apartment, he could clearly see its benefits and wished he could have arranged for one to be installed at Quantock Cottage. The best he had been able to do was obtain the agreement of the station master that should Caroline need to place an urgent call, she could use the station telephone. It was an advantage of the cottage being so close to the railway, and also the reason electricity had been available to it and the Saddington's cottage. George closed his eyes and waited for the conductor to arrive and inspect his ticket.

Caroline decided not to go straight home, but to take a walk down to the sea before lunch. Unlike the sandy beach at Blue Anchor, Helwell was not attractive to day trippers and those with greater leisure time on their hands. It was stark, rough and a little muddy when the tide was right out.

The rock pools fascinated Caroline. She poked around in them, exposing a crab here or a starfish there, teasing the anemones and occasionally finding a tiny fish. She was absorbed in this occupation when she heard a crunch of footsteps approaching across the pebbles.

"We meet again!"

"Good morning, Noah! Or is it afternoon now? I suppose it must be."

"You were the last person I expected to see here, I thought you were back in Chippenham."

"Cheltenham. Yes, I was, but then my friend Daisy found a cottage for me and here I am."

"Right here?"

"Yes, Doniford, just back along the lane. I didn't expect to see anyone else here either. Are there ships due again?"

"Not today, no, but this weather is playing merry hell with the channel traffic. I beg your pardon, I speak to women so rarely I forget my manners."

Caroline stood up and smoothed her dress down. The wind was again whipping her hair around her face and dark clouds were advancing from the west. Herring gulls flapped lazily along the tideline, oblivious to the erratic gusts. She took her gloves out of her coat pocket and put them on.

"I should be getting back for lunch."

"I have offended you, I'm sorry."

"Not at all," she smiled at Noah as a strong gust of wind blew her dress up at the front and she instinctively put her hands down quickly to catch the fabric, "I simply feel hungry and I have some tidying up to do now that Father has gone."

Noah glanced up at the clouds. "Would you permit me to walk with you?"

At the crab apple tree, they stopped. The first spots of rain had begun to dapple the road. Caroline suggested Noah might like to join her for some lunch and let the shower pass, but he declined.

"I don't think it will be a shower, I'd be better off getting back to Watchet. I'm glad you are here again though. Perhaps on a brighter day, we could have another picnic, on the beach?"

"I would like that. It's your turn to provide the food and drink though."

"It's a deal. You'd better get inside; you'll be drenched in a minute. I'll look out for you when I'm walking this way!" He turned up his jacket collar and set off towards Doniford village.

Caroline hurried indoors. She stood for a moment, her back against the inside of the front door. Her stomach had fluttered again when she had first seen Noah on the beach. She wanted to see him again.

8

A REPUTATION FOR THE RISQUÉ

It was to be the wettest summer in England for a hundred years. Caroline's hopes for an instant vegetable patch were dashed, though Ron cleared the four small beds of weeds and dug in some manure in preparation for late onions, leeks and cauliflowers. They tried lettuce, but the slugs ate the seedlings as soon as they emerged. The only success was the rhubarb; Vi supervised an impromptu cookery lesson in Caroline's kitchen where she instructed Caroline on how to make a rhubarb crumble, and then custard. Caroline felt absurdly pleased to be eating the results of her own labours later that day and resolved to visit the nearest library and take out some books on gardening and cookery.

Helen and Daisy arrived a few days after George had gone home, Helen having borrowed Tommy's car. The three women sat at Caroline's kitchen table around the teapot, with a plate of scones – Caroline's latest triumph – on offer.

"Do help yourself to a scone. I have some strawberry jam as well if you would like some."

"How delightful! Caro, one never pictured you as a cook."

"With Annie's help, and now Vi's, I shan't starve."

"Vi seemed to be a good egg when I called on her."
Daisy poured the tea.

"She is lovely, and her husband Ron has rather adopted
the garden. I think Father was relieved that I wouldn't be
entirely on my own in the wild here."

"Is there no one else nearby? Thank you, Daisy. I noticed
a Post Office on the way here but nothing else."

"Mr Bright runs the Post Office, and he sells the most
incredible collection of things in the shop. I am sure what
he doesn't have to hand, he would be able to get within a
few days. He would have got a radio for me, but Father and
I decided to go into Taunton for one instead. The reception
is not as reliable as it is in Cheltenham, but I have already
come to rely on it in the evenings."

"You must come to Minehead now that you are nearer. I
shall have a party, and you can both mix with the great and
the good of Minehead society."

"How is your political campaign getting along?" Caroline
cut open a scone and inspected the slightly doughy centre.
She hoped it would be safe to eat.

"The Council elections are at the end of August. I will
be standing for the Alcombe South ward as the Conservative
candidate, against a rather common little man who is the
Liberal Party candidate. He talks of nothing but relieving
the poor. The main concern for voters in the town is not
the poor, but the expansion of the commercial premises and
the potential for tourism. A real boon to the economy. I feel
confident I shall secure the votes necessary."

"It's all very exciting," said Daisy. "I've never known a
real politician before."

"Dunster has a parish council, does it not?" Helen
frowned.

"Oh yes, but that's not real politics, is it? Deciding the hire fees on the school room, and where to site the new public conveniences is hardly the cut and thrust of political debate."

Caroline watched her two friends with amusement. She felt sure Daisy had replaced Lady Victoria in Helen's affections and was curious as she knew Daisy had been involved with a young male painter a few years before. She couldn't ask the questions she had in her mind, despite feeling that Daisy was as much her friend as Helen's.

Before the two women left, Daisy promised to sort out some books for Caroline on a number of subjects and drop them off the following week. Caroline had also agreed to visit Minehead, and asked Helen to pass on a message to Tommy that Helen found rather cryptic.

"Are you sure that's what you want me to tell him?"

"Yes please. Say it again so that I know you have it right."

"You would like him to call on a day when it is not raining, and to bring a long coat?"

"That's it."

"I shan't ask what you two are planning. With Tommy it could be absolutely anything," Helen kissed Caroline's cheek as they embraced, "Within the law though, darling, please." She whispered.

Caroline established a routine to her days, overlayed with a routine for her week. She was aware of her luxury, not having to find conventional employment and having the whole cottage to herself. Determined not to become slovenly, she made herself get out of bed by seven each morning, and whatever the weather she walked to the beach and back. She was thankful for her wellington boots, as more often than not in those first few weeks, the rain was her companion. After breakfast she would clean, receive deliveries, and re-lay the fire in the sitting room if it had been lit the evening before. Afternoons were reserved for various activities depending on the day: on Mondays the laundry van arrived to collect and drop off the previous week's linen. So as not to miss it, Caroline worked on her knitting or pottered in the garden with one of the books Daisy had given her to identify plants. On Tuesdays Vi would visit for a chat and to help with whatever culinary adventure Caroline wanted to embark on.

Wednesdays were for sketching and painting. If it was dry, Caroline took her sketch book out to capture inspiration, and if it was wet, she would set up her canvas on a small easel in the kitchen and paint. On Thursdays after the laundry van had called in the morning she alternated between visiting Daisy when the Yarn Market was in progress and staying for the Women's Institute meeting, or either riding her bicycle or taking the train a single stop along the line to Williton. It was a slightly larger village than Doniford which boasted a small collection of shops and a café. Here she could chat to the lady who ran a yarn shop and solve any problems she encountered in understanding a pattern, or to the man who owned the shoe and boot shop who also did repairs and seemed to know everything about everyone in the local area. She could also have her hair washed and set, and trimmed when it needed it, in the bright and busy hair salon.

By the time Fridays arrived Caroline had usually accu-mulated several letters that required her response. She liked to write on Friday afternoons, to describe what she had done and seen during the week, and to have them neatly inserted into envelopes ready for Mr Bright to collect or for her to take to the Post Office on Saturday morning. Ron usually appeared on Saturday afternoons to spend a couple of hours in the garden.

"What did you want doing with that chicken coop, Miss?" He asked through the kitchen door as Caroline washed up her lunch things.

"Should I install some chickens?"

"Not if you're only going to be here for a year. Unless you'd want to eat them all when they go off lay in the winter of course."

Caroline thought of Bob and how he had wanted his own chickens. She wondered if he had them now.

"It rather looks as if it would fall down at any moment. Perhaps you could dismantle it and leave the wood and wire behind the shed?"

"Right-ho. The wood'll keep 'til we have more rubbish to burn. This weather is shocking! I'll take the run down but that'll be it for today I reckon."

"It was so sunny when I was here in March. Had it been like this I might have thought twice about taking this cottage!"

Ron removed his cap and scratched his balding head before replacing it. "You seem happy here though, if you don't mind me saying, and you've done Vi the world of good. She's missed having another woman to talk to. She'll be sorry to see you go, I know that."

"I'll be here until next June, Ron. She needn't worry about it until then. And she has been very kind to me with her cookery lessons. I wish there was something I could do for her in return."

"I've been thinking, it's Vi's birthday in a couple of weeks. She would like a nice painting of our cottage if you wouldn't mind having a go at it? Just a little one, and I can get it framed. But the cottage with some summer flowers, she'd like that."

The absence of an Anglican church in Doniford gave
Caroline a conundrum. She did not wish to join the
Methodist congregation; while she liked to hear their singing
if she happened to walk past during a service, their solemn
ways were off-putting to her. Although she did not feel the
need to go to church every Sunday, it had been an activity
she had grown up with and to not go at all left her with a
vacant period in her week that she felt uncomfortable filling
with anything else now that she was on her own. Her options
were limited. Williton had a substantial church and she knew
she could cycle there and back without too much exertion.
Watchet had a similar church, the main focus of the parish,
and also a small Fisherman's Church which was little more
than a small brick hall on the quayside. Both villages were
of a similar distance from Doniford, but Watchet was up and
over a hill, and Williton was a more level route. Caroline
chose Williton two or three times and found the service
to be joyful and welcoming. The more time she spent in
that village, the more she liked it there. If it were not for its
distance from the sea, she would have considered living there.

Caroline had taken her sketch book to the beach one
Wednesday, in a break between rain showers. She was growing
frustrated with the weather, having to light the sitting room
fire to help dry damp clothes in July was expensive and,
she had the notion, vaguely unhealthy. The sea was on its
way in, and a rumble of untidy waves sucked at the pebble
beach and rolled the stones with a monotonous tone. She
did not venture very far on to the pebbles but sat on one of
the raised rocks and set about sketching some of the pool
creatures. She had an idea of painting them in a series of small
canvases, with one creature on each, and then all together as
a collage on a single larger canvas. Her recent two seascapes

had been sold immediately at Elsa and Bobby's gallery and Elsa had written to encourage her to send more sea-related works. She had also mentioned yet again the clients who would pay for more intimate subjects.

Caroline was engrossed in the detail of a limpet shell and did not hear footsteps over the noise of the sea.

"Good afternoon! I hoped I would find you, though I would have knocked on your door if you hadn't been here."

"Good afternoon, Noah. Yes, I am here most days for a short while, even when it is as tempestuous as this!"

Noah looked out across the sea. "There is worse further out. It will be here in an hour or so. What are you drawing this time?"

"The creatures in this pool. I was hoping for a starfish, but there are none here. What do you have there?" She had spotted that Noah had a satchel with its strap across his chest, it looked full, but his binoculars were hung around his neck.

"My promised picnic. As I said, I hoped I would find you. There is one problem in that it requires cooking. I had hoped to treat you to a fire here on the beach but not today and this won't keep much longer."

"What is it? A fish? We can cook it at the cottage."

"Not quite a fish, but if you don't mind me using your kitchen to prepare it, it will be a feast."

They walked together the short way back to Quantock Cottage. It occurred to Caroline that had she any neighbours closer in proximity than the Saddingtons, there would be curtains twitching and gossip all around the village by the next morning. She chuckled to herself as she opened the front door and Noah followed her inside.

"What's funny?" He asked.

"I was just thinking how scandalously I am behaving. Allowing a young man into my home without a chaperone."

She glanced at him with a smile as she wriggled her feet out of her wellingtons.

"Oh, I wouldn't worry," replied Noah, hanging up his coat. "I'm not a young man anymore." He sounded weary for a moment, as if he were much older than his 31 years.

Caroline showed Noah through to the kitchen, and he asked her for a sheet of newspaper to put on the table, and a large pan of water to boil on the range. Only then did he reveal what was in his satchel.

"A crab! But it is enormous – and still alive! Goodness, how on earth does one kill it?"

"Same way as you would a lobster, though none of the boats brought any in this morning. We'll put him in the pot and then we'll need some nutcrackers if you have them to get at the meat."

"Alive? But isn't that cruel?"

Noah looked at her with a blank face. "No more than eating it in the first place."

It was an education for Caroline. The crab was cooked, and then Noah expertly used a small knife and the nutcrackers over the newspaper to extract the meat from the animal. Caroline made a pot of tea and cut and buttered some bread while Noah worked. Then she sat and watched his hands move with confidence and skill as they removed the pieces of shell. His skin was rough, his fingernails short but clean. Caroline picked up the crab's main shell and studied it, the roughness of the outside and the smooth white interior.

"Can I keep this?"

"Of course. I only damaged it a little on that edge."

Caroline stood up and put the crab shell on the mantlepiece above the range, standing it on end next to the mantle clock.

By the time they were ready to eat, the rain had started again, and the wind whistled around the outside of the cottage. Caroline had eaten crab before but had never seen it prepared or even considered for more than a moment the animal that provided it. Noah told her of the boat that had brought it in to Watchet harbour that morning. The *Marionette* was registered at Minehead but had landed her catch at Watchet to have it loaded on the early train headed up-country. The crew had reported rough conditions in the Irish sea and Noah had received similar reports from boats that had fished there during the night further south in the Atlantic. The men had all looked haggard and ready for their beds as soon as their cargos were offloaded and packed in the waiting crates.

"Their reports help us understand the weather, along with the forecasts. The Meteorological Office don't always get things right, and we rely on the ships coming back in to know what's on its way."

"And that's how you seem to know when the rain will come?"

"That and the dark clouds in the sky, yes." He said with a rye smile.

"It was a delicious meal, even if it wasn't quite a picnic, thank you."

"My pleasure. I wanted to see you again. I wanted to make sure you were alright here by yourself, but I can see you are managing quite capably."

"Father helped me arrange things when we first arrived, and my friends have helped me since then. The Saddingtons are a Godsend, truly I would not have managed without them. Do you know Ron?"

"The name rings a bell, but I can't say where from. Anyway, I'd better be getting back. It won't do for the gossips to see me leaving too late!" He pushed his plate a little further across the table but held Caroline's gaze.

"No." Caroline replied quietly. "No, we mustn't give the gossips any encouragement. So, I shall invite you to lunch on Sunday. Will you come?"

"I will. Service finishes at eleven, I can be here for midday unless that is too early?"

When Vi arrived later that week, Caroline was keen to go over timings for a successful roast dinner and suitable desserts. A crate of beer was ordered and delivered from Mr Bright, along with extra cream and vegetables and a pork shoulder joint. Caroline had her hair washed and set on the Thursday in Williton and purchased a set of napkins and a tablecloth. She did not have a separate dining room so the kitchen table would need to be suitably dressed for the occasion.

Dressing herself was rather more complicated. Caroline did not have a large couture. Sunday lunch was not an occasion that called for evening dress, or for her favourite short black beaded dress. That left an assortment of woollen and crepe skirts and dresses which were perfectly suitable for tea with Daisy Clare or shopping in Williton, but for entertaining a young man? Not so young, Caroline corrected herself as she stood in front of the open doors of her wardrobe. Her eyes fell on the pair of Freddie's trousers that she had kept after wearing them when visiting Midge and wore often around the house. They had felt so comfortable and practical. She shook her head sadly; not for this occasion. She really did want to make a good impression, and this surprised her.

Finally, she decided on a bottle-green woollen dress with long sleeves, a tied belt and wide collar edged with cream piping. Carefully she applied a little make-up, far less than Helen would have recommended, but more than she had ever seen Daisy wear. She looked at her nails. She kept them short and neat but rarely wore polish. They would do.

Three hours later, Caroline stood over a tray of potatoes that refused to crisp up in the oven. She pushed her hair away from her face and set about turning each potato over once again in the melted fat. Caroline had roasted potatoes before without incident, and she couldn't understand why these particular ones were misbehaving. She turned the final one as there came a loud knock on the front door. Shoving the tray back into the oven portion of the range, she hurried to admit her guest.

Noah stood on the doorstep clutching a small bunch of wildflowers. It had only occurred to him on his walk over from Watchet that flowers would be a suitable gift, and as it was a Sunday and no shops would be open, he had no alternative but to pick a few that caught his eye in the hedgerows. The wet weather had encouraged an abundance of growth.

"Good afternoon, do come in."

"Good afternoon. These are for you; I hope you don't mind their commonness."

"Not at all! Please, make yourself comfortable in the sitting room while I put these into a vase."

Noah did as he was bid. He inspected the new wireless set, a superior model to the one his parents owned, picked up the novel that Caroline had left on a side table and then put it down again. He took the photograph from the mantlepiece showing Caroline and an older man who could only have been her father, then replaced it next to the small clock and eventually stood at the window looking out towards the sea. It was the most natural position for him to take up, almost as if some force was compelling him to always turn his face to the water.

"Can I get you something to drink? I have sherry, or a beer if you prefer?" Caroline hovered beside the walnut drinks cabinet that held a bottle each of dry sherry and brandy.

Noah turned to face her, becoming silhouetted, "A beer if I may?"

"One moment." Caroline disappeared. Noah sat on one of the upholstered chairs and tried to relax. He felt strangely on edge; he was reluctant to admit he was nervous and wanted to make a good impression.

Caroline returned with two open bottles of beer that she had had the foresight to stand with four others in a bucket of cold water outside the kitchen door.

"Cheers!" she said with a smile as she took the upturned glass from the top of her bottle and poured the beer in to half full.

Noah did the same but chuckled to himself as he did so.

"What's funny?"

"We normally say that when we're about to take a drink."

"Oh of course, how silly of me."

"And I hadn't expected you to join me."

"I rather like beer. In fact, I much prefer it to sherry. I first tried it when I visited my friend Midge and really, I don't see why people think of it as a poor person's drink."

"Perhaps people don't know any better?"

Caroline looked up from her glass. She detected a note of annoyance in Noah's voice and realised that she may have unintentionally offended him.

Noah realised at the same moment that he had been a little quick with his retort and saw the hint of a frown on Caroline's face.

"I didn't mean …"

"I'm sorry … "

They spoke at the same time, stopped, both looked away from the other and then back. Noah tried again.

"Lunch smells wonderful."

"Thank you. I hope you like pork, though I've had a little trouble with the roast potatoes."

"It will make a welcome change from fish, and I am certainly hungry."

They smiled at each other in silence for a moment, which began to stretch on beyond a comfortable interlude.

This is ridiculous, Caroline thought. We have talked so freely before when we have met, what on earth is happening now?

Think of something, anything! Noah was also racking his brains for a topic of conversation.

It was Caroline who realised the issue first. She had a flash of memory from when she had stayed with Lina and Albert in Malvern just before Christmas the previous year. They had been in their drawing room with Helen and Tommy, and Caroline had realised then that Lina and Albert were acting as their parents had done before them, playing the parts they thought were expected of them as hosts in their large, comfortable house.

"Why don't we go into the kitchen? I can keep an eye on the carrots while we talk."

It worked.

They both felt more comfortable around the kitchen table. Noah asked what Caroline was painting and she uncovered her easel to show him her large study of rock pool creatures. They stood side by side at the kitchen window and Caroline listed the vegetables that Ron had planned to grow for her.

"I know where I have heard their name now. Ron Saddington used to take the services sometimes at the

Fisherman's Church on the quay. Stopped when his son was killed."

"Was that in the war?"

"No, no, Jeffery was out on a boat. He got caught up in the gear and went overboard."

"Oh dear. I noticed a photograph on their mantlepiece the other day when I went to take back a cake tin. That must have been Jeffery. Was he their only son?"

"Their only child, yes. It hit them both very hard. Ron took to the bottle for a while I'm sorry to say. Understandable I suppose. He came round in the end, doesn't touch a drop now as far as I know. But he's never returned to the church."

"Death affects people in very different ways doesn't it." It was a rhetorical statement and Noah heard it as such and didn't reply.

Over lunch they talked more about their brothers. Noah learned that Caroline had not had a conventional introduction to Cheltenham society due to her mother's reaction to Freddie's death. Caroline learned that Noah had always hoped to be harbour master at Watchet but following the death of his brother he had been asked, then persuaded, to take up the vacant role of coastguard. The two roles were not so different in everyday terms; both assisted with the daily running of the harbour and both were equally respected by the boatmen.

The difference came when there was some peril or accident at sea or around the coast. Then the coastguard came into his own, taking control of any rescue operation. At one time or other, he had also been responsible for preventing smuggling although there was far less activity of that kind now.

Over apple crumble and cream, Caroline asked, "Have you been involved in many rescues?"

"A few. I'm more likely to arrange assistance to meet a boat bringing an injured crewman ashore. A little further west and the Atlantic would bring far more storms and more danger."

"But we do get bad weather here. By here I mean away from the Atlantic. The storms we had over Christmas time were terrible."

"That was what we call a hurricane. The force of the wind was above ten. I thought we might have had a storm a few days ago but it veered north."

"How do you know? How can you tell where a storm is going?"

"We have charts, we receive information from ships out on the water, and we have our eyes when all else fails."

"You mean your binoculars? Of course. So that's why you walk up and down the coast so much, you are keeping an eye on the weather as well as the ships."

Noah smiled at her and nodded. "Tell me about Cheltenham. I've never been further north in this country than Warminster."

"I will but let me clear these things away first. I have coffee if you would like some?"

"I would prefer tea."

While they waited for the kettle to boil, they went out into the back garden where the roof overhung the kitchen window and afforded a little shelter so that Noah could tap out his pipe and smoke.

"This is a nice cottage," he said, drawing deeply as the tobacco glowed in the bowl. "But you're only staying a year?"

"I only have the arrangement for a year, yes. I might be able to stay longer, if I wanted to. I didn't want to commit for too long in case I didn't like it here."

"Does commitment frighten you?"

Caroline was caught off guard at the directness of his question. It wasn't a subject she had paid much consideration to, despite James' proposal and Bob's quiet persistence. The kettle began to sing on the range and delayed her answer. After filling the teapot, she went back outside. The rain had started to fall again; Noah seemed oblivious to it.

"No."

"Good. It doesn't do to be frightened of things."

As Noah strode out along the coast path later that afternoon, he considered the woman he had just left on her doorstep. He had danced with a few local girls over the years, taken them to concerts and even one or two to the cinemas in Watchet and Minehead. Always he had lost interest after two or three dates and had eventually been replaced by a younger and often more rakish model. He knew he had a reputation as a serious man, whose first and only love was the sea. It was not one he had bothered to dispute. Caroline was not like the local girls, though he was struggling to explain why.

He glanced out across the bay as a squall blew rain into his face. It was convention. Caroline did not seem to be weighed down by what society expected of her. And yet she was no rebel, he was sure of that. She would not deliberately court danger or scandal, but he imagined they could easily find her with her openness. Of course, she was older than the local girls had been, but so now was he. It was only then that he wondered if he should have accepted her invitation to lunch as they had been unchaperoned. Caroline had not appeared to feel that one was needed. If she was not intending to stay in the neighbourhood, perhaps she was less concerned about any damage to her good name?

The question then was, should he invest his time, his emotions, in a woman who could up and leave him in a few months' time?

Caroline stood at her sitting room window as Noah had done a couple of hours before and looked out at the rain. He would get wet through on his way home. He must spend a good deal of his time wet through. She would have liked him to stay a while longer, yet at the same time, she felt she needed some time to digest all they had talked about over lunch. They hadn't even arranged a time to meet again, she realised.

For a Sunday afternoon in July, it was as gloomy as October. Caroline made a fresh pot of tea, brought it back into the sitting room on a tray and settled herself next to the radio with her knitting. She had finished the blue jacket for Mary Rose's baby boy Mark and had now begun the same pattern for a third time in pale lemon yarn for Annie's baby. The announcer gave the weather forecast with a neutral and dispassionate voice as Caroline sipped her tea. She wondered if Noah was listening too.

Monday dawned as if the summer had never been in any doubt: the sky was the bluest cornflower hue with not a hint of cloud. Tommy whistled to himself as he drove along the coast road towards Doniford, his long raincoat folded neatly on the passenger seat. He had understood the message that Helen delivered from Caroline immediately, but the weather had conspired to keep him away until now.

It had not kept Tommy and Christopher apart. Indeed, the mist-shrouded moors had enabled them to meet and spend time together with less fear of being seen than on a bright sunny day. They had walked miles from where Tommy parked the car, discovered abandoned stone huts and secluded groves of stunted dripping trees, and returned to the car tired but satisfied. The difference now was that Tommy no longer sketched Christopher. They had learned that lesson.

Helen had provided directions and Tommy found Quantock Cottage with no difficulty. He pulled into the grassy drive and switched off the engine, then sat and looked at the property for a moment. It was as he had imagined and felt that Caroline could never be unhappy in her own little cottage here. As he was getting out of the car, Caroline emerged from the side of the house, wiping her hands on her apron.

"Tommy! How lovely to see you! You must forgive me I'm sure I look a fright. I've been beating a rug while the sun is out."

"You look as pretty as ever. I hoped it wouldn't be inconvenient my turning up unannounced like this, but Helen said you don't have a telephone."

"Come round to the kitchen. It's not inconvenient in the slightest. If we go anywhere, I shall need to remember to leave Vi a note. I wouldn't want her to worry if she received no reply to her knocking."

"Well, I have my long raincoat, which I must say was a most excellent secret code. Helen gave me such a queer look this morning when I left with it!"

"I know she wouldn't mind, but I didn't want to embarrass her in front of Daisy."

"Now, she's a funny sort."

"Tea? There's still some in the pot…. Did you mean Daisy is a funny sort?"

"I do. Absolutely not the type Helen would normally go for. Well, you've met Vic of course. And I'm not sure what to make of Daisy if I'm completely honest. I would never have thought…" His voice tailed off without finishing the sentence.

"I think I know what you mean," said Caroline, pouring the rather stewed tea into two cups on the kitchen table. "I'm sure Daisy told me she had been involved with a man some years ago, a painter I think, French or Belgian or some such. But she does seem to have rather captured Helen, don't you think?"

Tommy nodded in agreement.

Caroline suggested that they walk down to Helwell Bay so that she could make some sketches. On her explorative walks she had discovered a small, sheltered cove. With Tommy positioned close to the rocky backdrop, she would be able to keep an eye out for any approaching ramblers in both directions. The sea was calm and on its way out, the blue of the sky reflected almost exactly in the water.

"This is a magnificent spot. Did you have any preference to a pose?" Tommy had started to remove his clothes while Caroline arranged a rug for him to sit on. She had been uneasy about this moment, despite her enthusiasm to paint a life model again. She couldn't help but blush and fussed with the rug to avoid looking at her friend.

"I thought if you could take a classical pose, perhaps to sit with one leg out in front and the other bent at the knee, and rest your arm on your bent knee? Would that be comfortable?"

"I should think so. If it will give you what you think your patrons are looking for." Tommy grinned. He could see Caroline's embarrassment and couldn't help but find it endearing. He sat down in the position Caroline had described, keeping the raincoat close at hand should it be needed.

"Like this?"

Caroline braced herself and looked directly at Tommy. She was relieved to see he had arranged himself exactly as she had suggested and neither of them would be uncomfortable.

They spent the next hour and a half in the cove. Caroline grew more confident and directed Tommy to sit or stand as the sun climbed overhead and the shadow placement progressed. After a while she forgot to keep checking the approaches on either side of the cove for visitors, her eyes flicking between Tommy and her sketch book, her hand working as quickly as possible to capture as much detail as she could. For his part, Tommy was an excellent model. After watching the sea for a while and the gulls that bobbed gently on its surface, he closed his eyes and took his mind away to Christopher. It had an effect on him that he realised just in time would embarrass Caroline, and instead simply listened to the gulls and the ripples of waves in the distance. Once when he was facing towards the west he noticed a glint up on the hill above the water, but then it was gone and he paid it no further attention.

"I think that will do for now, you can get dressed again." Caroline closed her sketchbook and put her pencil back into her little wooden box. "It must be almost lunch time. Are you hungry?"

"Aren't I always?"

"I have some cold pork and cold roast potatoes from yesterday's lunch, they would make a sandwich with some chutney."

"A feast! Who would have thought that sitting by the sea would work up such an appetite?"

"Perhaps you should have been more in the shade, you do look rather pink," she said with concern.

"A healthy glow. Helen can smother me in calamine lotion this evening if I've burnt too much. And after lunch I insist on giving you that driving lesson. The weather is perfect, and I noticed how straight the road is by your cottage. I'll turn the car around and you can drive down to the railway station and back again."

"I'm really not sure."

"Nonsense! Once you get the hang of it, you'll be desperate for your own motor car. Why, Daisy had a try out last week when she came over, and she was a natural." Tommy suspected that Caroline would not want to be left out.

After lunch, Caroline tied a scarf around her head to keep her hair in place and got behind the steering wheel of Tommy's car. Tommy had already started the engine and given Caroline a detailed description of which pedal did what. He got into the passenger seat and instructed Caroline to pull away. The car lurched forwards and then stopped abruptly.

Caroline looked with a worried expression at Tommy, who was trying not to laugh.

"Never mind old girl. Let's have another go."

They reached the railway station after several lurches and stalls. Caroline got out of the car while Tommy turned it around. The station master came out to see what was going on.

"Good morning, Miss! Lovely day for it. Off anywhere nice?"

"Back home now I hope, Mr Evans. My friend is teaching me how to drive, though I'm not sure I'm making much progress."

He sucked his teeth in the universal male manner which conveys that whatever sight is in front of them is not one they particularly approve of, or feel is worthy of further effort. "And why would you want to do a thing like that? With a perfectly good train line practically on your doorstep."

"My friend insists I will enjoy it once I get the hang of it." She leaned in closer to Evans, and in a conspiratorial stage whisper said, "I much prefer the train."

They winked at each other, before Tommy gestured for Caroline to take the wheel again.

The slow journey back to Quantock Cottage was less jerky than the outward trip. As the car reached the cottage, Caroline asked if she could keep going for a little bit further. Tommy readily agreed, less concerned now that Caroline might forget to steer in the right direction. They proceeded with determination past the Saddington's cottage and slowly reached the edge of Doniford village. Caroline's smile was genuine, the experience of being in control of the vehicle was one she had never expected or thought she would enjoy as much as she was.

After pulling up outside the Post Office, Tommy again turned the car around as the lane was narrow, and then Caroline took the wheel once more. A little more speed this time as they passed the cottages and headed back to the railway station.

"Can I try turning around this time please?" Caroline felt it couldn't be as difficult as all that.

"Let me get out first, and I'll guide you. Look in the mirror as well and turn the wheel in the direction that you want the car to go."

Caroline looked at him blankly. "Of course." She said and crunched the gear stick into reverse.

A few moments later they were on their final trip back to Caroline's cottage after she had negotiated a seven-point turn in the space outside the railway station. She turned the car into the grassy driveway and came to a gentle stop.

"I knew you'd be an excellent driver once you had a chance!" Exclaimed Tommy. "A little more tuition and you'll be racing Helen around the countryside."

"Oh no, I don't think so. It's jolly good fun but I can get around perfectly well as it is using the bus and train services, and my bicycle."

"Wait and see. In a few days I fully expect to receive a letter asking me when I can take you out for another lesson!"

"Do you really think so? I simply couldn't afford to purchase a motor car in any case."

"From what you've told me about those life paintings, you would have more than enough if you sold them all." There was no hint of jealousy or pride in Tommy's voice. He had come to have affection for Caroline as if she were a sister and wanted the best for her in all things.

"Thank you for coming to pose for me Tommy. I can't imagine ever actually asking someone to do that. And I'll admit I did feel awkward at the start, but I think the sketches will give me plenty of reference material. Would you like to see the paintings before I send them off to London?"

"I would indeed. Now, don't forget, Saturday week, Helen's party at the house for her cronies. Come over in the afternoon and change before everyone else arrives, and of course you must stay the night at least. I'll run you back whenever you're inclined and if you've got a painting ready, I can take a look then."

When the delivery boy had been and gone the following day, Caroline decided the weather was simply too nice to stay indoors with her knitting. It occurred to her that if she did have a motor car she could simply hop in and set off in any direction she chose. She chuckled to herself, remembering Tommy's prediction. Instead, she put on her hat and gloves and a light cardigan, put her purse in her shopping basket and walked to the station to catch the next train to Watchet.

David Escott, harbour master at Watchet for nearly thirty years, closed the harbour office door with a bang and turned to go down the outside steps. The captain of the *Merry Jen*, Charles 'Chancy' Pritchard raised his head at the sound of

the door as he climbed up the stone steps and stopped when
he saw Escott.

"I wouldn't go in unless you have to, Chancy. Noah got
out of bed the wrong side this morning and no mistake."

"Noah? That doesn't sound right. Bad news, d'you think?"

Both men returned to the bottom of the steps as they
talked.

"I've no idea but he's been like it since I got in. Come
to think of it, he was sullen yesterday afternoon as well."

"Maybe a chance he's sickening for something." Chancy
pondered, illustrating why he had acquired his nickname.
There was always a chance of something as far as he was
concerned.

Escott knocked out his pipe on the wall of the boat
house and refilled it with tobacco. "Could be. Could be
that young lady he went to see at the weekend. Could just
be the weather."

"What young lady is that then?"

"Over to Doniford, not long moved in so I'm told.
Artist type."

Chancy nodded as if he knew all about the 'artist type'.

"I was just going to let you know we'll be another hour
loading before we can get away. I was going to check the
forecast with Noah but is there anything I need to worry
about?"

"You're headed to Cork? This high pressure is moving
quickly through, you should be alright getting there but
coming back will be rougher."

Noah stood at the large bay window of the harbour office
and watched Chancy and Escott in conversation below. He
felt claustrophobic. He needed to feel the wind on his skin.
The clock on the chimney breast said twenty minutes past
two. Noah decided to give the charts another half an hour

and then he would take his binoculars and walk up Cleeve Hill. Definitely not towards Helwell Bay.

He knew the name of the wrench his stomach had felt the morning before. The feeling that had stayed with him after he had turned away and walked back towards Watchet; stayed with him all day and into the evening no matter how much he tried to smother it with work, exercise, even two pints of bitter in the Anchor Inn. That had raised eyebrows; he was known as a single pint man. That feeling had kept him awake into the small hours. He did not like it. Caught by surprise at the strength of it, he was disgusted with himself for his inability to get it caged and under control.

Caroline left the station and walked through the winding streets of the little town. She marvelled at the confectionary in the baker's shop window and went inside to buy herself an iced bun sporting a glacé cherry on the top. Outside, she said good morning to a couple of elderly ladies dressed in black crepe, lace and ribbons, as they inched their way towards the bakery. Caroline knew she would end up at the harbour, she knew she wanted to see Noah again. She had no real idea of what she wanted to say to him; once again, trying to plan her thoughts around him led to them evaporate into the air. Better to just say whatever came to her in the moment, she decided.

On the quayside, fish and crustaceans were laid out for sale. Caroline cast a critical eye over each variety without really knowing what she was looking at. In the end, she played safe with three gutted pilchards wrapped in newspaper. There was no more delay to be found. Caroline turned and walked towards the harbour office. Several pairs of eyes followed her progress along the harbourside and up the stone steps.

Noah did not look up from the chart when he heard the door open. The office had been unusually quiet, and he had become absorbed in the lines and numbers in front of him.

Caroline cleared her throat. "Hello Noah."

He carefully placed his pencil and compass on the chart and raised his head. There she was again, in the very last place he expected to see her.

"I thought I would just call in to say good afternoon as I happened to be in Watchet. If you're busy I can leave you to your work."

Noah stood up, remembering his manners. "Won't you sit down?" He didn't know what else to say. He had been rationalising what he had seen through his binoculars with the knowledge that Caroline was an adult woman who had every right to spend time with anyone she chose, even in the most unusual circumstances, and now here she was in his office, wishing him a good afternoon as if nothing had changed. Yet of course, she did not know that he had seen her with that other man. Noah realised that Caroline was looking at him expectantly from the hard wooden chair near the fireplace.

"Can I get you something to drink? There's a pot of coffee on the stove, though we've no milk."

"No, thank you. Are you quite alright? You look as if you were in the middle of something, perhaps I should go."

"No! No, it can wait." He sat down again. He had to tell her, had to find out what was going on. "I saw you yesterday. On the beach."

"Did you?" Caroline frowned. "I didn't think anyone else was around yesterday."

"I wasn't actually on the beach. But I saw you. Both of you."

It took a moment for Caroline to understand fully what Noah had said. She saw the binoculars on the desk next to the charts and realised the full extent of his words. She remembered Bob's reaction to the life paintings she had made in Cornwall, how he had called them obscene at first but had tried to understand how Caroline had enjoyed the fluidity of line and shadow. A sense of defiance rose up inside her and she lifted her chin slightly, looking directly at Noah.

"I was sketching Tommy. It is not only watercolour landscapes that the gallery has been able to sell on my behalf."

"Sketching. Your... friend. Did he sketch you?" Noah's voice was hard, clipped.

"Tommy is an artist yes, but he was modelling for me. You met him on the quayside, don't you remember? He offered to pose weeks ago, and we had been waiting for a dry, sunny day..."

Noah stood up abruptly, knocking his chair backwards. He strode around the desk and went to the window. Looking out at the harbour he asked again, "Did he sketch you?"

Caroline felt angry and didn't understand why. She stood up too and took four steps towards the window, bringing her to Noah's shoulder.

"He did not. He has not."

"Has anyone?" Noah turned to face her. He realised now that he did not want to share the intimacy of company they had experienced together in Caroline's kitchen and on the beach walking. He wanted that for himself, with her.

Caroline understood the meaning of his question. She chose to answer him literally. "No."

They stood facing each other for some seconds in the large bay window of the harbour office. Fishermen on the quayside glanced up and noticed them. One or two stopped their loading to watch, reminded of the moving pictures they had seen on a big screen. Everyone knew that at such a point in the story, the leading man would take the leading lady into an embrace, or (to the delight of the female members of the audience) kiss her. When Noah turned away from the window to pace the office floor, his audience on the quay let out an audible groan of disappointment.

Inside the office the atmosphere was close. Noah felt out of his depth. The strength of his feelings had taken him by surprise; it had never troubled him before to find that he had been replaced in some girl's affections by another man. He could not reconcile the Caroline he thought he had come to know with this brazen behaviour as a carefree yet attractive young woman with her evident disregard for moral standards. Being unchaperoned with him was one thing; being alone on a beach with a naked man was quite another.

"How long have you known this friend?"

Caroline stepped away from the window, back towards the fireplace. "Two, nearly three years I suppose. He is married to a very dear friend of mine."

"Married? Dear God, do you care nothing for propriety?!" Noah was growing more confused by the minute.

"Please, Noah, there is nothing of that nature between Tommy and I. He and Helen are happily married. He simply offered to be a life model for me. I could hardly have asked anyone else!" She took another step towards him. She could not explain the nature of Helen and Tommy's marriage without breaking a confidence. She would not do that. "The poses were all tastefully arranged. I only discovered my ability with the human form last year, and it's not a subject that I have had any opportunity to return to until now. Don't you remember the sketches of Tommy in my book?"

Again, they stared at each other. A thousand words swarmed around Noah's brain; each one would sting if it could escape through his lips.

"I should go." Caroline reached to pick up her basket, and Noah caught her other arm as she did so.

"No, I'm sorry. I don't know … it's not…"

Caroline left the basket on the floor. She was now only a few inches from Noah; he had not let go of her arm and passed his free hand over his face in frustration. Caroline touched it gently with her fingertips.

Noah tried again to marshal his words. "It's not something I expected to see. It caught me off guard. Of course, you are free to behave however you wish. I have no right to…"

"Noah, why not come and see the paintings when they are finished? Before I send them on to London. They are art. I'd like you to see them." Her slender fingers against the rough skin of the back of his hand reminded her of Max. She closed her eyes for a moment. When she opened them again, Noah's face had softened. His blue eyes were less fraught.

"I'm sorry, Caroline."

"I understand. Truly. I really should be getting along though, there is a train at twenty minutes past four."

9

JUST LIKE OLD TIMES

Annie Jenks was delivered of a son on the morning of Sunday 24 July 1927. Caroline received a letter from her father on the following Wednesday, informing her that the child would be christened on Sunday 30 July, and asking if she might stay for a few days either side of that weekend. Naturally, her father omitted to mention the name or birth weight of the baby. Caroline had not missed George as much as she feared she would, except in the evenings. Then she missed his company, even though they had often spent an hour or more in silence either listening to the radio or reading.

After telephoning Cheltenham and leaving a message with Sara that she would be arriving on the Thursday and would stay until the following Tuesday, Caroline made her arrangements to leave Quantock Cottage. She called on Vi to let her know so she would not be concerned to find the cottage locked up and quiet. She informed Mr Bright so that he might keep any letters while she was away and stop them cluttering up the doormat. He also offered to take in her laundry as she would not be home in time to meet the van herself. With all of her other regular deliveries suspended, Caroline packed her suitcase and returned to the town of her childhood.

Ferris hurried out of the glass doors at Norwood Court when he saw the taxi pull into the driveway. He ushered Caroline into the apartment building and carried her case up the two flights of stairs for her before returning to the taxi to pay the driver. Sara came out of the kitchen into the hallway as Caroline entered the apartment.

"Nice to have you back, Ma'am. Cup of tea for you?"

"Yes, thank you, Sara. How are you? How is Annie and the baby?"

"We are all well, thank you Ma'am. Little Victor is a lusty one, got a right pair of lungs on him!"

"Victor? So, Jacob chose that over George. I can't wait to see them. And the Christening is at St Mark's?"

"Yes Ma'am."

Caroline smiled at Sara's use of 'Ma'am'. She was used to being addressed as Miss but knew Sara had been trained to address all of her female superiors in that way.

An hour later and George had returned from the Building Society. Sara served their dinner and then left father and daughter to their reunion. George was keen to hear about everything Caroline had seen and done since he had left her in Somerset, and Caroline was careful to not speak too much of Noah. She focused instead on Vi and Ron's contributions to her education in the ways of household management. George was satisfied that she was coping on her own.

He had some news of his own. Annie and Jacob had asked him to be Godfather to Victor, and as a further honour, the little boy would also take George as a middle name.

"How lovely! You are not Godparent to anyone else, are you?"

"I was, years ago, to a son of a friend. The boy did not live beyond his fifth birthday, some disorder of the lungs."

"I'm sorry to hear that. Sara says Victor has no such affliction."

George chuckled. "No, apparently not."

Before visiting Mary Rose and the children at the vicarage the next day, Caroline called in to see Agatha Kettle. For an extra three shillings a week, Sara had taken to making Agatha's lunch each day before starting on the cleaning and dinner preparations for George, and Agatha had quickly grown fond of the young girl. Miss Kettle was keen to bring Caroline up to date with the goings on at Norwood Court.

"Naturally, one doesn't like to gossip," she started as she poured the tea. "But there have been things one sees, things one hears."

"Anything in particular?"

"Well. I have a suspicion, nothing more mind you, but a suspicion that Mrs Bassett is having an affair."

Caroline dropped a sugar lump into her teacup and stirred thoughtfully. "She is no longer in mourning."

"No indeed. However, my suspicions are that it might be with Mr Monk."

"Matthew? Surely not! Whatever makes you think that?"

"We have known for some time that Mrs Bassett has been staying elsewhere most weekends. We also know that Mr Monk does not return here from the air base now until Saturday morning. Last weekend, they arrived together."

Caroline stopped mid-sip. "Together?"

"Yes! In the same taxi. For the few moments that I happened to see them together outside, and walking into the building, there was a certain look, an expression. I could be wrong of course, but I have always had a feeling for that sort of thing."

"But what about Rebecca, Mrs Monk?"

"She spends the majority of her time with Captain McTimony, perhaps she has not noticed anything out of character."

"And how is the Captain?"

"Ferris tells me there is no real improvement. His speech is still absent, he had a small amount of movement in his hands, enough to grasp items, but he is still incapable of taking care of himself. I fear he will remain an invalid. Such a shame for such a vigorous man."

Caroline left Miss Kettle's apartment in a contemplative mood. She strolled through the Suffolks under the shade of the horse chestnut trees and along Lansdown. The air was heavy, as if rain was once again on its way. By the time she reached the vicarage, she was thirsty and perspiring. Mary opened the door with Mark against her shoulder and Angelica peering out from behind her leg. As soon as Angelica saw Caroline she shrieked with joy and raised her arms to be picked up.

They all went through to the garden where a table with a jug of lemon water and glasses on a tray and chairs were set out on the lawn. Angelica brought a procession of dolls and teddy bears to show Caroline from the rug that was spread out next to the table, but eventually contented herself to sit at Caroline's feet and play quietly. Caroline presented Mary with the jacket she had knitted for baby Mark, who gurgled and snuffled for a while before settling down to nap. The garden was full of scents from the lavender, roses and snapdragons, with bees and butterflies waltzing from flower to flower.

The women talked for almost two hours while Mark slept and eventually Angelica lay down and napped as well.

Philip was out visiting his list of ill and infirm parishioners and Mary said he would be sorry to have missed her.

"I shall see him on Sunday though, at the Christening."

"Of course. And will you come to tea afterwards? Mark will wear his new jacket in your honour."

Caroline could not refuse.

Saturday was even more humid than Friday afternoon had been. Caroline and George took a late morning trip into the town centre and had lunch in a café on the Promenade. Afterwards George went to browse in a bookshop, while Caroline caught the tram to Prestbury. She had thought of Bob frequently since she had left Somerset and was keen to try and see him. She guessed that as the football season had ended (according to Ferris) he would be at home on Saturday afternoons.

Bob was in his small back garden when Caroline knocked on the front door. He was constructing a chicken run out of some timber off-cuts and wire that a neighbour had donated. Wiping his face with a handkerchief, he walked through his kitchen and hallway and opened the door.

"Hello! I thought I would surprise you with a visit."

Bob was caught completely by surprise and took a moment to remember his manners. He ushered Caroline inside and into his sitting room at the front of the house, brushing the seat of the only upholstered chair in the room for her to sit on. It was a spartan room. With the exception of his mortgage, Bob was not one to ask for credit and would be adding to his furniture as and when he could afford the items he needed. A few pieces had been donated by friends and family around the town, and he was as comfortable as he could wish to be.

As it faced north, the sitting room was cool compared to the humid outside. Caroline accepted Bob's offer of a glass of water rather than tea and picked up the newspaper that was on a side table by the chair. It was open on the advertisements page.

"Are you going to buy some chickens?" She called to Bob.

He returned and handed her the only good glass he possessed. "Yes, I've been working on the run. Would you like to see?"

They went into the garden and Caroline was impressed at its neatness despite the inclement summer the country had experienced that year. Unlike her own bare vegetable plot, Bob's was lush and green. Tomato plants were held up with string; runner beans twined around hazel branches and carried pretty pink and white flowers where the beans would eventually develop. In one corner stood a compost heap surrounded by corrugated iron sheets, and in the other was the half-finished chicken run.

They talked about chickens and vegetables for a while before retreating out of the heat and back into the sitting room. Then the conversation faltered.

"And you're only staying for the weekend?" Bob asked for the third time.

"Yes. Only for Annie's baby's Christening and then I shall be returning to Doniford. It's strange, I still don't feel I can call it home just yet."

"Home is where the heart is, so they say."

"They do, yes. I think my home is by the sea, but I'm not sure if it is completely at Doniford. There are so many other seaside towns after all."

There was another silence.

Then Bob said, "Lottie is expecting. Eric is doing well in his new post. I didn't think they would waste much time starting their family."

"That's wonderful news! You must give me their address before I go. I hope she is not experiencing any sickness."

"Not that I've heard. Mother goes over by train every Saturday, she's there now, I expect she'll stay with them for Lottie's confinement."

"So many babies. And so much nicer when one can hand them back to their mothers. Angelica was quite insistent that I play with her dolls when I visited Mary yesterday, as if I had only arrived to see her!"

"But you'll want one of your own one day…?"

Caroline looked at him and saw the hope still in his eyes. It would always come back to this she realised, and though it didn't make her uncomfortable, it did make her a little sad. She wanted Bob to have his own family to fill his own house.

"Certainly not in the near future, no." She said as gently as she could.

Caroline stayed for another ten minutes, trying to keep the conversation light and asking Bob about his plans for the kitchen and the front garden. Eventually she stood up to leave.

"I'd better be getting along. I'd like to spend as much time with Father as I can while I'm here."

"Let me get a scrap of paper and write Lottie's address for you then." Bob disappeared once more into the kitchen and reappeared with a stub of pencil and the torn off back of an envelope. He wrote his sister's address carefully and handed the paper to Caroline.

"Thank you. Well, take care won't you Bob. And good luck finding your chickens."

"And you be careful too. Especially if you're driving a motor car." He smiled, and Caroline felt better about her visit.

The Christening was a much smaller affair than Annie and Jacob's wedding had turned out. The weather still had not broken and ladies fanned themselves with whatever they had to hand. At the end of the service, the Godparents assembled around the font; George was joined by Annie's sister Julia and Jacob's brother Colin, and Victor George Jenks announced his acceptance into the Christian community with his now customary lusty cry.

The congregation who had been invited, and several who had not, formed a procession through the new housing estate at St Mark's to Annie and Jacob's house. Neighbours on either side had been laying out plates of sandwiches and pies, and making tea in a variety of pots and urns to feed and water the party. Caroline and George joined the throng, Caroline carrying a small silver brush and comb set for Victor as his Christening present in a white box tied with a pale blue ribbon. There were no speeches, no formality at the Jenks' house, but after an hour George managed to draw Annie and Jacob to one side for a moment while Victor was being handed around various relatives.

"Caroline and I shall be leaving shortly, but I wanted to give you this." He handed Jacob a small envelope. "I have taken the liberty of opening an account for Victor at the Building Society, and as a gift I shall deposit five pounds each year into it. The account details are in the envelope, should you wish to also deposit any monies. When he is twenty-one, it should provide a sum that he could use towards his education, or a motor car or perhaps to see some of the world. It will be his choice."

Jacob quickly calculated the amount that Victor could hope to have when he reached twenty-one and started to protest that it was too generous an offer. Annie didn't bother to try and add up the sum; she threw her arms around

George's neck with many thanks nearly knocking him over before crying tears of joy and in turn hugging Caroline too.

As they walked back towards the railway station together, Caroline linked her arm through her father's and said, "That was a very generous thing to do for little Victor."

"He will not always be little. If he survives childhood, he will need all the assistance he can get. It is quite possible that Annie and Jacob will have many more children, but I shall not be Godfather to them all. It is a responsibility that I take seriously, as I know you do with Angelica and Mark."

"I can't imagine what the world will be like when Victor turns twenty-one. That would be … nineteen forty-eight. It seems such a long way off."

"We must all hope that his generation do not have to sacrifice as yours has done, my dear."

That evening, after returning from tea at the vicarage, Caroline knocked on Galina Bassett's apartment door. Galina had learned that Caroline would be visiting for the weekend and had asked George to extend an invitation to listen to music with her as the two women had done many evenings before. Caroline sat in the familiar apartment and sipped the vodka that Galina had poured for her.

Galina lit a cigarette and breathed out the smoke over her shoulder away from Caroline. Then she turned and fixed Caroline with an intense look.

"There is someone you have met?"

Caroline was taken aback. "How did you know? I mean there is someone who I have become acquainted with, but how could you possibly know?"

Galina smiled. "My dear Caroline, I did not know. However, the easiest way to find something out is to ask, is it not?"

Caroline blushed at being taken in so easily, and then chuckled to herself. "That was rather mean."

"I apologise. But now I want to know about him. Does he have passion?"

"Galina, really!"

"Perhaps that is too crass. Is he interesting?"

Caroline gave as detailed description of Noah as she dared, without allowing herself to be drawn into commitment to attraction. Galina listened, nodded, sipped her drink and smoked. When Caroline had finished, Galina drained her vodka and put the glass on the coffee table.

"This man is an improvement on the film maker. I do not think he is as interesting as you clearly do, but I am not embarking on a relationship with him. He would have to be very handsome in any case. But I watch you describe him, and I see that you are interested in him, and this is a good thing."

"I agree James will always put his work first above everything else. Noah is also committed to his work, but I don't think it drives him in the same way that James is driven. There is something reserved in Noah I think, but I don't know what it is. I suppose he is rather conventional though, and responsible."

"And is that what interests you? That is not a good thing. When the moment comes that you find out what this Noah is holding back from you, the interest will disappear. Then what?"

Caroline considered for a moment. "Perhaps that will depend on what it is that he is holding back? And by then, I might care less."

Halfway through her second glass of vodka, Caroline decided to ask Galina about Matthew Monk. She was sceptical about Miss Kettle's observations, but she had remembered how Matthew had looked at Galina when they met at Vaughan Rickard's party, and the concern on Rebecca's face.

"Have you found anyone you find interesting recently?"

Galina drew deeply on her cigarette as Borodin's *Symphony number 2* swirled around them. "There is someone… who is decreasing in interest, though not yet to the point where I am no longer interested at all." She looked directly at Caroline, challenging her to say more.

"I would not like to be the wife of someone who was unfaithful."

"Yet you would be the mistress of an unfaithful husband. One situation cannot exist without the other."

Caroline looked at her shoes, feeling chastised. Galina knew about Max, in the vaguest terms and in the strictest confidence.

"There is a difference of some importance," Galina softened, "in that it is perhaps more immoral to continue something that could have been a single, spontaneous act."

"In either case, the woman, the mistress, is always painted in harsher colours." Caroline welcomed Galina's concession.

"Always. We are not meant to enjoy sex. Which is of course ridiculous, but where we have been liberated with the right to vote, we remain enslaved to men in so many ways. And do not imagine for one moment that my love for my husband has diminished in any way. No one, ever, could take Marius' place in my heart. But he is no longer in my bed, and being an independent woman allows me certain luxuries. Affairs are one such luxury."

Caroline nodded. The need to depend upon a man for security, income or a home universally led to women taking up with men who they would otherwise not give a second glance. She had not considered it a luxury before as Galina described it, but she could see now that it was. She thought about Noah; Caroline had the luxury of becoming involved with him because they liked each other, and not for any other reason. For so many women such as Annie or Lottie, if they wanted to leave their parent's home, they would only be able to do so if bound – metaphorically or religiously – to a man.

When Caroline returned to her father's apartment later that evening, having consumed more vodka and her eyes stinging a little from Galina's cigarette smoke, she could hear the rain falling outside. It was still humid, but a breeze had accompanied the rain and Caroline slept soundly. She dreamed of being surrounded with jewels of many colours and sizes, so many that she could not climb over them to reach the figure standing in silhouette some way off.

The topography of Helwell Bay was such that a stream locally known as The Swill, and officially as Doniford Stream, flowed out into the Bristol Channel a little way to the east of the main beach. This was not unusual around much of the coast of England; various streams, rills, cuts and rivers emptied their contents into the wider bodies of water. Heavy rain would often swell these rivers, leading to flooding of the adjacent farmland. While the tidal rise and fall along the coast of the Bristol Channel is normally within a relatively small range, the combination of rainwater swelling the rivers and an occasional high tide at the same time sometimes led to more significant flooding.

Noah had spent much of the weekend that Caroline had been in Cheltenham studying his charts and receiving weather reports. A very large low-pressure system had been deepening as it made its way across the Atlantic Ocean and Noah was concerned. He had been watching the clouds, sensing the subtle changes in the wind and temperature, and had come to the conclusion that the tides would be high enough over the next two or three days to cause some flooding in Watchet. The harbour wall would keep the worst of the swell away from the town, but the water would find its way into the harbour and further into the homes and businesses that were on the streets immediately behind the harbour office.

He had done his best to warn the townspeople. It had been difficult before the rain began, but as the wind picked up people begrudgingly took heed and started to move their possessions either upstairs or to friends and families' homes further into the town. Escott had sent some of the larger boats down the coast to Minehead to minimise the damage to those left at Watchet. Too many boats in the harbour would lead to the smaller ones being crushed and sunk.

Noah's own few possessions were safe above the boat-house. He slept on a narrow bed in a room next door to the harbour office. A small kitchen space and a toilet with a hand basin had recently been installed, but there was no bath. Noah made do with washing himself daily and took a weekly bath at the Anchor Inn in an upstairs room that was usually made available to visiting fishermen. He felt it was no great hardship to exist this way, given the conditions he had endured at the Western Front. However, he was conscious that he was getting older and eventually might want more comfort than the room provided, particularly if the range of movement in his leg decreased.

The rain fell across Exmoor and the Quantocks unimpeded. On ground that was already sodden, little more could be absorbed and soon the pools stretched further and further, joining each other and forming shallow lakes. The wind increased and an occasional low rumble of thunder vibrated in the heart of the granite boulders that were scattered across the landscape.

Caroline stared out of her carriage window as the train rocked and clinked along the tracks towards Taunton where she would need to change. The sky was solid grey, the trees were being buffeted by the wind and although the window was not streaked with rain it was clear that it was falling heavily. An elderly man read a newspaper opposite Caroline, and regularly blew his nose into his handkerchief. His grey overcoat was worn at the elbows, and he smelled faintly of camphor and shoe polish.

It had been a good weekend for Caroline. She was happy to see Annie and Jacob settled with little Victor in their new home, and to hear that Lottie was also expecting a baby. Sara was an agreeable housekeeper for Caroline's father George, and Caroline had very much enjoyed spending time with him again. Their relationship seemed to have changed subtly and while she could not put her finger on exactly how or why, she thought it something to do with her new-found independence. They had agreed that George would spend Christmas with Caroline that year, travelling down on Christmas Eve and returning to Cheltenham the day after Boxing Day. Neither of them had relished spending the day alone.

At Taunton Caroline had some cheese on toast for lunch in the station tearoom while she waited for her connecting train. She watched the other customers while she ate, wondering where they were heading and why. Four soldiers sat at one table, nursing mugs of steaming tea and smoking while they talked quietly. They were in uniform and looked as if they had been marching for a week. On another table a mother was cutting up small squares of bread for a toddler, while his older sister with her hair tied in pigtails with red ribbons swung her legs on her chair and prodded her own sandwich suspiciously. In the far corner, a young couple sat, leaning close towards each other across the table, holding hands and whispering earnestly to each other. Caroline studied them furtively over her toast. They appeared to be on the verge of an argument, each one attempting to withdraw their hand now and then but held fast by the other.

A woman in a pale blue overcoat and a matching hat approached Caroline and asked if she could share the table. Caroline agreed, saying she had almost finished. The woman was heavily made up with pale blue eye shadow and bright red lipstick badly applied. She ordered a toasted tea cake and a pot of tea, and then asked Caroline if she were travelling up the line or down.

"To the coast actually."

"Do you know, it has taken me all morning to get this far from Exeter? Honiton has trees down everywhere and of course around Sowton is flooded terribly. I really don't know that I shall reach Southampton today at this rate. Shocking weather for the summer, such as we've had, don't you agree?"

"Yes, it has been rather wet. Is it very bad further west?"

"One should say we are used to it by now, dear, but all the same I don't remember such flooding. They say the Barbican at Plymouth was flooded last night and there is a ship on the rocks at the Lizard. No one hurt thank goodness, but still a worry for all down there no doubt. My sister lives in Southampton, that's why I am headed there, and she says…"

Caroline let the woman continue uninterrupted and wondered what Noah was doing at that moment. Would he be up on the cliffs watching the weather and looking out for ships in distress? Or would he be in the harbour office with his maps and the radio receiver?

Noah was battling his way up Cleeve Hill in the wind and rain. He wanted a good look at the sea and to keep an eye out for any ships that were off course. One had come into the harbour that morning unexpectedly, with its engine needing attention. They had been heading to Fishguard with a load of china clay from Cornwall but had decided to take shelter at Watchet where one of the crew had relatives and let the storm pass while the engine was repaired. Their report of the sea state around Cape Cornwall confirmed Noah's concerns that the worst was still to come. It was as he reached the spot on the hill where he had first met Caroline that he suddenly thought of the Swill.

The river Washford ran through the centre of Watchet and out into the harbour through a brick outlet constructed by the Victorian townsmen. It was already threatening to overflow at Stoates Mill. The families who lived along its course were used to keeping their best possessions upstairs and Noah had not had to convince them to take any evasive action. But the Swill would often flood in the winter when there had been heavy rain inland. It would creep across the lane that led from the railway station to the beach and smother the fields for days. The railway, having been laid on sleepers set on a raised bed, was rarely flooded, but the residents of Doniford could not always reach the station.

If the tide was particularly high, there was a possibility of it reaching Quantock Cottage and Helwell View, and Noah couldn't remember when Caroline was due to return home.

10

BLOWN IN ON
THE STORM

Caroline stepped onto Doniford Halt platform at twenty minutes to four. The rain was still falling solidly, and she carried her umbrella ready to shield herself from it. She intended to walk the short distance to Quantock Cottage, have a cup of tea (which never tasted as good in cafés as the first cup made by the newly returned traveller to their own kitchen), then go out again to inform Mr Bright and Vi and Ron that she was safely home. As she walked through the ticket office, Mr Evans the station master called out to her.

"I wouldn't walk if I were you, Miss, the Swill is across the road. If you can wait a few minutes, I will telephone up to Bright and ask him to send the taxi down for you."

"That does seem rather extravagant Mr Evans, it's really not very far."

Evans looked at Caroline's feet. "You don't have your wellingtons packed?"

"No. Oh I see, perhaps a taxi would be a good idea then."

"Yes Miss, and even with your wellingtons, I doubt you'd

keep your feet dry. In any case, you can't see where you're walking, so you'll be best off waiting here."

Fifteen minutes later Caroline was deposited outside her gate along with her case, a bundle of letters, a cotton drawstring bag containing her clean laundry and a basket of provisions that Bright had sent with the taxi driver. She was happy that it had saved her the walk to the village and had appreciated Evans' intervention as the taxi drove cautiously through the water just outside the station yard.

While the tea was brewing, Caroline unpacked the basket of food then took her case upstairs to sort out her clothes. As she closed the wardrobe door, she glanced out of the bedroom window. The wind threw another splash of rain against the glass and thunder followed. Caroline peered through the distorted pane. The tide was evidently in, and much further in than she had seen it before. The spray from the closest breakers was visible over the hedge at the far end of the field across the lane. She shivered and pulled her cardigan closed across her chest, crossing her arms to keep it there. Part of her wanted to put on her wellingtons and coat and take a closer look, but the more sensible part pointed out that she was currently dry and there was a pot of tea in the kitchen that really shouldn't go to waste. The sea would still be there in the morning she said to herself as she descended the stairs.

The electricity went out just after Caroline had switched the radio on that evening to listen to the news broadcast. She sighed, switched the set off again and used a spill lit from the kitchen range to bring the small oil lamp from the sitting room to life. The wind was gaining strength and Caroline was reminded of the storm the previous January that she had been kept awake by. Was the roof of Quantock Cottage securely tiled? She hoped so. Caroline decided to assemble a bucket and a large enamel basin in the hallway just in case they were needed; she would take them upstairs when she went to bed.

For August, it was dark and gloomy at eight o'clock. Caroline was thankful for the small fire in the sitting room as without it everything quickly felt damp. She had picked through her letters earlier, opening the ones she thought were less important first and discarding those that were advertisements. This left two handwritten envelopes and Caroline knew who each was from. One, postmarked Malvern, was from Lina. Caroline read the three small sheets of neat handwriting first, noting that Lina was suffering with morning sickness and had engaged a nurse ready for her confinement. Her doctor had said he thought twins were a possibility and Lina was apprehensive about the birth. Caroline refolded the letter and put it back into the pale cream envelope. She liked Lina, but she found her curiously old fashioned and often wondered at her lack of interest in the world outside of her comfortable home. Her husband Albert was now a politician, yet Lina was happy to be excluded from his work unless she was entertaining his influential colleagues.

The other letter was in a pale blue envelope with an exotic stamp on the front and Midge's familiar hurried handwriting. Caroline had written to Midge in the first week she took up Quantock Cottage and had eagerly hoped for a quick reply from her friend – as quick as the African postal service allowed.

23 July 1927, Tanganyika
Dear Caroline,

Some sad news to start with I'm afraid. Marie-Claire is dead. It all happened so suddenly, I still have some difficulty believing that it is true, but it is. Last week we were cleaning out some old supplies in one of the huts in the compound, and Marie-Claire gave a shout. She had been bitten, we think now by a spider. Within two hours she had a fever, and by morning she had died. The bite on her hand swelled up enormously and turned quite black. The menfolk described something similar from their time in the trenches, but it was absolutely disgusting, and heart-breaking at the same time. We had only been friends for a few months, and even with the language barrier, I very much enjoyed her company.

We are waiting to hear if her parents want her remains shipped back to France or if she is to be buried here in the compound. There is a small cemetery, about a dozen graves in a small corner. There are no headstones, only simple wooden crosses that the brothers carve the name of the person into. No dates either. I shouldn't like to be buried here if anything were to happen to me.

I had been meaning to write and tell you about a recent trip Marie-Claire and I had made to a larger compound on the shore of Lake Tanganyika. We were attending a service of thanksgiving led by the Bishop and several clerics. The whole of our compound went in four large carts, driven by mules and local men. It was quite a spectacle to see so many people pouring in from all directions to the arena. We were seated on the ground for much of the service, but to hear the voices of all assembled raised in song and prayer was extraordinarily moving. We met several regional clerics at the meal afterwards, and one will be visiting our compound in a few weeks. His name is Oliver Gregson and he is an Oxford scholar.

A Tanganyikan girl has been brought in to help me, her name is Kanoni and she has as much English as Marie-Claire did when I first met her. Kanoni is a curious girl, I have no idea how old she is, no one seems to know for certain, but I would make a guess of perhaps 10 or 11 years old. Skin and bone, apparently only one dress to her name and no shoes, and they say she walks six miles to and from the compound every day. I am attempting to teach her some basic English, which can only help her in life. She is bright enough, and incredibly hard working for one so young.

Mother says the river is very high again this year and has flooded at Reading twice. If you are so close to the sea, is there a risk of you being flooded in your little house as well? I do hope not! It is most unpleasant; the water takes forever to recede and the mud it leaves behind is so difficult to clear up. I suppose it would be sand rather than mud if one lived near the sea.

I have a letter from Luke, just a short note really. He is engaged to a young nurse that he met at the hospital. I wonder if all of my brothers will marry nurses. Does that mean I should marry a doctor do you think? Mark is coming to our compound in a few days' time and I shall see him for a whole week. I am very much looking forward to that. It feels like forever since I saw him.

Do tell me more about Vi and Ron, they sound absolutely precious! I must write to Helen next, do you see much of her now you are living closer? Can you imagine her as a politician? The idea is rather amusing.

Looking forward to hearing from you
Much love
Midge

Caroline folded the letter and replaced it in the envelope. She shook her head at the thought of Luke being engaged so quickly to a young nurse. How her lovers positively pined away when she rebuffed them! She felt sorry for Midge, to lose Marie-Claire so soon after the two had become friends. Africa sounded a vibrant but rather dangerous place and Caroline had no desire to visit there.

She stood up and went to the sitting room window. Midge's comment about sand being an issue if the sea flooded the land had made Caroline feel uneasy. She peered out into the grey evening; the far hedge that enclosed the meadow closest to the sea was now being washed at its base by the water. It took a moment for Caroline to realise the water level would only have to rise by a couple of feet before it would advance across the meadow and be lapping at her front gate.

As she stood biting her lip nervously, Ron appeared pushing a wheelbarrow along the lane and into her front garden. Caroline went to the front door and opened it as he was about to knock. The strength of the wind surprised her; it had got up significantly since she had arrived home.

"Brought you some sandbags!" Ron shouted over the noise. "If you close the door, I'll pile them up against it. Might not need them, but better safe than sorry."

"Thank you! But what about the kitchen door?"

"No, you'll need to keep that free in case the sea gets this far, you don't want to trap the water in the house."

"Is it likely to, do you think? I had never considered we might be flooded until today."

"Have been before a few years ago, but it's not a regular thing. We're a bit higher up than you, it's never reached as far as us. I still put sandbags around the front door though, just in case. Go on now, close this and I'll see you're alright."

Caroline did as she was told. She looked at her wellington boots in the hallway and moved them to the second step of the stairs. Perhaps she should move some things into the spare room. No, surely the sea wouldn't reach her little house – it was August after all!

In Watchet, Noah was also handling sandbags. He had assembled a small group of men who were busily shovelling

sand from the builder's yard near the railway station into
empty coal bags. These were then loaded onto small carts
pulled by ponies and taken down the winding streets to
the houses near the river and harbour. Noah knew in his
heart that if the sea wanted to wash through the town, a
few bags of sand would do little to stop it, but they all felt
they needed to do something to defend their homes. He had
filled a few bags early on, but his leg and side had begun to
hurt, and he swapped with a young baker's lad called Jim
who now shovelled the sand into the bag while Noah held
it open. Noah felt old. He was now thirty-two. The damage
to his body that the war had inflicted troubled him more
when low pressure systems swept over-head and he knew
that this was as deep a depression as any they had known
during the summer for many years. All of the men's faces
were creased with concern and grime from their occupation.
They sweated profusely.

Despite the hard labour, Noah and the other men found
a sense of camaraderie in working together. They had done
so before when the town had been threatened with flooding.
It reminded Noah of being in the trenches with his fellow
soldiers. He usually tried not to remember those days; it had
taken him many months to quell the dreams and flashbacks
from his time at the front and he did not want them to
return. The rhythmical scraping of shovels and thump of full
sacks were echoes of the sounds that had become familiar
in France. Noah stood up for a moment while Jim went
for a fresh sack. The rain fell onto his skin as it had on the
Messine Ridge.

The tide was at its highest and had already breached the
wall by the harbour office. The road behind dipped lower
than the harbour wall and those few properties that stood
there solidly built of stone with walls three feet thick in

places had water a good ten inches deep inside their lower floors. Beyond that row of houses, the town rose gently and few others expected to be inundated the further they were from the river. Noah thought most would be safe that night, but the higher tide would be the following evening.

Caroline spent a restless night. Once it was dark outside, it was almost impossible to see how far across the meadow the sea had encroached. She stood at the bedroom window in the dark a couple of times and tried to make out any sense of a ripple or shimmer, but the moon was hidden by thick clouds. She went back to bed hoping that Ron was right and the sandbags would not be needed.

Wednesday morning was as grey and wet as the morning before. Heavy clouds lumbered their way eastwards up the Bristol Channel, tipping torrents of rain across the whole of the south-west of England. Caroline was awake at a little after six and immediately went to the bedroom window to survey the outlook. She breathed a sigh of relief as the meadow appeared to be only partially covered with water. Looking down into the front garden there seemed no evidence of invasion during the night. So far, Quantock Cottage remained untouched.

The electricity supply was still off. Caroline was thankful for the kitchen range and fed it more coal as part of her morning routine. After breakfast Caroline pulled on her wellingtons, an overcoat, and an old but serviceable sou'wester hat which she had discovered in the cupboard under the stairs, and went out to investigate the status of her surroundings. She did not get very far. Doniford Lane, the road that she had driven down only a few days before in Tommy's car to the station, was now impassable to all but the most sure-footed horses and wagons. Even then, Caroline thought, horses would shy at such an unknown depth of water. She could see the station buildings on the other side of the expanse of water but would not be able to reach them.

Caroline turned and walked a little way back towards her cottage to where the road forked and led to the sea. Here the river was almost across the whole road but not quite. Caroline skirted the water, hoping it would recede rather than completely flood her route while she was further from home. Mud and sand covered the road as it became a track to the beach; it was slippery and Caroline only went a little further before deciding she did not want to end up sprawled out across it with no one to help her stand up again. She picked her way up the bank that supported the meadow hedge to see what state the beach was in. Grasping hold of a sturdy but stunted Rowan tree, Caroline looked out at the water.

Reflecting the dark clouds above, today the sea looked as dark as wet slate, with peaks of white foam being whipped across the channel. The wind was still strong and roared in her ears. Thankful for the chin strap on the sou'-wester, Caroline squinted to keep the rain out of her eyes. The beach at Helwell Bay was normally covered with large pebbles and further out it turned to muddy sand. The rocks buried closer to the usual high tide mark acted as natural groins and prevented the pebbles from being moved too much along the coast. This morning, large numbers of pebbles were piled up against the stretches of rock and even more against the rise of cliff where Caroline had sketched Tommy. It reminded Caroline of the craters she had seen on newsreels of the war, the irregular arrangement on an aspect that would usually have been much flatter.

Caroline turned and looked across the top of the hedge into the meadow. Again, what had originally appeared to be flat now displayed a number of pools of standing water, and several large pieces of tree. Other bits of flotsam and jetsam were strewn across the meadow and beach: lobster pots, pieces of rope, broken wooden crates, all sporting patches of creamy-brown sea foam. While she stood clinging to the tree, Caroline determined the tide was on its way out. She knew it came in and out roughly twice each day but had not taken the trouble of finding out exactly the pattern of the tides.

Crows and gulls patrolled the meadow, picking over the seaweed for bugs, crabs and small fish. Caroline watched them for a few moments, noting how they generally avoided each other unless one found a tasty morsel. Then they would squabble loudly, though the wind and sea were still louder in Caroline's ears. Amongst the larger birds, a magpie strutted and scuttled. Every now and then it tried to take off, only to be blown further back from its starting point.

Caroline returned to Doniford Lane and kept going past her own cottage and up to Vi and Ron's. They welcomed her inside and offered her tea and toast. She accepted the tea and spent an hour with them asking what she should do in case the tide was higher that evening. Ron advised her to move any rugs and valuables upstairs, along with as many buckets as she could find – some filled with coal for the bedroom fireplace, and others empty in case of a leaking roof or a more intimate requirement. Caroline nodded; the bathroom was a luxury but it was also downstairs. Vi was concerned that Caroline was on her own.

"You are more than welcome to stay in our spare room for a few days, dear, isn't she Ron?"

"Of course! We can move your best bits of furniture upstairs and then you can pack a case and come back here."

"Thank you very much, both of you, but the sea only came a little way across the meadow last night and I'm sure it will be alright."

Vi and Ron exchanged glances. Vi said "If that's what you want, dear. But you can knock on our door any time, you know that."

Noah had spent the morning working a hand pump to try and lower the water level in the lane behind the harbour office. A long tube had been laid to the harbour wall and men and women with large brushes were attempting to sweep the mud away with the water. Escott approached him carrying a tin mug of hot tea.

"Going down much?"

Noah shook his head. "Not that you'd notice, but at least it feels like I'm doing something. Thanks. Much damage?"

Escott had been inspecting the boats sheltering in the harbour. "A little, mostly where the fenders had come untied. I've heard the trains are only running as far as Taunton this morning, and Exeter is cut off."

"These summer storms are so unpredictable. For a while I thought it would move towards Ireland, as you know."

"So did the boys at the Met. Anyone who thinks it's an exact science is a damned fool. We just have to deal with whatever the sea brings."

"Tonight will be the test."

"Ahh. Reckon we'll have another couple of feet before dawn. Those new gardens in Minehead will be swamped, I always said they left them too open to the elements. You're looking tired, boy. Leave that now and get some sleep before the next tide. No one will think badly of you for it and if they do, I'll put them straight."

Noah rubbed his face with his free hand feeling the stubble on his cheeks. "I might take an hour's nap. Then I need to check there is nothing out in the channel heading our way."

An hour turned into three. Noah woke hungry and feeling as if he had only slept for twenty minutes. He washed, changed his sweater and ate a small, cold meat pie before collecting his binoculars, satchel and coat. He climbed Cleeve Hill, leaving the road and taking the footpath as close to the edge of the cliff as he dared. Reaching his preferred spot, he lifted the binoculars to his eyes and scanned the horizon. With the rain and low cloud, the horizon was considerably closer than usual. He had known it would be difficult to see anything, despite being in his elevated position. Turning towards Minehead, he could see the beach at Blue Anchor but the town to the west was obscured.

Noah remembered Caroline standing with him on the same spot, excited to see so far with his help. He really should find out whether the Swill had burst its banks, someone at the railway station would know. He packed his binoculars into their case and started back towards Watchet, blown to stumble regularly by the wind.

On returning to Quantock Cottage, Caroline decided to roll up the rugs on the ground floor and carry them up to the spare bedroom. She had appreciated Ron and Vi's offer of help but was reluctant to seem an incapable townswoman. If she intended to make her home near to the sea, she would need to be prepared to deal with a flood occasionally. After the rugs, she stood with her hands on her hips in the kitchen. She wondered how high the water might be if it breached the sandbags at the front door. A couple of inches? A foot? What else was at floor level that could be damaged?

There was little in the kitchen that needed moving once Caroline's easel was safely stowed in the spare bedroom. In the sitting room, Caroline took the books from the lower shelves of the bookcase and piled them up on the spare bed. The furniture was not hers, and had no sentimental value, so she resolved to leave it all where it stood. The radio was the one valuable item, and with a little difficulty she carried the cumbersome box up to her own bedroom and stood it on the floor by her bed and near to the electricity socket. She plugged it in to make sure that it was still working, and then realised there was still no electricity and even if there had been there would be no programmes until the news at six o'clock. She turned it off again. Caroline felt nervous. The rain fell incessantly, the wind roared, a train rumbled into the station at the bottom of her garden. It was almost two o'clock and she had not eaten lunch. She would make do with an apple as she was not particularly hungry, but to pass the time she would peel some potatoes and carrots to have with a lamb chop as an early dinner.

A rumble of thunder. Caroline counted, "One, thunderstorm, two thunderstorm, three thunderstorm, four." A flash of lightning. She looked at the clock on the mantlepiece and decided to put her knitting to one side and start dinner. It was ten minutes past five. She had been working on the second sock for her father's Christmas present and still had to concentrate hard on the pattern as she knitted on four thin needles. Caroline went to the sitting room window again, but as yet there was no sign of sea spray over the far hedge. Reassured, she went through to the kitchen.

Noah dripped rain across the ticket office floor.

"Oh yes, burst a couple of days ago. Can only get in and out of the yard with a cart now. Evans is alright, and the trains are still running as far as Taunton." The station master at Watchet shouted over the sound of the thunder through the ticket office window.

"So there would be no point in taking the train to Doniford?" Noah asked.

"Not unless you've got webbed feet!"

Noah shook his head and smiled his thanks to the station master. The train would have taken just ten minutes, he could have checked on Caroline and been back in Watchet for high tide.

Why on earth had she taken a house so remote? It made no difference to him now how hard it rained, he was wet through. Back at the harbour, where temporarily they could get into the office again, Noah wearily climbed the stone steps. Escott was sat at the desk, speaking into the telephone.

"…No…..Well that can't be helped…No…..Then you'd be a damned fool! Keep them there for another day and let this one move on….There's no room I tell you!…Nothing past Taunton at the moment…Right. I'll let you know in the morning. Goodbye."

"Bristol?"

"Cardiff. Got a Captain who wants to drop his load here."

"Why here?"

"Doesn't want to go any further west in all this!" He waved his hand towards the window. "Let's hope he stays put for another twenty-four hours."

"What's the cargo?"

"Coal. Oh I know, we need it, but I don't want a wreck on my hands tonight any more than you do. A big wave and the load could shift, it'd go down in minutes just like the *Arabella Jane* did in 'twenty-two."

"Anything else on the water?"

"Not that I know of. That barge that was on its way from Bristol has put in at Clevedon until this storm passes. A few trawlers along the Welsh coast but nothing this side for us to worry about." He studied Noah. "But you are worried, aren't you? What is it, lad?"

"Doniford Swill has burst. I thought I might go over and check on Ron Saddington and his wife, you know they live near the station there."

Escott nodded. He was no fool. He knew the Saddingtons would be unlikely to need any assistance and Noah was not exactly a family friend. The cottage nearer to the station was more at risk of flooding. He looked at the clock on the wall. "By the time you get there, it'll be close to high tide. Nothing more to be done here now."

"I won't be any longer than necessary."

"Take as long as you need, boy. The sea is your remit, the harbour is mine. I'll cope."

Noah knew, on paper, that was the way of things. Yet in reality, the two men worked as a team. He put his dripping satchel and binoculars on the table and went back out into the storm.

The coast road, Noah judged, would be safer than the coastal footpath and he'd be less likely to stumble over and twist an ankle or worse. Still, as he climbed up from the town and above the railway, he was buffeted and at times made to stand still by the wind. If he had been able to measure the strength, he would have known the gusts were reaching 70 miles per hour. Not for the first time he questioned what he was doing. He did not have to leave Watchet, he could have changed into dry clothes and stayed in the harbour office until or unless the sea breached the harbour again. The boat had been taken out of the boathouse and tied up at the rear of the office building, ready to rescue anyone who needed help if the town flooded more extensively. He should be there to help, but something was driving him towards Caroline. He had to make sure she was safe.

It was a short but steep climb. As he reached the top of the rise, the wind took his breath away and roared in his ears. It began to hail. He thrust his hands into his pockets to protect them but found walking even more difficult as his arms were no longer providing momentum. His legs felt unusually heavy and despite the hard road surface he stumbled occasionally. The hail grew in size and intensity. The road was white with it, icy pellets stung his face. Noah felt as if he were starting to suffocate; the noise, the sensation of being covered, the pain now growing in his hip and leg. He lurched sideways, slipped and fell against the hedge, down on one knee. He swore and remained there for some moments until the hail eased and the sound of it quieted. With mud on his hands and trousers, he struggled to get to his feet again and kept going, breathing hard.

Caroline was in her bedroom once again for a better look at the approaching sea. The hail had obscured her view for some minutes, and she felt the cold draught from where the window frame did not quite fit the opening in the wall. She made a mental note to stuff it with newspaper before the winter. There were a few moments of calm at the end of the hail shower. Everything had been covered in tiny white balls the size of peas. It looked surreal in August, yet it did not feel like August at all.

The calm broke as another gust of wind assaulted Quantock Cottage full on. The sea was now against the far meadow hedge, the spray and dirty foam lifting over it as it had the day before. It was mesmerising, Caroline felt she could not look away. If she could stay there watching, perhaps the sea would not cross the meadow and surround her. She shook her head and scolded herself for having such an infantile notion. But still, she thought, a watched pot never boils. She looked across to the bedside clock; another hour before the radio broadcast would begin if the electricity would only return by then. It was disorienting to have such bad weather for so long in the summer. Caroline had pictured herself enjoying long warm evenings sitting in the back garden surrounded by flowers and birdsong when she first thought of taking the cottage. The grey skies were oppressive, the rain confining and the wind headache-inducing. This was not the summer she had imagined.

Noah reached the edge of Doniford and leaned against a field gate for a moment to steady his legs. He was shaking and felt cold and heavy. He could hear the sea mingled with the wind's continued roar, and despite the pain in his side and back, and legs that he could barely lift to take steps in any direction, he pushed himself away from the gate and continued along the lane. Naturally, Noah was the only human outside. A few homes had faint lights glowing in their sitting rooms and front parlours, but the majority in the hamlet were dark. A dog barked as he passed, safe inside its kennel. A newspaper was wrapped around the corner of a corrugated iron shed, plastered there by the wind and rain. A shed door swung and creaked on its hinges. Noah thought he could hear gunshots. He stopped in the middle of the lane, swaying a little, trying to distinguish each sound and decide whether he could really hear it or if it was a product of his memory. Satisfied that the gunshots were imagined, he started off again.

His teeth were chattering. Was it really that cold? Focus on the road he told himself, one foot in front of the other, as he had in France. He left the hamlet behind, and Helwell View became visible through the horizontal rain. The trees that lined one boundary bent violently away from the house towards the railway line behind the cottage. A piece of cloth, perhaps a tea towel, was caught in the branches, bright white against the grey surrounding it. Noah knew Ron and Vi would be safe from the sea; Helwell View was built on a rise in the land with a pathway leading up from the road that incorporated several steps to the cottage.

Only a few more yards to Caroline's front door. The effort of standing straight when the wind constantly blew from one side was almost overwhelming. The hail began again; Noah was once more convinced that he could hear gunfire.

Caroline was in the kitchen when she heard a thump against the front door. She hurried into the sitting room and tried to see what had made the noise through the window but as the window was flush to the cottage wall, she could only see directly in front of her. The hail was still crashing down and everything had turned white again. She went into the hallway and called out but there was no reply. Caroline went up to her bedroom and looked down from that window. She let out a gasp when she realised the crumple of clothing and boots slouched over the sandbags was a man. She hurried back downstairs, put on her wellingtons and coat and went out through the kitchen and around the side of the cottage.

Noah heard Caroline as if she were at the end of a long tunnel, calling his name. He felt hands touch his face. He looked up but could not trust what he was seeing. He understood that he was being urged to get up, but he wanted to sleep. Now that he was semi-reclined, his legs had stopped trembling and he was starting to feel warmer, although the word feel was perhaps an optimistic one.

Caroline shouted at Noah, turned his head to face her as he lay against the sandbags. His eyes were open, she was relieved to see, but what on earth was he doing out in such a storm! She tried to pull at his coat, encouraging him to get up. The hail was stinging her legs, hands and face. She couldn't just leave him there, she had to get him inside. Caroline was about to take off and run to Ron and Vi when Noah moved his arm and began to try and push himself off the sandbags. Caroline did her best to get her hands under his armpits, then wriggled herself under his arm so that she could support him better. Slowly they staggered back around the cottage and into the kitchen where Noah sank onto the chair by the range, dripping across the kitchen floor from head to toe.

Caroline stood in front of him, her hands again either side of his face to tilt his head upwards.

"Noah, can you hear me?"

"Caroline?" His thoughts were slowly martialling themselves into some sort of order. He was no longer outside. The rain and hail no longer lashed his skin. The crashing in his ears was fading. But the pain in his side and legs was still there. Pain was good, his Captain had told him as they carried him out of the trench; pain meant he was still alive. Noah's head swum, he leaned to the side and vomited on the floor.

Caroline had moved just in time. She took the tea towel from the rail on the range and wiped Noah's face. He seemed to be waking out of his stupor, and she talked to him quietly, gently.

"We need to get you out of those wet clothes and into bed. Do you think you can manage the stairs? Let me help you stand... that's it, now let's have your coat off... good, now just move this way a little so you don't slip."

Noah stood and his legs began to tremble again. He shrugged out of his coat and then gripped the kitchen table for a moment, fighting the urge to vomit again. His senses were returning and he was deeply embarrassed. This was not how he had imagined his arrival at Caroline's cottage would be. He allowed himself to be manoeuvred out of the kitchen to the bottom of the stairs. They were too narrow for two people to climb side by side and in the end, Noah ascended on all fours and used the banister at the top to help him stand again.

Caroline steered him into her bedroom, the bed of the spare room being covered with books from the sitting room and pots and pans from the kitchen. The years of nursing her mother would have some use after all, she thought as she unlaced Noah's boots and took off his sodden socks. She still had no idea why Noah had walked to Doniford in such bad weather, but she focused on the task at hand; removing his clothes and getting him covered up with sheets and blankets to try and stop what she observed to be shivering. Noah was co-operative, ready to abandon his embarrassment for the moment and lay down on a soft, dry bed. Though every item of clothing was wet, Caroline spared Noah the indignity of removing his underwear. She noticed the scars on his arms and shoulders and thought no more of them; she had seen similar on many men as they had worked with their shirt sleeves rolled up on a hot summer's day.

An hour later Caroline sat in the kitchen waiting for the kettle to boil again. She had left Noah to sleep, carried his wet clothes downstairs and washed out his trousers and socks before hanging everything on the clothes horse in front of the range to dry out. The woollen fabric would take some time and was currently still dripping onto newspaper on the floor beneath. The rest of the kitchen floor had been cleaned, and a basin placed beside her bed just in case. It had been a distraction from the storm if nothing else! The kettle began to sing; she retrieved it with a tea towel folded over the handle and poured the water onto the tea leaves in the pot on the table. Then she placed the small saucepan of carrots and potatoes onto the range top, and the tray with two lamb chops into the small oven space.

While the tea brewed, she went to look out of the sitting room window again. There had been no more hail, but she was shocked to see that the water was half-way across the meadow with the waves clawing their way over the hedge. Foam was blown around the field and clung to the hedge that bordered the lane to the beach. It was only then that Caroline understood Noah had been concerned for her well-being and had driven himself to walk from Watchet on her behalf. She was indignant; what an idiotic thing to do! Of course she would be perfectly alright, even if the cottage did flood – and it still might, a small voice in her head told her – she would be able to take care of herself. Now she had to take care of Noah as well. She hoped that he wouldn't need a doctor, that would require her to go out in the storm and walk up to Doniford. Goodness, how ridiculous he had been. And what of Watchet and the fishermen? What use was he upstairs in her bed when they would surely need him back at the harbour?

She stopped herself mid-rant. He had been worried about her safety, not his own. It was Caroline's turn to feel ashamed.

11

REALITY SETS IN

Noah dreamed. He was under the earth again. Mud was in his mouth, his ears, his eyes, pinning his arms and legs in unnatural positions. He tried not to breathe, but he had to open his mouth and he could taste the mud, feel it stick to his tongue, trickle down his throat. He tried to move his arms, tried to reach above his head, not knowing if that way was up. He tried to kick his feet, as if he were swimming, perhaps he could push his way out to the surface…

Caroline turned away from her bedroom window as Noah began to move under the covers. He kicked and writhed; he had been laying almost on his stomach with one arm underneath him. Caroline crossed the room and was about to put her hand on his shoulder when he jerked and gasped himself awake. He lay for a moment breathing heavily, licking his lips. Then he rolled awkwardly onto his back and looked up at Caroline. It took him a moment to remember where he was.

"Would you like a drink of water? I think you were dreaming."

"Please." His voice was hoarse.

Caroline held the glass to his lips, and he sipped just a little before falling back on to the pillow again. He closed his eyes and Caroline thought he was going back to sleep. She put the glass back on the bedside table and was about to go through to the spare room when Noah spoke.

"I'm sorry."

She turned back to the bed. "There is really no need to be. Get some more sleep and see how you feel tomorrow." She pulled the blankets up over his shoulder. The room was in deep shadow but she noticed the stubble on his face.

Noah considered saying more, but he was so very tired.

Caroline got into the spare bed. It was only a quarter to nine but there was nothing more to be done that day. She would hear Noah in the night if he needed anything as she had left the doors open. The sea had reached almost to the near hedge that stood between the meadow and the lane and if it decided to come in, Caroline thought as she opened the novel she was reading, so be it. She tried to read but found she couldn't concentrate. She turned out the lamp and wriggled down the bed. The sheet smelled a little musty, but she did not want to sleep in a chair when there was a perfectly good bed to be had.

Thursday morning.

Caroline lay in the spare bed hardly daring to breathe, straining her ears to hear any watery noises coming from below. There were none. The wind still blew, but with much less ferocity than the night before, and the rain fell gently against the window. It occurred to Caroline that the wind must have changed direction; the rear windows of the cottage had not been blasted with rain like the front windows during the storm. She rolled over, pushed off the covers and shuffled her feet into her slippers. She had left her dressing gown in her own bedroom on the back of the door, so she put on her cardigan from the day before and went downstairs.

There was no water on the hall floor. Caroline let out a breath of relief. She went into the sitting room and could see no sign of sea invasion in the front garden. There was foam on the meadow hedge on the other side of the lane, and it hung like ugly blossom on the crab apple tree by her garden gate, but there was no evidence of the tide on the lane itself. Caroline smiled to herself; they had weathered the storm. It was almost seven o'clock. She shovelled some more coal into the range before using the bathroom, then began to prepare breakfast.

Half an hour later, Caroline carried a tray up to her bedroom and nudged the door open further. Noah looked at her from his place on the bed.

"Good morning. How are you feeling today?"

Noah smiled weakly. "Embarrassed. Humbled." He glanced at the tray. "Hungry."

"Are you able to sit up?"

Slowly Noah raised himself and dragged his body to a sitting position. He moved to one side of the bed so that Caroline had room to sit there as well. Caroline moved some of her things on the dressing table and transferred the teapot and rack of toast before passing the tray to Noah. Then she retrieved the teapot and poured out two cups. There were scrambled eggs, fried bacon and tomatoes on two plates and a saucer with a knob of butter.

"Try not to eat too quickly now." Caroline said as she dropped two sugar cubes into Noah's teacup.

They ate in almost silence. Noah tried to chew each mouthful as many times as possible realising that he had hardly eaten anything beyond the meat pie over the past two days. Caroline got up for the toast and poured a little more tea. When they had finished every morsel, she took the tray from Noah's legs and put it back onto the dressing table.

"Your coat is still rather wet I'm afraid, and your trousers are damp, but your shirt is dry. I can iron it if you'd like."

"I shall need to excuse myself. I don't know if I can rely on my legs just yet."

"Do you want to try?"

Noah considered his situation. "I am only wearing my underclothes. I don't remember getting undressed…"

"You needed a little help. I couldn't have you soaking the bed by keeping them all on. Here, if I stand in front of you, you can hold my hands to stand up. Then if you feel able, take a few steps."

They conducted their strange waltz across the bedroom and along the short landing, before Caroline suggested that Noah descend the stairs backwards. She collected the breakfast tray and followed Noah into the kitchen. It occurred to her that if she had neighbours other than Ron and Vi, she would be feeding the scandalous gossip which would no doubt be roaring around the countryside about her. Having had Noah to stay overnight, unchaperoned, and seeing him gingerly crossing the kitchen in his vest and shorts. Did she care? She decided she did not.

Noah emerged from the bathroom and Caroline persuaded him to return to bed for a while longer. He did not protest, and slowly climbed the stairs with his hands on the treads. Caroline washed up the breakfast things and then took his shirt, socks and trousers up to him.

"I don't think you should put these on just yet. I do have a pair that might fit you though." Caroline put the clothes on a chair and opened her wardrobe. She pulled out Freddie's trousers.

"Why do you have a man's trousers in your wardrobe? Or is that another thing that I should not ask you about?"

"They belonged to my brother." She said simply. Their eyes met for a moment before Noah looked away.

"I'm sorry. I seem to be apologising a lot. You just behave in ways so extraordinary. Everything you do is so beyond what one expects of a young woman today."

"You make it sound as if I'm misbehaving." Caroline laid Freddie's trousers on the end of the bed and sat down.

"I don't mean to, I'm sorry..." They both laughed quietly. "Caroline, can we go back to when we ate the crab in your kitchen? Can you forget how stupid I have been since then? I don't quite understand why I reacted so to seeing you with your friend, but it seems that when we forget about other people, we get along so much better."

"You mean, like sitting here in my bedroom with you in a state of undress?"

"I do. I know you, but I don't know if I will ever completely know you, and I think... I think that is what attracts me to you."

He was about to say more when a grimace of pain crossed his face.

"What is it? Are you alright? Should I find a doctor?"

"No, no I shall be alright in a moment. I get pains, in my side and legs, there seems no reason for them though the doctors say it is damage to my nerves. If I can lay down for a moment, it will pass." He slid down the bed on to his side, with his head on one pillow.

Caroline turned around and lay down on top of the covers, her head level with Noah's on the second pillow.

"You see," he said with a smile, "no other woman would do that."

"I want to see your face when I talk to you. And after all, it is my bed." They smiled at each other for a moment. "I saw your scars."

"I got off lightly. Others suffered more."

"I have seen." She did not want to think of Max, but he came to her mind regardless. I will not compare them, she told herself resolutely. "Don't talk about it if it's too painful."

"The dreams are as bad as the real thing."

"You were dreaming last night."

"Sometimes it's as if I am dreaming when I am awake. Thankfully not as often as when I first returned home, but sometimes…"

Caroline put her hand on Noah's arm. They were no longer smiling. They moved closer, Caroline still on top of the covers, Noah still underneath, until they were embracing. They stayed there for some time.

They talked quietly, colouring in some of the conversations they had had previously. Caroline explained her teenage years and how they had been enclosed. It went some way to explain her naivety, Noah understood. She had been exposed to very little that had caused her mother to comment in disapproving terms within Caroline's hearing. The tea party circles on Thursday afternoons had bored Caroline so she had never really listened to what was being said. In his turn, Noah talked about his older brother Peter, about the sea and its moods, about the responsibility of his position. This last point, at almost eleven o'clock, prompted him to release his hold of Caroline and attempt to sit up.

"I need to get back to Watchet."

"You can't walk that far; you can hardly make it down the stairs."

"I can't leave Escott to do everything. They will have had more flooding."

Caroline sat up and swung her feet off the bed. "I will take my bicycle to the Post Office and telephone from there. You can go tomorrow if you are stronger."

Noah did not argue.

Caroline returned from the Post Office and informed Noah that she had spoken to Escott and explained that Noah was unwell and would not return to work until the following Monday.

This time Noah did argue. "Monday?! No, that's far too long, I can't just leave my post."

"Escott said you are to take your time to recover. He was really very good about it all. I explained that I was on my way to ask the doctor to call and that if you were not able to return on Monday, I would telephone him again."

"You lied?"

"I did not! I called on Doctor Bentley and he will be here later this afternoon. We have enough provisions, and Mr Bright seems to think the electricity will return by tomorrow so we will have the radio to entertain us." She smiled, "and I would like you to stay until you are better."

"You really don't care about your reputation, do you?"

"I have no reputation to care about. Oh, but I had quite forgotten! I am expected at Helen and Tommy's on Saturday for her party!"

"Perhaps we'll be able to walk to the station by then, and I can get the train to Watchet."

"Or you could come with me? If you feel able. If not, I shall have to tell Helen that I won't be able to attend after all." Caroline did not sound to Noah as if she would be terribly upset to miss the party, but he did not want to be the reason for her absence.

"I'm sure after another good night's sleep I shall be back to my old self."

Doctor Bentley did not share Noah's optimism. He diagnosed nervous exhaustion and prescribed a week at least with as little exertion as possible, much to Noah's displeasure. When the Doctor had gone, Caroline brought an armful of books for Noah to read while she set about making bread, some scones and a thin broth from the lamb chop bones and some vegetables in the kitchen.

So it was that they lived in domestic solitude for another day, as the waters slowly receded around the railway station yard and the beach re-emerged from beneath the waves. It was as if they had always been together; neither felt uncomfortable in the other's presence. Thursday evening Caroline had fallen asleep again on top of the covers beside Noah but woke when it was dark and returned to the spare room. On Friday night, Noah was recovered enough for Caroline to spend the night back in her own bed, and he moved to the spare room.

By Saturday Noah was in need of a shave and some clean clothes. "I cannot arrive at a stranger's house for a party looking like this!" he protested.

"If we go at lunchtime, I'm sure Tommy will let you borrow his shaving things, or you could visit the barber when we arrive in Minehead."

"It's been a while since I was last in that town. I remember there is McIlroy's, I could purchase some more appropriate clothes."

Caroline realised she had no idea whether Noah was a pauper or an heir apparent. Noah seemed to read her thoughts.

"I have a little put by. In truth, I don't need to spend much and as you know I sleep at the harbour office."

"You have no other house?"

"It has never been necessary. I spent so much time in the harbour office when I came back from hospital, I never got round to finding my own place."

"And your parents? Are they close by?"

"They live just outside Porlock now. Used to have a bigger house in Watchet but when Father gave up fishing, they moved to a smaller cottage that used to belong to a great aunt on Mother's side. I suppose I could take their spare room, but it's a way from Watchet. I shall inherit one day, but both are in rude health."

Caroline once again cycled into Doniford and requested the services of the brothers who operated a motor car as well as a horse and cart as a taxi. They arrived promptly at one o'clock, and ferried Caroline and Noah across the flooded railway yard. The trains were running almost to time, and they arrived in Minehead at a little before two. Caroline was concerned that Noah would tire as he walked through the town, but he assured her that he was well enough not to require a taxi at that end of their journey as well. She left him at McIlroy's and continued to Helen and Tommy's house.

Daisy Clare had already arrived. They embraced and chattered as Caroline was shown up to the room she had stayed in previously.

"Actually, Helen, I'm afraid that a friend of mine will be joining us shortly, I hope that's alright. If you don't have the room, we can absolutely find a hotel, it's still early."

Helen's face slowly broke into a smile. "Darling Caro, of course you shall have the larger room across the landing and your friend can have this room! Unless, of course ..."

"No, two rooms please. I'm sorry I couldn't let you know sooner; it's really been quite a week."

"Then we shall require tea and sandwiches so that we can hear all about it. Come along Daisy, let's go and see what Mrs Rich can magic up for us!"

When Caroline had explained the events of the week, and Helen and Daisy had pronounced their happiness for her, Caroline asked after Tommy.

Helen lit a cigarette before she answered. "He has gone to collect Christopher."

"Really? Christopher will be at the party tonight?" Helen noted the concern in Caroline's question.

"He will. Tommy was insistent. He feels it is highly unlikely that anyone here in Minehead will know Christopher, and he promises to behave himself. I believe he will, he knows how important this evening is to me."

Caroline was going to say more, but the sound of the doorbell jangled through the house.

"I wonder if that is your young man?" Daisy speculated.

Mrs Rich opened the door and showed Noah into the front sitting room. Noah's transformation caught Caroline by surprise.

Helen stood and offered Noah her hand, "Good afternoon, Mr Kingston, I am very pleased to meet you. May I introduce Miss Daisy Clare? And I believe you are acquainted with Caroline."

"A pleasure, madam." Noah kissed Helen's fingers lightly and then turned to Caroline. "We are well acquainted," he said with a smile.

Caroline was entranced. Noah looked debonaire in his new suit, clean shaven and with his hair trimmed and greased back from his forehead. Dashing, she thought, and rather like a film star.

"You'll take tea, Mr Kingston? It's a little early for anything else."

Caroline shot her friend a look, knowing full well that Helen had no real objection to champagne for breakfast if the mood took her.

"Thank you, yes, and please call me Noah. This is a very fine house you have. Is your husband at work?" He took the cup and saucer that looked tiny and delicate in his hands.

Helen lit another cigarette after Noah declined one, "My husband is an artist. He is collecting a friend who will also be joining us this evening."

"Of course, an artist like Caroline." Noah smiled at Caroline and she felt her face turn pink. There was something in the way Noah said the word 'artist' that made her feel uncomfortable.

"And Miss Clare, Caroline has told me about you too, you have a bookshop in Dunster?"

As they chatted, Caroline was impressed with how at ease Noah appeared. She was pleasantly surprised that he remembered much of what she had told him about her friends. Daisy was also impressed with Noah and asked him several questions about the weather reports and charts that he used for his work. Helen remained reserved, as if considering Noah's suitability, the way a parent might.

"How many guests will there be this evening?" Caroline asked Helen while Daisy and Noah stood at the drawing room window and discussed cloud formations.

"One hopes for thirty. Mrs Rich has been an absolute Godsend; the canapés are being prepared as we speak. When Tommy returns, I shall ask him to supervise the drinks provision in each room."

"He is very good at making cocktails. Thirty is rather a lot."

"One needs to make the right impression with the right inhabitants. With the election only a few days away, every moment counts. I really should be out canvasing but ensuring the influential votes tonight is my priority."

"I noticed the placard on the front lawn as I arrived. I saw two posters on my way through the town as well."

"The ward I am contesting is not on your route here from the station. We have spent weeks handing out leaflets and such-like in Alcombe. I was quite hoarse last week from the speeches I had to give. Really it has been far more work than I had anticipated, but I do think the people of Alcombe appreciate my efforts."

The party was a huge success for Helen. She made her entrance down the staircase once all of the guests had arrived, wearing a royal blue backless evening gown in satin and chiffon, to a round of applause. Alcohol flowed, with Tommy as mobile barman between the rooms mixing cocktails on demand for all. Christopher's introductions had been brief, as he and Tommy arrived after the first guests had been admitted. Mrs Rich and two other young women of her acquaintance served the canapés and other buffet morsels while dressed in black and white uniforms. Daisy hovered on the edge of various circles, desperately trying not to talk too much or too loudly but listening intently.

Noah felt more tired than he had admitted to Caroline. He made his drinks last as long as possible before allowing his glass to be refilled, often bringing the glass to his lips without drinking any of the contents at all. It was a trick he had learned from a young sergeant who had disliked gin and brandy but so desperately wanted to be accepted by his men. He chatted to guests, who were superficially interested in his employment, just as he was superficially in their political leanings. Noah had always been able to fit in with any social circle; his time in the army had been marked with frequent instances of being taken into the confidence of officers younger and older than himself. He was aware that he was not accompanying Caroline as he might otherwise have done if the hosts were not well known to her. Now and then he would glance across the room to check on her, and to appreciate her from a distance.

For her part, Caroline had adopted the role of Christopher's attendant for the evening. Recognising that Tommy would need to support Helen, and that neither she or Christopher would know any of the other guests, Caroline felt they could sit and observe the company together. She also wanted to know more about the object of Tommy's affections. They sat in the conservatory together, which had been illuminated with many small candles and lamps for the evening. Caroline wore her short, black, beaded dress. She was the only female guest with her calves on display.

"How did you and Tommy meet?" She asked, draining her second Sidecar.

"In Exeter, at the jazz club in the Mint. We were both with other friends. Got talking at the bar and, well…" He spoke with a soft, slightly effeminate voice. Sitting with his legs crossed and smoking, he reminded Caroline of a photograph she had seen of Oscar Wilde. Christopher had similar dark hair, worn a little longer than one would expect of a chemistry teacher. His hair was his only distinguishing feature. His face was bland with no freckles or pockmarks, he was of average height and build. His suit was grey tweed with a matching waistcoat. Caroline wondered if his outward appearance had somehow been cultivated to enable him to blend into academia rather than stand out.

"You teach chemistry?"

"I do. While I was at Durham I taught first year students occasionally and took some of the classes at the Grammar School when they needed cover. Once I'd graduated, I applied for the position I had previously at the Exeter School. Then, thankfully a position came up at the University when I had to leave the school."

Caroline was aware that every sentence had nuance. She wondered if Christopher had been forced to leave Durham. She decided not to ask. Instead, she said, "Tommy is enjoying himself, don't you think?"

"Tommy always enjoys a party."

"And you do not?"

"Not as much, no. I prefer singular conversations. Your friend Kingston also seems to be well suited to this atmosphere."

"Doesn't he? Have you ever been to sea, Christopher?"

"Oh no. I once tried punting on a river. It didn't end well. I'm afraid I'm rather uncoordinated." He blushed. "Have you travelled?"

Caroline was relieved to be asked a question at last. "Not abroad, no, but I do like to visit places in this country. I've spent some time in Dorset, last year I went on an art holiday in Cornwall, and I went up to Blackpool when Helen and Tommy were married, that was rather fun to see the illuminations."

Christopher crossed his legs in the opposite direction. "Yes, Tommy has explained Blackpool to me." He looked as if he were suffering a spasm of pain, the grimace on his face caught Caroline by surprise.

"I say, are you alright? Shall I get you another drink?"

"No, no thank you, a little indigestion, I think. Please, tell me more about Dorset."

The guests started to leave just before midnight. By one in the morning, only those staying at the Gersen-Fisch residence overnight remained. Helen looked radiant, Tommy flopped down in the chair next to Christopher and handed him one more cocktail.

Daisy covered a yawn with her hand as she joined the others in the conservatory.

"I'm pooped! Helen you have been magnificent this evening, dear. Alcombe South could do no better than to have you representing them." Daisy said sleepily.

"Thank you. I have had similar assurances from one or two notable guests this evening. Tommy, would you mix me a dry vermouth?" She took his seat as he vacated it. "And have you all enjoyed yourselves?"

It was agreed that everyone had. Caroline could see Noah was tired, and she made their excuses before Tommy could press any more alcohol on them. They left the two couples in the conservatory and slowly climbed the stairs to the first floor.

"Have you really enjoyed yourself this evening?" Caroline had her hand through Noah's arm.

"It has been a long time since I was in such illustrious company. I'm not sure I have as great an interest in politics as the other guests, but it has been enjoyable, yes. How about you?"

"I found it difficult to keep up with some of the discussions."

"Does that include those with Christopher?" There was no jealousy in Noah's question that Caroline could detect.

"He plays his cards very close to his chest. I suppose he has learned to."

"I won't pretend to agree with that lifestyle, Caroline. Tommy is a pleasant enough chap, but I rather think I would prefer to limit my dealings with him and his kind."

They were at the top of the stairs. Caroline removed her hand from Noah's arm. "I'm sorry that you feel that way."

"Now don't take on so. I am speaking for myself. I can see how fond you are of them all."

"I have known Helen since school. I would not give up my friendships based on their romantic choices."

"Caroline, I am not asking you to. I am simply saying that I prefer not to pursue them." He could see that she had drunk enough to make her sway slightly and took a step back away from the top of the stairs. "Can I walk you to your room?"

Caroline nodded. It was less than ten steps along the landing to the bedroom she had been allocated. They stopped again at her door.

"Noah. Sensible Noah." She put her arms around his neck.

"Sober Noah. Come along now, put yourself to bed and we can talk about it more another time." He disengaged himself and opened the bedroom door for her. Then he kissed her hand and guided her into the room before closing the door behind her. He smiled to himself and went into his own room.

On the train back to Doniford Halt the next day, Caroline sat next to Noah in the carriage as they pulled away from Minehead. It was after lunch, Helen having insisted they stay for the midday meal having slept so late with no breakfast. Tommy had already left to drive Christopher back to Exeter, and Daisy would be leaving later that afternoon.

Caroline sighed. "I was rather drunk last night. I'm sorry if I behaved inappropriately."

Noah put his arm around her shoulders. "All is forgiven. I think we are equal in our embarrassment now, don't you?"

"I don't wish to seem uncharitable, but I really don't know what attraction Christopher has for Tommy. I tried all evening to talk to him, but he was very closed off."

Noah rubbed his chin thoughtfully. "Perhaps he simply wasn't interested in you? These academic types often have difficulty talking to women you know."

"I tried to be interesting, and to be interested in him."

"Don't take it to heart. You are interesting Caroline, at least you are to me. Daisy is a curious woman, don't you think?"

"Daisy is such a pet! Rather dotty, but jolly good at practical things."

"She is intelligent, she understood instantly when I explained how the clouds change formation with the different weather systems. Helen has a different kind of intelligence; she can certainly command an audience."

"Helen likes to be in charge. She likes things her own way. But she is generous with it. We made an unlikely trio at school, but somehow we all rub along together."

"The third in your merry band is Midge, the one in Africa?"

"Yes, dear Midge. She is rather like Daisy, very practical and matter of fact. I do hope she is baring up. Poor Marie-Claire, her death sounded simply ghastly."

"The blackness you mentioned sounds rather like the gangrene men developed in the trenches."

They sat in silence for a while, until they were approaching Watchet. Then Noah removed his arm from Caroline's shoulders, stood up and opened the carriage window. He shouted to the station porter as the steam swirled around the platform.

"Will you take a message to Escott? Let him know I shall be back at the harbour tomorrow."

He sat back down.

"The doctor said a week's rest."

"Caroline, I simply cannot leave my post for that long without making proper arrangements. I was an idiot to get stuck in the storm the way I did, but I really feel alright again now."

"Then promise me you will travel back by train and not walk. And that you will remember to eat regularly."

"I will if you promise me you will come to the cinema with me next weekend."

Caroline's face lit up. "Oh, could we? In Minehead?"

"We have a small picture house in Watchet you know. If you don't mind getting the train here and back by yourself that is?"

"A picture house in Watchet? I had no idea! How perfectly thrilling!"

"You are a funny thing." Noah chuckled to himself.

12

VOTES FOR WOMEN

Helen stood at the window of the drawing room. It was twenty minutes to eight; overnight showers had left the street outside washed and dripping, but now the sun was breaking through the clouds. A fine day would mean a better turnout. Helen knew she faced an uphill struggle to secure the Alcombe South ward, and fine weather could help.

Her main opponent, Mr Joseph Royston Shoesmith, was the Liberal party candidate. He had won the seat from the Conservatives two elections ago, then lost it to Helen's predecessor. He had campaigned hard on improving the health and amenities of the residents who lived on one side of the ward in ramshackle housing. The other side of the ward consisted of newer housing of better quality, filled with young families of mainly clerical office workers aiming to better themselves and propel their children onto an even higher standard of living. It had been these residents that Helen appealed to over recent weeks, talking to them about further employment opportunities, and against the expansion of smaller housing units that would encourage the lower classes to move in.

At the local hall, Helen had attended Mother and Baby groups, the Women's Institute meetings, the Mother's Union meetings, National Council of Women meetings, Girl Guide meetings, Allotment Association and Residents Association meetings. She spoke about the need for investment to create jobs, improvements to road surfaces, the introduction of a new omnibus route through the ward, and promised to intercede on behalf of the Allotment Association with the local council to cap the plot rents. She had talked with enthusiasm about a planned parade of shops which would include a hair salon, and a post office, and would save the residents a walk of two miles into the centre of Minehead for those amenities. She had done all she could to be pleasant, benevolent, authoritative and personable.

The Shoesmith campaign had naturally focused on her sex, and how unsuitable she would be as a relatively young woman with little political experience to represent the ward. There had been remarks, some whispered and others far louder, about her not being a 'local'. Shoesmith was also not from Minehead but had lived on the edge of Alcombe for the past twelve years. There had also been one or two comments that had concerned Helen more than she had shown, about Tommy and the nature of their marriage. A note had been left for her after one meeting that had used the word 'unnatural' though with no direct accusation. Her agent had dismissed it as 'the usual dirty tricks campaign tactic to be expected of the Liberals' but Helen had felt the cold grip of fear, nonetheless.

Helen watched the postman make his way along the street. He waved as he saw her watching him unlatch the gate and she smiled without warmth. Mrs Rich scuttled into the hallway and collected the envelopes, sorted them quickly into those for Tommy (which she left on the hall table) and those for Helen which she took into the drawing room.

"Will you require luncheon today, madam?" She asked, holding the letters out for Helen to take.

"I really have no idea, Mrs Rich. My husband is unlikely to require anything as the sun has finally appeared. Perhaps you could make up a plate of cheese and pickles and leave it for me? Miss Clare will be here shortly, and we shall dine out this evening whatever the outcome of the day."

"Very good madam. And may I wish you good luck for today."

"Thank you, Mrs Rich. I feel I may need every wish you can muster."

It was a close-run thing. Helen stood with her agent and Daisy Clare on the stage of the meeting hall in Alcombe as the results were read out by the Returning Officer. She felt sick, would have sold her soul for a double gin with no tonic, and nervously played with the catch on her purse. Daisy clapped politely after each result was announced, her gloves sending clouds of dust up into the air.

"…Shoesmith, Joseph Royston, Liberal candidate, two hundred and eighty-seven votes. Gersen-Fisch, Helen Margaret, Conservative candidate, three hundred and seventeen votes…."

A cheer went up from the rear of the hall where the Conservative party and Primrose League members had gathered. Helen had been elected. Her agent shook her hand vigorously.

"Well done! Well done indeed. Do you have your speech ready?"

"I rather thought I would keep it short, Michael."

"Yes, excellent idea. Don't forget to mention the plans for the new school."

Helen stepped forward at the behest of the Returning Officer.

"Thank you, everyone for your support this evening, and throughout the campaign. My thanks also to Mr Shoesmith and the other candidates who put forward such persuasive arguments and created a spirited competition. I believe the people of Alcombe South will benefit from my representation of them, not least in our drive to secure a new grammar school for the area and the extension of the omnibus route. Supporting professional families in Alcombe South is key to the prosperity of all. Thank you to my wonderful agent Mr Benhall, and my dear friend Miss Clare, for your unfailing support. Sleep well tonight my friends, for tomorrow we have work to do!"

More applause, which Helen acknowledged with a brief wave of her hand. Photographers called to attract her attention and Helen gave her best smile to the flashes of light before stepping off the stage. Daisy was on the verge of tears, overwhelmed by the occasion and so proud of her friend.

"Michael, would you be a lamb and make sure that I have a list of all of the committees that Mr Carmichael previously occupied. And if the Education sub-committee is not on the list, please speak to the chair of it and let them know I shall be very interested. Is the councillor for North Alcombe on that one, do you know? I saw him at the rear of the hall, perhaps you could arrange a meeting between us for next week?"

"Absolutely, although I do think you should consider again engaging a permanent secretary. I do have all of the councillors to look after. Perhaps Miss Clare could assist for the immediate future?"

Daisy was helping Helen with her coat. She looked directly at her friend. "Of course, I should be honoured to assist as your secretary, although I couldn't possibly take on more than two days each week. I do have the bookshop to take care of…"

"I shall need someone to see to the correspondence, it has already increased substantially. Daisy if you would be able to spare me some time until we can appoint a permanent secretary? I should hate to impose on Mrs Rich any more than we currently do."

"I can, but really Helen you will need an office."

"Leave that to me," said Michael, ushering them out into the warm night air. "I know there are rooms available above Rochester and Bincombe Solicitors in town that would make suitable office accommodation."

"Thank you, Michael. I have been thinking perhaps we could have one of the apartments above the new parade when they are completed? Would it not look more committed to be situated in the area one represents?"

"Well yes, particularly as you are not a resident. I shall make enquiries, but for now I do think the solicitors' office space will be most suitable. Can I walk you ladies into town?"

Daisy spotted Tommy finishing a cigarette next to his car and waved to attract his attention. "That's most kind of you but Helen's husband is here with his motorcar."

"In that case, I shall wish you a good evening and many congratulations once more Helen."

They parted and Daisy and Helen walked across the street to where Tommy had parked his car.

"Good evening, ladies! I hear congratulations are in order?" They all got in and Tommy turned the car around.

"Yes! Helen won, though with a smaller margin than we would have hoped for." Daisy had recovered from her emotional moment and was now animated and starting to feel hungry again. She looked at her watch. "Goodness, quarter past one!"

Helen yawned. Her mind was whirling with all of the meetings and information she would need to focus on.

Her research had been extensive in the run-up to the elections, but now she would be in a position to influence decisions. It was what she felt she had been born to do. Her mother's involvement in Plymouth's various committees and philanthropic enterprises had rubbed off on Helen, and while she had no desire to spend her own income on helping the poor, Helen felt she would be able to convince others to spend theirs on improving the ward she now represented.

Tommy glanced at his wife in the passenger seat. "I asked Mrs Rich to make some sandwiches before she went home and there is coffee in the kitchen. Well done, old thing."

Noah had returned to Watchet by train on the Monday morning. The Swill had receded enough to show a narrow strip of road between Doniford Lane and the station yard. The suit that Noah had bought in Minehead hung in Caroline's wardrobe; Noah had nowhere to store fine clothes above the boathouse and did not want to have to explain their appearance. Escott had looked him up and down when Noah walked into the harbour office and had remarked that he still looked green around the gills.

"The doctor said I should rest for a week, but I couldn't impose on my friend's hospitality any longer. I need to see the latest charts, are they those?"

Escott stood up and indicated to Noah to take the chair at the desk.

"They are. Message from Cork came in earlier, clear weather there and the wind is now from the north. That depression has moved through and high pressure is building again. We can hope for a stable few days at least. Let things dry out some. Welsh boats are all out of the ports now and that barge is on its way from Clevedon. All back to normal."

"A northerly isn't normal for August though" Noah said with a frown.

"We take what we're given." Escott stood expectantly, waiting for Noah to elaborate on where he had been. After a few moments looking at the paperwork, Noah looked up.

"Thanks for holding the fort here. I'll be alright as long as I remember to eat occasionally and not pretend that I am some kind of Chaplin character who keeps going no matter what accident befalls him."

"What you need is a good woman to go home to – and a good home. One more than a storeroom over a damp boatshed." Escott raised his eyebrow, "And I think you have at least one of those."

Noah put down his pencil and compass.

"Her name is Caroline. She has taken the cottage near to Doniford Halt on a year's agreement. Yes, she is a good woman as you put it, an extraordinary woman. But also, an independent woman. We have much in common but equally much that we disagree on. I'm not sure how she would feel about marrying a coastguard, but I suspect that marrying anyone is not a priority for her."

"Who said anything about getting married? Unless you want children of course. Oh I may be an old stick in the mud, but on this I am certain. Too many young people these days rush into a marriage and then find it's not all they thought it would be. If you've found a woman who doesn't want a ring and wedding bells, I say don't push for them until you're ready. If she's got means of her own, what's to stop you finding a little place together? See how things work out?"

"I would never have put you down as such a modern man!"

"Practical, my friend. I've seen too many men regret marrying the first girl they fell for. And too many take risks at sea because they don't want to go home. And of course, there are plenty who meet later in life and settle down without the paperwork, so to speak. Divorce is an expensive thing and a nasty business all round."

"What about you and Mrs Escott? You spend as much time in this office as I do."

Escott tapped out his pipe into the fire grate and started to refill it with tobacco. "Gert and I were each other's second choices. You know she is a butcher's daughter. Engaged to a lad who used to go out on the *Princess June*. Went overboard, never found. Around the same time, I was courting a young girl from Williton, Martha Feltham. Beautiful thing she was, long auburn hair and green eyes. In service at Meeson Hall out at Five Bells. Tripped carrying a tray of something and fell from the top of the stairs to the bottom. Broke her neck."

"I'm very sorry to hear that."

"Well, it was a long time ago now. Fact of the matter is, both of us didn't fancy the idea of being engaged again. We courted for a year or so, and then her father sat us down and said if we were serious, then he would put up some money for us to have a home, but we'd need to be married first. Gert and I talked it over and worked out we had enough saved between us to get a small place without her father's help. So that's what we did. She was old enough then to do as she pleased. I signed the papers. Her father was furious of course, but there was nothing he could do about it. Gert fell pregnant and we got married, as we always said we would. But the little mite wasn't meant for this world, he only survived three days. If not for him, Patrick we called him, well we probably still wouldn't be married now. People assume after a while in any case. Gert has always been Mrs Escott to those she's met since we took the house."

It was, Noah thought, the most he had ever heard Escott say in one sitting. He appreciated the older man's counsel.

"Gert would never have inherited the business, that was always going to go to her brother John. So it wasn't as if we were being cut off from anything by not marrying. And I've heard that some of these war widows lose their pensions nowadays if they marry again, so don't be surprised if more women decide not to in years to come. I spend time here because Gert looks after her mother. She'll have to come and live with us sooner or later, but for now Gert spends a lot of her time there, so I spend mine here. Saves on coal."

"Didn't people gossip?"

Escott laughed and lit his pipe again. "Of course they did lad! We knew they would. We thought we would let them; did the butcher some good having all those upset women commiserating with him and buying an extra ounce of beef or dozen eggs while they were at it. Didn't do us any harm in the long run, besides one or two who said our Patrick's death was judgement on our sinful ways. We're not overly religious, and the talk stopped eventually."

"So what you're telling me is, as long as Caroline and I can weather the inevitable storm, we should do what we feel suits us best?"

"I am. Take both families into account but ignore them if you two feel strongly one way or the other."

As if on cue, the office door opened, and Chancy Pritchard entered.

"Come to sign the papers for those extra crates we brought in yesterday. I don't suppose there's a chance of looking the other way just this once?"

At Quantock Cottage, Caroline occupied herself convert-
ing her growing number of sketches into artwork to send to
London. The change in the weather prompted her to borrow
Vi's mangle which Ron transported in his wheelbarrow, and
wash out the linen from both beds as well as some other
sheets and pillowcases from the airing cupboard. Though
she could have sent it all away with the weekly laundry van,
she wanted the physical exertion of the activity. Finally, she
thought as she looked out of the kitchen window at the
billowing white items on the washing line, this is how I
hoped it would be.

Without the rain clouds, the days were pleasantly warm
and long. Flowers opened, bees and other insects busied
themselves about the garden. Caroline moved her easel
from the kitchen into the garden most days for the better
light. She kept time by the to and fro of the steam trains as
they passed the end of her garden. Vi visited once or twice
a week and the two women would sit in the garden and
drink tea. As Vi was a woman of regular habits, Caroline
made sure her artwork was of a suitable subject matter on
those days.

By the time Caroline caught the train to Watchet for
her cinema date with Noah, the Swill had returned to
within its natural limits and the railway yard was almost
clear of water though not of mud. They had arranged to
meet at Watchet station and instead of their usual direction
towards the harbour, Noah guided Caroline west to a small
hall that had been converted to show films. It reminded
Caroline of the hall at Budleigh Salterton and she sighed
at the memory of that weekend she had spent with Helen,
Tommy and Midge.

"Are you alright?"

"Yes, just remembering another hall similar to this one."

"I bought a quarter of bonbons, would you like one?"

They were joined by around thirty other inhabitants of the town, leaving the hall half empty. The show consisted of a news real that was a week old and had come from Minehead, followed by an old movie called *Down to the Sea in Ships* which starred William Walcott and Clara Bow. It was a film much appreciated by the audience, who applauded, cheered and cried "boooo!" at appropriate intervals.

Afterwards as they walked back towards Watchet station, Caroline asked Noah if he had ever seen a whale.

"Not up close, no. I hear they beach themselves sometimes further west, around Cornwall, but not here."

"It was interesting that several of the characters had to pretend to be someone else in order to do what they wanted to."

"Yes, I thought that would intrigue you."

"Of course, all acting is pretending to be someone you are not. It's a lot of fun."

"You have done some acting before?"

"Yes, when I stayed in Dorset a couple of years ago. I'd forgotten I hadn't told you about it."

"I would love to hear more, but your train is due."

"Would you like to come over next weekend? Come to dinner on Saturday perhaps? Though not if the weather is terrible of course!"

They both smiled. "I will come for dinner on Saturday. And if the weather looks bad, I shall telephone to the post office and ask them to deliver a message to you."

Two weeks later Caroline was in the kitchen, feeling invigorated by her early morning swim. She was adding the finishing brush strokes to a painting of Tommy, in green and blue watercolour with charcoal, when the postman knocked on the front door. She wiped her hands on a cloth and hurried along the hall.

"Telegram for you, Miss."

"Thank you. Could you take a letter from me, please? It has a stamp."

"Of course, Miss."

Caroline swapped the telegram and two other letters with the letter she had finished the evening before. When the postman had left, she returned to the sitting room and opened the telegram.

YOUR FATHER ILL STOP COME
QUICKLY STOP

Its brevity was alarming. A cold stone of fear dropped from Caroline's chest into her stomach. She looked at the mantle clock; forty-five minutes until the next train up the line was due. She picked up her knitting, the novel she had been reading, and the other two letters, and hurried upstairs to begin filling a suitcase. Twenty minutes later, she returned to the kitchen, turned the easel to face the wall and covered it with a sheet. She hastily wrote a note for Vi which she tucked into the outside of the kitchen window frame. She wrote another to the milkman and left it in the top of a bottle that she had to empty and rinse so that there was something to hold the note. After a final look around to make sure she hadn't forgotten anything, she put on her coat, hat and gloves, picked up her case and hurried down to the station.

Ferris was trimming the hedge beside the row of garages at Norwood Court when Caroline's taxi pulled into the gravel drive. He hurried over to help with the luggage and held the glass door open for Caroline to enter the apartment building.

"He is in the hospital still, Miss. Mrs Bassett suggested that I send the telegram to you, though I don't exactly know the nature of the illness."

"What happened?"

"It seems that he told young Sara yesterday morning that he felt unwell but would go into work as usual. Then one of the clerks found him in his office, white as a sheet and running with sweat. They called for a doctor who arranged to admit him. Mrs Bassett was just going out when the message came, that's how she came to suggest the telegram."

They had reached the top of the building and Ferris, a little out of breath from talking and climbing at the same time, set down Caroline's case and wiped his face with his handkerchief.

"I do appreciate you sending it. Do you happen to know which ward my father is in?"

"I'm sorry to say I don't, Miss."

"No matter, I shall make enquiries. Thank you, Ferris."

Caroline was surprised to find Sara in the kitchen of the apartment.

"When Ferris said he was going to send for you, I thought you might want some dinner when you got here ma'am." The girl was crimping the edge of a beef and potato pie as she spoke.

"That's very thoughtful of you, Sara. Could you make a pot of tea? I have some telephone calls to make."

No one seemed to be particularly concerned for her father, Caroline thought as she unpacked her case in her old bedroom. She washed her face and hands quickly, then retrieved her address book and began her telephone calls. She tried Doctor Riley first, only to find that he was at the hospital. She tried there next and spoke eventually to the matron who informed her that George was awake and would be able to receive visitors that evening between six and eight. She would give no further details and hung up abruptly when she felt the conversation was at an end. Caroline was reassured that her father was not in imminent danger of demise, reasoning that had he been the matron would have told her to come straight away.

Her next call was to Mr Bright at Doniford Post Office. His official voice was comforting. As Caroline explained briefly why she would not be at home for a few days, he relaxed somewhat and assured her that all deliveries that passed through his hands would be held for her, and if she would be so good as to telephone again when she had a date to return, he would have everything brought to Quantock Cottage to meet her. She thanked him and hung up the receiver.

Her final call was much shorter. She telephoned the harbour office at Watchet and left a message with Escott to pass on to Noah. They had arranged to have lunch in Williton on Saturday, but Caroline felt she would stay in Cheltenham at least until after the weekend. There had been another moment of jealousy from Noah when Caroline had told him of her month-long stay in Dorset with James and the company of actors. Caroline had explained the chaperone arrangements and the exhausting nature of their daily schedule. Noah added this information to his growing mental file of 'Unconventional Caroline' and tried not to assume anything more than what he had been told. Yet Caroline had immediately understood his change of mood. She had found it irritating and wondered if he would be against her doing the same thing again should the opportunity present itself. She suspected he would.

Her telephone calls completed, Caroline put her address book away and returned to the kitchen. The tea things were on a tray on the dining table and Sara was peeling carrots.

"I'll leave these in the saucepan on top, ma'am, ready for you to have when you want them. The pie will be forty minutes or so. I'll stay 'til it's done, but you can have it cold later. You'll be off out to the hospital shortly I expect?"

"You are a gem, Sara. How is Miss Kettle?"

"Worried for your father, ma'am, but fit as a fiddle otherwise. I'm sure she'd like to see you if you have the time."

"I will call on her tomorrow morning."

"Will you be wanting dinners made up while you're here? Or other meals?"

"I think I can manage my own thank you, though we shall continue to pay your wages as before. My father did that on Fridays I believe?"

"Yes ma'am. That would be very kind of you."

"I will know how long I intend to stay after I have seen Father this evening."

September was warm and dry, so unlike the preceding months of 1927, and after her long train journey Caroline decided to walk to the hospital. Evidence of the winter storm was still visible in the form of stumps of trees and piles of logs. Rooves had mostly been repaired; the new slates standing out bright against the older weathered ones. When she reached the hospital, Caroline asked first to see Doctor Riley. He came to meet her in the reception area and showed her into his office.

"You are looking very well, my dear! Please have a seat."

"Thank you. It has been a long day, but I came as soon as I could. How is my father? What exactly is wrong with him?"

"Have you heard of diabetes mellitus? Your father has developed it. The level of sugar in his body is too high.

This causes patients to go into a shocked state and can lead to other complications such as blindness."

"I see. Is there a cure? Or some treatment?"

"Medicine is advancing all the time. Only a few years ago doctors in Canada arrived at a treatment using a chemical called insulin, though there is still some debate on its effectiveness. The Germans are favouring a treatment called horment, though again it will be some time before its effectiveness can be established. Your father seems to have responded to the insulin we gave him yesterday; I should think he can go home tomorrow as long as his urinary sugar level is where it should be."

"But will it happen again?"

"Oh undoubtedly. In fact, I am surprised that it hasn't shown itself before now, it's quite unusual that a man of your father's age should suddenly develop diabetes. I rather think he has had it for some time at low levels. From what he has told me, his diet has changed over the past year and this could be one factor in the condition."

"You mentioned blindness, is that likely?"

"I am inclined to give your father a sight test before he leaves us. Blindness is common as we age, my dear. Diabetes can hasten the onset. He will need to change his diet again to remove as much sugar as possible."

"But he is not going to die?" Caroline could feel the tears welling up and rummaged for her handkerchief.

"No, my dear. He was lucky that his clerk summoned help quickly, but now I think he is stable, and we should be able to keep him that way. Would you like to see him now?"

As she walked back towards Norwood Court later that evening as dusk fell, Caroline felt tired but reassured. George had been alert and seemed to understand the nature of his condition. She had agreed to stay for a week, to help Sara rearrange the grocery provisions and satisfy herself that George was indeed fit enough to return to work. He had been adamant that she should not prolong her stay and insisted that a week would be more than sufficient.

"Do not think I am unwilling to have you back home, my dear, but I will not have you give up your recent freedom to nurse me when I do not require it."

Caroline had patted his hand and tried to smile. They both knew she would give up everything at a moment's notice if George did require it.

They fell into an easy companionship once again. George was encouraged to take a walk around the Park each day, and Sara quickly understood the changes that needed to be made to his diet. He would need to find an alternative to his habit of taking lunch at a café in the town, and Sara suggested vegetable soup which she would make in a large batch every two or three days. A small primus stove in his office would enable George to heat it up.

Caroline took advantage of her situation and visited Mary Rose and the children. Mark was in good health and finally putting on weight, though Angelica had a cough that made her gasp for breath. Mary was concerned that the district nurse was not taking it seriously, and asked Caroline if she thought it would be better to speak to a doctor. Caroline said she would see if Doctor Riley would call as he would be taking dinner with her and George that evening.

Annie Jenks brought her baby son Victor to visit Caroline and George one afternoon, after the invitation was passed on through Sara. No longer constantly crying loudly, Victor was also putting on weight and kicked his legs vigorously when laid on a blanket on the sitting room floor. Annie admitted to administering a little glucose in water once a day to Victor, as recommended by the district nurse, and gripe water in the evenings. It had made all the difference, she said, and meant he would sleep for six hours at night rather than two. Annie looked exhausted, but Caroline felt she was in no position to offer any advice and instead complimented Annie on being a conscientious mother.

The day before Caroline was due to return to Doniford, she took the train to Stroud to visit Lottie. It was not a trip she had made before and was pleasantly surprised at the journey through picturesque valleys and tree-lined cuttings. At Stroud station Caroline engaged a taxi to take her to the address Lottie had given on her letters. It was a short enough distance that Caroline could easily have walked, had she known the route.

Lottie answered the front door, red-cheeked and breathing hard. She squealed with delight when she saw Caroline on the doorstep and welcomed her in. The house was furnished in a similar style to that of Caroline's old home at Glencairn Road with dark wood and wildly-patterned wallpaper that had started to peel in a few places. The wooden floors were scrubbed and had thin rugs to soften the noise of footsteps rather than for decoration. Built at the end of the previous century, it had four bedrooms and two reception rooms in addition to the kitchen, scullery and outside toilet. To Lottie and Eric it was a palace, and neither had any qualms about filling the bedrooms with their family as soon as nature allowed.

Lottie took Caroline on a tour of the house while the kettle came to the boil on the kitchen stove. A cot was disassembled in one of the bedrooms. Lottie explained they had been given it by a neighbour and Eric had promised to put it together on his next day off.

"It's still a while before we'll need it of course, and Mrs Coleford next door says it's bad luck to bring a cot in before the baby is born, but Eric and me don't go in for old wives' tales like that. I need to see it put together so I can start making the sheets and blankets for it."

It became apparent that Lottie and Eric were in a constant state of criticism from Mrs Coleford next door.

"We're civil of course, have to be when you're neighbours and share a garden wall. But she finds fault with just about everything I do and say. Even told me I was hanging the washing up the wrong way the other day! Eric says it's just because she's on her own and wants to help, but I told him, my washing habits have been good enough for my granny and my mother, and they'll be good enough now. The wrong way round indeed. Lummy!"

The women looked at each other across the table and burst into laughter.

"It is so good to see you again," Caroline said when they had recomposed themselves. "When is the baby due?"

"January." She looked down at her stomach. "I feel like a whale already, mind you. Eric has twins in his family, he's been teasing me that we'll have triplets."

"That would certainly fill your bedrooms."

Caroline left Lottie waving on her doorstep and walked back through the town to the railway station. She stopped along the way to purchase a few items, realising that she should take advantage of the opportunity before she returned to Doniford. She was beginning to pine for the relative quiet and less structured existence she had grown used to in her own home. Stroud, like Cheltenham, was noisy and more sombre-looking with its stone buildings and inhabitants who seemed to live life with gritted teeth. The town did not leave a good impression on Caroline; she wondered if Lottie would remain her cheerful self if all her neighbours were like Mrs Coleford.

On their final evening together, Caroline and George sat listening to the radio in the sitting room. He had announced that he would be returning to work the following day.

"You will do as Doctor Riley says, won't you, and telephone him the moment you feel weak again as before?"

"Now Caroline, don't fuss so. I am fully aware of the need for action should I begin to feel ill again. My new spectacles will be ready next week, and with this new diet I feel much better."

"Sara says she will be making similar changes to Miss Kettle's lunches, having understood why you have needed them."

"I rather think at Miss Kettle's age, one should be afforded leniency in one's meals. You are satisfied that I will be in capable hands with young Sara?"

"I am. She is so like Annie in many ways, and yet so much more … modern I suppose."

"Annie has promised to bring Victor to see me on Saturday afternoons while the weather is fine. It will be most pleasant to see the little boy grow."

"I do hope Doctor Riley has been able to see Angelica. Mary has never got along very well with the district nurse."

"From how you describe the girl's symptoms, it could be whooping cough. Do you not remember having it when you were young? I think you were seven or eight years old."

"No, I didn't think I had had any illnesses like that. I don't remember ever being ill."

"Your mother and I were blessed with robust children, certainly."

Freddie's presence filled the silence for a moment. Both Caroline and George were thinking of how healthy and full of life he had been.

13

TO THE HEAVENS

As arranged, Caroline had telephoned Mr Bright to inform him of her return. This meant that the local inhabitants became aware almost as quickly as if Caroline had sent them individual telegrams. Noah had telephoned Bright two days before her arrival to see if he had any news, and learning of Caroline's intended return, felt a sense of relief that he would see her again soon. All too often young women went to the aid of a sick relative and ended up staying at their bedside for years. However much he wanted to see her he did not want to impose on her as soon as she arrived. Instead, he bought a bunch of flowers at Watchet railway station and paid his three pence to ride to Doniford Halt in the morning. He left the flowers and a note for Caroline to meet him on the beach the following morning at her kitchen door.

If only the whole summer had been as warm and bright as today, Caroline thought as she floated on her back in the sea. It was calm, and the tide rocked her gently while a gull soared above her. She had felt the need to swim as soon as she had woken that first morning back at Quantock Cottage. Not knowing what time to expect Noah at the beach, she had packed a breakfast and her current novel along with a towel into her rucksack. Rolling onto her front, she noticed a fishing boat out in the water before swimming slowly back to the shore.

She had dressed in a light cotton dress and cardigan and was brushing her hair when she spotted Noah on the cliff path heading towards her. A flutter in her stomach made her giggle. How silly, she thought, I am nearly twenty-four and still giddy as a schoolgirl. She arranged her bathing costume out on the rocks to dry, humming a tune that she had heard recently but couldn't remember where. Ten minutes later Noah crunched his way across the shingle and sat down beside her.

"Good morning. Isn't it glorious today?" She said, shielding her eyes from the sun to look at him.

"All the more so for seeing you." Noah grinned and pulled a bottle from his satchel. "Would you like some ginger beer?"

"No thank you. I saw a boat out there. Did you?"

He took a mouthful and swallowed, then replaced the cork in the bottle. "Yes, it's Chancy coming back in, the *Merry Jen*." He looked out across the water. "Look, there are two more to the right. We're expecting several back today. High tide is at just before two this afternoon so they will wait outside the harbour until it's high enough for them to dock and unload."

He stopped as he realised Caroline was looking at him and not the sea.

"I have missed this." She said quietly.

"You've only been gone for a week. How is your father?"

"The doctor thinks he has diabetes. I don't know how dangerous it is, I rather got the impression that Doctor Riley didn't want me to worry. Father has returned to work today, and Sara, she's our daily, will look after him and make sure he is eating the things he should. Annie is under instruction to telephone if he seems unwell again, under the guise of taking Victor to visit him at the weekends."

"Victor?"

"Annie's baby, the one I went to the Christening for. Father is his Godparent."

"And Annie is Sara's sister? You see, I am slowly piecing together the jigsaw of your life away from here."

Caroline chuckled, "I suppose it is a bit of a puzzle."

"It sounds as if you have a network of spies to keep you informed at any rate."

"Oh, thank you for the flowers, I almost forgot! Did you walk both ways?"

"It was no trouble. I caught the train here and walked back. Like your father, I suspect there are spies who would tell tales on me if I were not looking after myself."

"I shouldn't want you to become ill again."

They looked at each other for a moment, smiling.

This is a different passion, thought Caroline.

This is what I need, thought Noah.

"I can't stay here for too long this morning, and I will walk back along the road. Your friend Helen has been in the newspaper again while you've been away."

"Really?"

"I thought you might want to see it." Noah pulled the folded front page of the *Western Mercury* from his satchel and handed it to Caroline.

She read the column that accompanied a large photograph of Helen quickly, then handed it back to Noah. "I should go and see her. Although I suppose Daisy will be there."

"This kind of thing, it doesn't sit well with people Caroline. Shall we walk back to your house?"

"Yes. The day suddenly feels cloudier."

Mrs Rich opened the door to Caroline the following day as a light rain began to fall over Minehead.

"Come in, Miss. Mrs Gersen-Fisch will join you shortly."

Caroline went into the drawing room and took off her hat and gloves before sitting on the edge of a chair to wait. The house was silent. There was no clock in the drawing room Caroline realised. She was sure there had been before, to one side of the mantlepiece. There was a gap there now in the ornaments.

Helen opened the drawing room door, entered and closed it behind her. Her make-up was applied heavily, her dark hair sleek and freshly cut. She wore a beige two-piece outfit with a long chocolate brown silk scarf. She stood with hands behind her back still pressed against the door.

"Helen, darling, I had to come."

Caroline swept across the room, her hands held out. Helen meekly placed her hands into Caroline's. She allowed herself to be led to the sofa, where the two sat. A box of cigarettes and a lighter were on the coffee table and Helen reached for them while Caroline spoke again.

"I only saw the newspaper yesterday, I have been back to Cheltenham, Father was taken ill. I hoped Daisy has been with you."

Helen exhaled. "Is your father recovered?"

"Yes, yes he has returned to work. If you don't want to talk about it all I quite understand. I just had to come and see if there was anything I could do."

"Everything has already been done. Or undone, if one cares to look at it that way. I don't know what you read in the press. Michael, my agent, did his best to fend off the reporters, but they are like a pack of hounds when they get the scent of scandal."

"It was a short piece, Noah showed me. It said Tommy had been arrested in Exeter along with three other men. It didn't explicitly say why. It made more of him being your husband and there was a picture of you, I assume taken recently when you were campaigning."

Helen reached for the ashtray and tapped her cigarette into it. "Caro, I have tried to be sympathetic to Tommy's affair. No one could have been more tolerant. Despite my deepest intuition that Christopher was no good for him, I went along with his wishes, agreed to the pretence, even welcomed Christopher into my home.

"Tommy and Christopher went to a club last week, a club for men. I have no idea who those other two were and I have no wish to know. What I do know is that Christopher was indiscrete, the man cannot hold his drink at all, and the group were overheard. The police were called, there was a scuffle, and all four were arrested. Thankfully the charges were of drunken assault – I say thankfully in the meanest terms you understand. Tommy was fined and released the following day."

"Good gracious! What did he have to say for himself?"

"He blamed it on the drink of course. He kept saying how everything was sorted out and no one knew about he and Christopher. I'm afraid I quite lost my temper with him. I was standing by the fire as he went on about how bad he felt for Christopher and how it would affect his position at the University, and before I knew it, I had thrown the mantle clock at him to shut him up. It's always poor Christopher! No matter the damage to my political career and reputation, no matter that we might have to move house again, to start again, no matter that I despise Christopher!"

She was shaking with anger. Caroline had never seen her friend so deeply upset before. This was quite unlike the blazing row Helen had had with Lady Victoria in London; Caroline could see now that that had been no more than petulance from Helen whereas this was a wound that was fresh and deep and painful.

"Shall I ask Mrs Rich to bring us some tea?" Was all Caroline could think of to say.

"Darling, if I drink any more tea, I shall develop a Chinese complexion!" She stood up and crossed the room to the drinks trolley. "Have tea if you would like, but I shall have a Gimlet."

Caroline went to find Mrs Rich, and when she returned Helen was sitting back on the sofa with a large gin in her hand and her eyes closed.

"Helen, where is Tommy now?"

"In purgatory I should think. I have no idea. I doubt he is with Christopher, at least not in Exeter. He left after I threw the clock at him. I think he took a case."

"Perhaps he has gone to his father's?"

Helen shook her head. "He would be sent away with a flea in his ear. He might have gone up to Blackpool, possibly to get some cash from his dear uncle. He could be anywhere and frankly, darling, I care not where."

"You can't mean that, Helen. He could be in a ditch somewhere!"

"Can't I? Caroline, I have kept to my side of our agreement. I have been reserved, I have been careful. For heaven's sake, I have even lied to Mrs Rich, though that all went out of the window when I had to explain the broken clock."

"You mean she knows about ... you and Daisy?"

"Good Lord no! She knows Tommy has some unreliable friends of a certain persuasion, but that he and I are married for better or worse."

On cue, Mrs Rich appeared with the tea tray. She set it down, hesitated for a moment when she saw Helen's half empty glass, and then left the room.

"No doubt she will now think me an incurable lush on top of everything else."

Caroline poured her tea. As she stirred in the sugar she said, "So, what are you going to do now?"

"Do? About Tommy?"

"About everything. Tommy, your seat or ward or whatever it's called, all of it."

Helen visibly pulled herself together after knocking back the last of her drink. She placed the glass firmly on the table and looked directly at Caroline.

"Tommy will surface eventually with his tail between his legs. I have been holed up here for days and left Daisy and Michael to look after things at the office. At least there are no press on the doorstep now, it seems I am yesterday's news at last. What I shall do, is face the world again. I shall refuse to discuss my husband's affairs and focus on my work for Alcombe South. Drink up your tea, and we will surprise Michael with a visit. If you can face being seen in public with me?"

Caroline smiled. "Of course I can. You have done nothing wrong Helen."

Tommy had driven to Malvern, to see Lina and Albert. Lina had given birth to twin girls two weeks before. Both little more than four pounds at birth who mewed like kittens and had been confined to Lina's bedroom until they put on at least another pound in weight. Albert had been more concerned for his wife than for his daughters. He had been disappointed that the babies were both girls, as had his father and father-in-law, and had hardly looked into their lavish cribs since they had been born. They had been christened at a day old, with the Very Reverend Maudley wiping a finger of holy water from a flask across each tiny forehead in the presence of Albert's valet and cook. Albert had promised Lina a much larger party to celebrate at Christmas.

Tommy's arrival was exactly the distraction that Albert had needed. Lina was Tommy's distant cousin, and he spent some time with her on his first afternoon at the grand house overlooking the Priory parkland. He dutifully cooed over the girls, Amelia Phillipa and Veronica Josephine, who were being rocked by their nurse in their cribs, before joining Albert in the library.

The men took advantage of the better weather during September and spent hours on the golf links above Malvern and fishing in the Teme Valley. Albert said he had no need to return to Parliament for ten days or so, and Tommy was welcome to stay for as long as he wished. Tommy knew how fortunate he had been to have somewhere to run to. Helen's reaction had been understandable, he admitted to himself. As he sat on the riverbank holding his borrowed fishing rod Tommy ruminated on the events of the evening in Exeter.

He had been enthusiastic to go to the club in the Mint, it was where he and Christopher had met and was understood to be a sympathetic location for men of their kind. Christopher had been less willing to go but agreed and had been the one to strike up a conversation with the other two men. What had their names been? Tommy could not remember. Christopher had drunk far more than usual, that Tommy did remember. Two or three times he had suggested Christopher slow down, and Christopher had at one point replied with "you are not my wife!" a little too loudly. Had that been the cause of the police turning up? Tommy still really didn't know.

Turn up they had, and as Christopher was man-handled
to his feet he had swung at one of the officers. One of the
other men had joined in. Tommy had stood in shock, held
firmly by a policeman, watching the spectacle which was
over in no more than two or three minutes. They had been
bundled into a police van and thrown into cells overnight.
The following morning, swift justice was delivered as one
by one they were taken before a Magistrate. Tommy had
paid his fine immediately, returned to where he thought he
had left his car the evening before. He finally found it two
streets away, and had driven back to Minehead.

He had not attempted to contact Christopher. He did not
know if he wanted to. He could see now a pattern that he had
been blind to previously. Christopher was careless. He had
been the one to leave the sketches lying around his cottage
at Budleigh. He had been the one who had had to leave
Durham after spending too much time alone with a younger
student (or so Christopher had said). He had been the one at
the club to drape his arm around Tommy's shoulders.

Tommy felt the fishing line move in his hands but ignored
it. Before he met Helen, he too had been indiscrete. A close
shave with the law had led his father to all but banish Tommy,
with the words "do whatever the hell you like but keep
our name out of the courts and out of the press!". His
allowance was predicated on those conditions. The time that
Tommy and Helen had spent in London with their crowd
of acquaintances had had an effect on both of them; Tommy
had learned to be more aware of his surroundings and the
need to cultivate more meaningful friendships, and Helen
had finally been able to express herself openly. He considered
there on the riverbank that over the past year they had both
regressed to somewhat near their previous selves. Now he
had to make a decision. Would he continue on his current

trajectory and almost certainly face prison, poverty and chemical conversion? Or would he honour at least some of the commitment he had made to Helen in Blackpool and behave as one would expect a politician's … he chuckled to himself as he tried out both wife and husband to conclude his train of thought.

The fishing line had become still again. Just as well, thought Tommy, as I've no idea how to land a fish in any case. He looked across the water at the trees. A bank of alder and willow, heavy with the end of summer dust and swaying gently in the breeze. Tommy wished he had brought his paints; it would make an excellent study in contrasting colours. But was he also playing the part of an artist? Yes, he had sold some canvases through the gallery his friend owned, but was he a serious artist? Was he serious about anything? What did he know? What could he really do well?

He knew he needed physical exertion in order to sleep soundly. He had always been a fidget and was a bag of nervous energy at the best of times. He knew he could become obsessive; he recognised that in his pursuit of Christopher. Yet he loathed the thought of deliberate exercise and had little interest in animals. He had no formal training in any profession, his schooling had been dry and uninspiring with a religious thread that was not his own. He could see no clear pathway out of his current position.

Later over dinner, Tommy asked Albert if he knew of anyone who was looking to hire an unskilled, unathletic and unscholarly individual.

"Good Lord, don't tell me you want employment for yourself?!" Albert was genuinely surprised. "I thought you and Helen rubbed along alright with what income you have between you. Has the old girl been splashing out on new outfits and furs?"

"No, we live just about within our means. But with Helen finding her feet in politics, I'm at a bit of a loose end. I need something to occupy myself with."

"I see. Well, I must say, you're rather cut off from civilisation down there on the coast. And no doubt any role you might be interested in already has an incumbent. Dead man's shoes, so to speak. Have you considered investment opportunities?"

"Not really. I suppose I could tap the old man for a bit of cash if something interesting presented itself, but I don't see how that would necessarily keep me occupied. Simply handing the money to another party to do all the work wasn't quite what I had in mind."

"It doesn't have to be that way. Not all investors are the sleeping kind. I take it you don't fancy administration of a charity or good cause? Rounding up subscriptions for a hospital or children's benevolent fund?"

"No, that's really Helen's forte. That's part of my conundrum old chap, I have no idea what I want to do!"

Albert placed his knife and fork on his plate and dabbed his chin with his napkin. He was frowning, which Tommy understood to be his thinking-face. After a sip of his wine, Albert scratched his ear and said, "You're reasonably good with a combustion engine, correct?"

"I'm by no means a mechanic, but I can carry out rudimentary repairs."

"Don't mind getting your hands dirty?"

"Not at all. What are you thinking?"

"I do have an idea, but I don't want to get your hopes up just yet. Let me make one or two telephone calls in the morning and then if I'm right, I'll tell you over lunch."

Caroline and Helen walked into the centre of Minehead where Michael Benhall had secured temporary office space. Helen kept her eyes determinedly looking in front of her, knowing the little knots of women were gossiping about her as she walked past. Men behaved quite differently, she was surprised to find, with several raising their hats to her and wishing her a good morning. Caroline took her lead from her friend and walked as tall and straight as she could beside Helen. They reached the solicitor's building and climbed the two flights of stairs to the office. Michael was on the telephone as they entered.

"Yes, if you could that would be excellent.... I shall inform Mrs Gersen-Fisch of that .... No more than to be expected, no ......" He waved at the women to sit down, "Indeed, Mrs Johnson ....Yes, well, if there was nothing else, I really should be ... yes, yes, I see ....Yes, good morning, Mrs Johnson!" He replaced the receiver. "Helen! What a lovely surprise, how are you?" He stood up and came around the desk which was piled with letters and copies of newspapers.

"I have emerged, Michael. This is my dear friend, Caroline Munhead. She has given me the confidence this morning to resume my duties and take control once more."

"Good morning, Miss Munhead. And not a moment too soon if I may say so! Miss Clare has been assisting as agreed, but really she is not cut out for political administration."

"No, poetry is far more her style, though I appreciate her efforts enormously, as I do yours Michael."

"Is there anything I can help with, while I'm here?" Caroline offered.

"Can you type? Take dictation? I really should get back to the party office."

Caroline shook her head. "I've never tried I'm afraid."

"Well, that pile is this morning's post. Could you at least sort through and see what requires an immediate response?"

Caroline set about the envelopes, happy to be useful. Helen and Michael walked back down the stairs together talking, and then Helen returned and closed the office door.

"He is an absolute brick. Are you quite sure you don't mind helping for an hour or two?"

"Of course not. Perhaps I could try to use the typewriter, it might be useful one day."

"Yes, do. I shall catch up on the correspondence, although if the telephone rings, would you be a dear and answer it? Take a message and tell them I will reply at the earliest convenience. Unless it's the press, Michael says there have been a few calls from them and we are to simply say 'No, thank you' and hang up."

"I'm sure I can manage that."

Tommy returned to Minehead after a week in Malvern. He too had made telephone calls and written one or two letters while staying with Albert and Lina and was now feeling more in control of his own affairs. He had no idea how Helen would react to his plans, but as they did not involve Christopher in any way, he hoped she would approve. He had missed her. As he drove through the outskirts of Bristol, he mused at how little he had thought of Christopher over the past two or three days. Indeed, that had been the first time today that the man's face had tried to insert itself into his consciousness.

Mrs Rich had been putting on her coat ready to go home and welcomed Tommy by informing him that Helen was at dinner with the councillor for Alcombe North. There was a coolness in Mrs Rich's tone that Tommy had expected; her reputation would have been called into question as well as his own and Helen's.

"I can poach you a couple of eggs if you are hungry, sir." She said, giving every indication that she would prefer not to.

"No, that's quite alright Mrs Rich, you get off home. I can see to myself, and I promise to tidy up the kitchen afterwards." He opened the front door for her. "Thank you for looking after my wife."

Mrs Rich hesitated on the doorstep. She turned back to him and said, "It's not my place to comment on what happens here, sir, but your wife is an extraordinary woman."

"She is indeed, Mrs Rich. That is why I have returned. Good evening."

It was the following morning when they faced each other across the breakfast table that Tommy apologised and set out his plans.

"An airfield? Good gracious Tommy, what do you know of aeroplanes?"

"That's the beauty of it all, I shall learn from the fellows already there. The investment will be relatively small, they have several backers by all accounts, but they are happy to have me tag along and be useful wherever I can."

Helen sipped her coffee. "How far away is this airfield?"

"A little place called Thurloxton, between Taunton and Bridgwater. I'm going down there next week to meet them all. You could come with me! Make a day of it. What do you say?"

"And you have committed how much to this enterprise?"

"Three hundred at the moment. Albert has come in with five, though naturally he won't be getting his hands dirty."

"Naturally."

"And I've written to Father and uncle Cecil to see if they would be willing to add some funds. If I can raise a thousand, that would show serious intent. They already have some wealthy backers of course, and two aircraft that they are repairing."

"I'm afraid I don't understand Tommy, how would you recover your investment? How would the dividends be paid?"

"Granted it's all a bit sketchy at the moment, but taking passengers is the goal. You can fit ten people onto each aeroplane. Do you know, it's only just occurred to me that I could learn to fly!" Tommy's face lit up as he looked into space above Helen's head.

Helen finished her coffee. She was relieved to have Tommy home again but had heard him talk of outlandish ideas such as this before.

"Tommy, please, do let's be sensible for a moment. What you do with your money is entirely up to you, I have no opinion on that as long as our accounts are paid when they become due. I hate to rake over the coals, but we have had a narrow escape from a very serious situation. You could have been charged with indecency or worse. As your wife … as your friend, I do not want to see you in prison. I know you have no interest in politics, but I do, I am serious about embarking on such a career. It is difficult at the best of times being a woman in a man's world, but I cannot, can not succeed if you parade your sexuality without a care for the consequences. Darling, how you behave affects my prospects. You must see that."

"I do. And for the hundredth time I apologise for being such an ass. It is the very success of your campaign that has spurred me to this, don't you see? You have shown me that lounging around with my paints, while enjoyable, is not productive. Not sociable. It achieves nothing. While I was away, I came to understand that spending so much time by myself led to me being over exuberant when I finally came into company. I need to find a better balance of my humours, and it seems to me that working alongside a team of dedicated engineers and learning as much as I can from them could be the way to absorb some of my excitement."

"We would live more separate lives. Is that acceptable to you?"

"I rather thought it would be more acceptable to you. You said yourself just now, we are friends. I should hate to lose you as a friend Helen. If that means we spend a bit less time in each other's pockets, then I'm willing to accommodate that. I presume I shall have to find a hotel near the airfield for one or two nights a week, but really that will need to be discussed after I visit them."

"You really have thought it through, haven't you. What day will you be going down next week?"

"I thought Tuesday. You'll come? Do say you will. We can take Daisy too if you like, and Caro."

Helen tapped her fingers on the table for a moment. "No, just you and I. Let us treat it as a business trip, a fact-finding mission. You for your investment, and I for whatever benefit I can draw from the association. Agreed?"

September unfolded into warm days that ripened the final harvests across the country. Those who had persevered through the torrential summer were rewarded with plump berries, roots, pods and fruits. Lina and Arthur's daughters slowly gained the required ounces to enable their escape from the bedroom. In Cheltenham, Victor Jenks continued to thrive on his combination of milk, glucose and gripe water, and entranced all who knew him with his big blue eyes. Lottie continued to carry her swelling belly around the police house in Stroud, and while she could not be sure it would not be triplets, she became ever more convinced it would be twins she would present to Eric sometime after Christmas.

Caroline and Noah continued their unconventional courtship. Existing as she did in relative isolation, Caroline rarely heard the comments in Doniford village from the older women remarking on Noah's visits. Vi and Ron were on hand to quell the worst of the gossip, and to lend a hand to Caroline when she discovered a task which she could not achieve by herself. Her cookery skills improved steadily, and her next collection of paintings went off by train to London leaving her free to embark on another knitting project that might become a Christmas gift.

For his part, Noah found contentment that he had not realised had been lacking in his life. Unlike previous dalliances, Caroline was undemanding of his attention, did not hang around the harbour office day and night, and while not indifferent to his presence, seemed infinitely capable of existing without him. The smothering he had experienced before, often in the first flush of excitement in a relationship, was absent and he was able to savour the time they spent together and look forward to future times.

Noah also gave much thought to what Escott had told him, and about finding more suitable accommodation. It was true he had a sum of money saved in his Post Office account (his wages were rarely dipped into for more than food each week), and some bonds in the bank in Minehead that paid a small amount each year. Certainly enough for a house with a small mortgage. His parents were in good health so would not be leaving him an inheritance any time soon. He visited them every few weeks, taking a ride on any boat from Watchet heading along the coast. He had not yet told them about Caroline but had broached the subject of buying a house with his father.

Caroline changed her routine to swim in the afternoons as the mornings grew cooler and purchased a new red and white bathing suit from a catalogue she picked up in the salon in Williton. She regularly took tea with Daisy, feeling there had been some cooling of the relationship between her friends since Helen's successful election. Daisy seemed not to mind hugely. They talked about Caroline's paintings and Daisy's poetry, and sometimes about Noah. Once Daisy asked Caroline if she were serious about making a future with Noah, as that appeared to be the direction they were heading. Caroline considered for a moment before answering.

"I am waiting to feel that I love him, Daisy. I very much like his company, but I'm just not sure yet."

"And you haven't … forgive my crassness, but you haven't consummated the relationship?"

Caroline blushed a little as she chuckled. "No, Daisy we have not. Noah has been a gentleman throughout."

"Perhaps that would help you decide. Not everyone is compatible. And I am told that sometimes men change when they become married. As if the race has been run and the trophy obtained, so to speak. Of course, I am not experienced in such things, but how would you know exactly? That you love him, I mean." She looked intently at Caroline over the teapot.

"I would just know."

Tommy and Helen drove to the airfield at Thurloxton to meet the engineers. Albert had followed up his telephone calls with letters of introduction to the four owners of the enterprise, all former RAF servicemen: Peter Skelthwaite (Senior aircraftman, Technician), Rodney Cooper (Leading Aircraftman), Rupert Wallace-Farr (Chief Technician), David Rayne (Chief Technician). They called themselves the 'ground crew' but officially they had decided on the company name of Sunray Air. Peter had been to school with a cousin of Albert's, and recognised Tommy and Helen from Lina and Albert's wedding the year before.

The airfield was still mostly just a field. Work had begun to clear and level a runway through the centre, and to the eastern side stood a large hangar and three smaller buildings. Peter took Tommy and Helen on a tour of the facilities and to meet the others. He was enthusiastic and described the plans to refurbish the buildings to create a lounge area for passengers as well as constructing an observation tower, larger fuel store and a second hangar. Tommy was intrigued by Peter's expansive plans and asked several questions about the capacity for passengers, and the destinations that could be reached. Helen listened carefully to the conversation but commented with nothing more than appreciative noises.

In the hangar, Rodney, Rupert and David were at work on a half-stripped aircraft. Pieces of the aeroplane were strewn across the floor, and the tail section had been removed. It was a Dutch Fokker F.VII which could carry up to twelve passengers. A later model, the F.VIII, had crashed in Kent some six weeks earlier, and the ground crew at Thurloxton were intent on making modifications to the F.VII to improve its robustness. A second plane was covered with tarpaulins. A propeller rested against a wall and across the rear of the hanger stood a long workbench holding various tools, pieces of metal, wood and canvas. Helen was largely ignored as she wandered around the hangar looking at the mechanical debris. The men talked animatedly with their heads close to the engine, then stood at the hangar door and smoked as they discussed further possibilities of improving the aircraft's performance. When Helen joined them, Peter and Rupert suggested they move to the portion of the building that served as an office.

Over bitter black coffee, the men discussed the terms of Tommy's investment and return, and a schedule for his attendance at the airfield. There would be someone on site most weekdays, and Tommy could expect a return of five per cent at the end of the first full year of the operation of the proposed passenger service.

Helen had a question. "Forgive my interruption, but who will these passengers be? Why should someone wish to fly from here to Devon or here to Wiltshire when there is a perfectly reasonable railway service? Or indeed, motor cars." She smiled sweetly.

Rupert offered cigarettes all round. As he struck his lighter, he said, "It's true, air travel is no faster than the railway, but why squeeze into a stuffy carriage or risk your motor car breaking down when you can soar through the clouds in an aeroplane? You have to admit, dear lady, that the attraction of flight is glamourous."

Peter chipped in, "There are a considerable number of people around this area who are keen to fly regularly. If we can secure the option in Salisbury to refuel, we can continue to London. That's an attraction."

Rupert looked at Helen. He sensed that she was making calculations and would need to be won over if Tommy's money were to be secured. Appealing to her vanity would not be enough.

"The second aircraft will be more of a utility cargo transport. Letters and parcels, large but light items such as bicycles, perishable goods, all moved across the country and potentially to France or Ireland for a very reasonable rate."

"And you have pilots?" Helen asked.

"The four of us fly, we'd be happy to instruct Tommy if that's of interest to you?" Peter turned to Tommy.

"Rather! I'm willing to do anything useful."

"And your plans for the passenger lounge, do you have a designer in mind?"

"Not yet," said Rupert, "that is still some way in the future. We expect to have the utility service running by the end of this year, which will subsidise the passenger service for the first year or two afterwards. Do you know of any designers?"

"Oh Helen is a dab hand at throwing a room together, aren't you old thing?"

"Really? David is in talks with an architect chum of his about redesigning the space. Perhaps we could draw on your experience, Helen, once the structural work is done?"

In spite of her determination to remain outside of the investment, Helen found herself agreeing to meet with the architect on the provision that it did not encroach on her political work.

On their journey home, Helen was quiet.

"What an interesting bunch they were. What do you think, can you see the possibilities of Sunray Air?" Tommy asked.

"I rather think I can see beyond their current plans, dear heart. The limitations of the railway system, that it only goes where the tracks are laid and trains must remain on those tracks, could be exploited by air transport. The government is still discussing airships, and I think for the glamour aspect those are more appealing. But for cargo and a postal service, I can certainly see that an aeroplane would be more flexible. I wonder if there would be a suitable field on the edge of town that could be converted to an airstrip. Think what publicity that would bring to Minehead!"

28 September 1927
Cheltenham
Dear Caroline,

It is with profound sadness that I write to inform you of the death of our baby boy, Mark Philip, on the 24th of this month. As I write these words I can still hardly believe God has taken him home.

Mary is prostrate with grief. Celestine has come to help look after her and Angelica, but Mary will speak to no one, and hardly even to me. I fear she blames herself, although Celestine thinks she also blames the district nurse, Mrs Hammond, for not involving the doctor sooner than she did. When you visited last, I believe you witnessed Angelica's cough. She has recovered, thank the Lord, but it seems it was whooping cough. I see it around the parish with regularity, and I admit I thought it no more than a childhood illness. Yet, I now understand that in children as young as Mark, it can be fatal. It was so in our case.

I know you would have wanted to attend the funeral, but I conducted the service yesterday with only three or four parishioners present. The coffin was so small; it is never an easy thing to bury a child, least of all one of your own. I did not think Mary would want to prolong the laying out and Celestine agreed when she arrived that it would be for the best. Forgive me, Caroline, for not sending a telegram to inform you.

I know Mary will recover from this in time. The shock of the loss will eventually be tempered by the happy memories we have of our son from his brief time with us. Please do not feel the need to rush to comfort Mary in person, but perhaps a letter if you have a moment? It may help her begin to emerge from her stupor of grief.

You have been a good friend to Mary and I since we arrived at St Mark's. Please do let me know when you will

be in Cheltenham again and we would be pleased to have
you to dinner.
   Yours in Christ
   Philip

   Caroline held the letter in her lap for a long while. She
did not cry, as perhaps she might have cried had the news
been about Angelica. However, she knew the pain of loss
and she felt the weight of grief once more. Eventually she
refolded the letter and put it back into its envelope, then
placed it on the mantlepiece behind a china cow ornament.
She would not hurry to respond; she needed to find the
right words.

14

A CONFUSED MESSAGE

"Daisy! Can you stop for a moment?" Caroline called up the staircase at the rear of the bookshop.

She had caught the train to Dunster station and walked up into the village, through the blustery swirl of falling leaves in the middle of October. Daisy had been replaced by an agency secretary in Helen's office and now only visited Minehead on Fridays and occasional weekends if Helen was giving a reception or party. While she had enjoyed the intensity of the local political discourse, Daisy had frequently found herself out of her depth and was not sorry to return to her books and printing press. It was the latter that she was engaged at when Caroline entered the shop.

"Come up! I'll only be a few more minutes." Daisy shouted down to Caroline, who obediently climbed the stairs.

Gladstone the cat was sat on the windowsill looking out across the Yarn Market. He briefly turned his head to see who the visitor was, and satisfied that it was Caroline, he resumed his watch. Daisy continued to turn the press handle and posters deposited themselves in a tray near her feet. Caroline picked one up.

"What's this? A Spiritualist?"

"Yes, Penelope Smyth, she is quite renowned you know. I believe she is from Essex or somewhere near London and has caused a stir in the theatres there. It's rather exciting that she will be here."

Caroline read the poster out loud, "Mrs Penelope Smyth, the noted Spiritualist, will conduct a séance for a select audience at 7pm on Thursday 27 October in the Great Hall, Dunster Castle at the invitation of Miss Abigail Fines. Tickets on application from Dunster Castle estate office." The text was above an image of a seated woman with her head rolled back and a depiction of ectoplasm escaping from her open mouth.

"Have you ever been to a Spiritualist meeting?" Daisy finished cranking the machine handle and removed the printing plate.

"No. Mother went once or twice but Father didn't approve. Our cook, Mrs Monger, was a member of a congregation in Fairview I believe. I have read about them though. One couldn't not have, there seems to be a newspaper story almost weekly about a spiritualist found to be a fraud."

"They give the movement a bad name." Daisy frowned, "Mr Conan-Doyle has researched the phenomena extensively, and he believes there is some merit in Spiritualism."

"You don't believe in it all Daisy, surely?"

"I am of an open mind, my dear. I intend to enquire about tickets. Do you think Helen would come along?"

Caroline laughed, "Absolutely not! I know for a fact that Helen thinks it is complete tosh. Tommy could probably be persuaded though."

Daisy looked crest-fallen. She had hoped to invite Helen and Tommy as well as Caroline to a late supper after the séance.

She was aware that she spent most of her time with Helen at Helen's house and felt she was falling behind in her manners at not inviting her friends to visit her.

Caroline could see the disappointment on her face. "I didn't mean to be harsh, I'm sorry. Only I know Helen doesn't approve of these meetings because we had discussed it a while ago. There was one advertised when Helen and Tommy lived in Budleigh and she had been very vocal in her dismissal of it all." She looked at the poster again, "I could go with you if you like. I could ask Noah too. I have no idea how he feels about this sort of thing, but he can either say yes or no."

"Would you? I should hate to go by myself. There is quite the divide in the village about it, if I am completely honest."

"It doesn't say how much the tickets are."

"No, I rather think they will be somewhat expensive, in order to preserve the exclusivity of the evening."

"And it says at the invitation of Abigail Fines. I thought she lived in Tiverton with her father."

"She does, but she is very interested in the Spiritualist movement, and the castle will make such an atmospheric setting for it. Shall we go down?"

They descended the stairs to the shop floor.

"If you can secure a ticket for me, then I will go with you. I shall ask Noah on Saturday and let you know if he will need a ticket too."

"Excellent! And you must have supper here before you return to Doniford, both of you. The last train is at a quarter to midnight, I promise you'll be on it. Speaking of food, I thought we might have lunch at the Bluebell, shall we go?" She put her head into the stairwell. "Gladstone! Come a long now, I have to go out and so do you!"

That evening, Caroline sat at her kitchen table with sheets of writing paper in front of her. She had bought a sympathy card at the Post Office in Dunster, not wanting to leave her response to Mary any longer.

My dear Mary,

I was so terribly sorry to hear of your loss. Philip wrote to me after the funeral, and I'm afraid it has taken me a while to arrange my thoughts. I wish Mark could have stayed with you for so much longer. Even though he was only with you for such a short while, I know he was so very loved and he brought you both so much joy. I remember his beautiful eyes and the way he would suck on his fingers while you cradled him. For the time he was with you, he was an excellent little brother for Angelica.

I was glad to hear that Celestine was with you. I am sure that will have been a comfort, as well as helping with Angelica. If you should want to come and spend some time with me here, you would be most welcome. I have a spare bedroom and Angelica could play on the beach and watch the steam trains as they pass at the bottom of the garden. Take your time, and let me know what you decide, and of course I shall call on you the next time I am in Cheltenham although I do not know at the moment when that might be.

I shall keep you all in my prayers,
Your friend
Caroline

When Caroline asked Noah about his feelings on Spiritualism the following weekend as they walked out of Watchet up Cleeve Hill to look out across the Bristol Channel, his response was as vehement as Helen's had been.

"Utter poppycock! Charlatans, each and every one of them. They prey on other people's grief you know."

"I'm sorry you feel so strongly. I had rather hoped we could go with Daisy."

You're not serious?"

"Well, yes, I am. I've never been to a séance before, I should like to see what happens. Daisy seemed to think that if someone as respected as Mr Conan-Doyle approved then it couldn't be too awful."

Noah shook his head. "If you are determined to waste your money on such a carnival act, I think I should go along with you both. If only to prevent you making complete donkeys of yourselves! Don't expect me to respond if the woman starts asking if anyone has a biblical name though."

"I don't expect you to respond at all. I would just appreciate it if you came too." Caroline looked back towards the town. The day was overcast and blustery, but for once, dry. She held down her skirt as the wind lifted it indecently. "What are they building there, do you know?" She pointed to a patch of ground that had been cleared and had trenches dug in the outline of a building. It stood on an elevated position around two thirds of the way up the hill from the harbour.

They both stopped to look.

"New houses. There will be three to begin with, all detached. Escott was telling me about them the other day. They will have a good view of the channel from there."

"At least they won't be troubled by floods!"

"No, they won't" Noah said thoughtfully.

The castle Great Hall had been sensitively prepared for the evening's meeting. Chairs had been set out in rows, enough to seat fifty. Three more chairs stood to the side of the hall, perpendicular to those in rows. Opposite these, a long table had been set out with two large punch bowls and many glass cups, along with piles of napkins and rows of empty slender glasses that a butler would fill with champagne on request. On a raised dais, a grander chair somewhat like a throne had been placed. Its gilt arms and carved head piece shimmered in the light of the oil lamps. A heavy, black velvet curtain had been attached to a long pole set across the room behind the dais.

Daisy had bought three tickets at four shillings each, and clutched them to her chest as she, Caroline and Noah walked up the castle drive at twenty minutes to seven. Several motor cars were parked at the front of the castle, and footmen stood at the open door to receive the visitors. Caroline noticed Jack Herridge standing beside one of the cars, smoking. He saw her at the same time and stepped forwards to meet them.

"Good evening, Jack, are you well?"

"Good evening to you. I hadn't expected to see you at this ridiculous affair!"

"We are here to accompany Daisy. This is my very good friend, Noah Kingston. Noah, this is Jack Herridge, he is stable master here."

The men shook hands cordially.

"Is Abigail here, Jack?" Daisy asked, squinting as his cigarette smoke blew into her eyes.

"Oh yes. This is all her big idea. She'll make an entrance no doubt. I can't believe Old Andrew has approved of it all." Caroline heard the aggravation in his voice.

"We'd better go in. Good to meet you, Mr Herridge." Noah steered the women towards the footman and left Jack to finish his cigarette.

Once inside and relieved of their coats by yet another footman, they were shown into the Great Hall which was humming with muted conversation. Daisy introduced Caroline and Noah to two or three acquaintances. Then they took cups of punch and found three seats together with Caroline in the middle of her friends. A woman behind them was chattering to her companion about how she hoped her dear mother would come through with a message. Noah snorted and Caroline nudged him.

"Alright, I will keep mum!" He shook his head and crossed his long legs.

As a grandfather clock struck seven, a door to one side of the velvet curtain opened and Abigail Fines entered, escorted by a tall, young man in a tail suit and slicked back dark hair. Abigail smiled to her assembled guests, who clapped politely as she came to a stop in front of the dais. Her dark hair was piled up onto her head in coils and her slender neck was adorned with a single ruby pendent to match the rubies in her ears. She wore a red chiffon dress with a deeply plunging neck, underneath a flowing red velvet coat with golden embroidery at the cuffs and edges and a fox fur around her shoulders. She was beautiful and everyone in the room naturally fell silent.

"Friends, welcome to Dunster Castle this evening for what I am sure will be a unique and very special event. Please do take your seats." There was some shuffling and nudging, but the room quickly settled again.

"That's Norman Peterson, the polo rider. No wonder Jack's in a bad mood," whispered Daisy, "he's too handy with a whip on his horses by all accounts."

"For those of you unfamiliar with these meetings, I must ask that you all remain seated and silent unless you recognise yourself in a description or message given by Mrs Smyth. The lights will be dimmed, please do not come forward, simply raise your hand or stand up where you are. Mrs Smyth and her assistant will join us in a moment. When the meeting ends, Mrs Smyth will retire – please remain in your seats until she has done so. You will then be welcome to join us in the blue drawing room for further refreshments."

Another ripple of applause accompanied Abigail and her consort to their chairs at the side of the hall. When the applause had died away, and the room was silent again, the door opened once more, and two women appeared.

The first, it was apparent, was Mrs Smyth's assistant. Jennifer Crooke was a woman in her mid-forties, never married and a competent secretary. She was dressed in a grey woollen suit with a mustard-coloured blouse and wore thick glasses. Her salt-and-pepper hair was set in waves close to her head and she wore no make-up. Miss Crooke trotted in front of Mrs Smyth and plumped up the velvet cushion that had been placed on the throne-chair before stepping backwards and leading the guests in yet another ripple of applause as her employer and star attraction stepped up onto the dais.

Penelope Smyth, widow of some twenty years and now fast approaching sixty, was a tall thin woman. Her hair was white and ballooned around her in a mass of thick tresses that curled gently at the ends. She had piercing blue eyes and a tiny mouth painted dark red. It stood out against her pale skin and gave an impression of perpetually expecting to be kissed rather like a Japanese geisha. Her outfit was equally voluminous; a long evening dress in black covered with a full-length kimono-style coat in duck egg blue. The coat was exquisitely embroidered with exotic birds and flowers, silver threads catching the light. Having made her entrance, she took off the coat and handed it to Miss Crooke, before taking her seat.

The lights were dimmed. Mrs Smyth closed her eyes and began to breathe deeply. Those in the hall who had seen her before understood that she was attempting to summon her spirit guide, said to be a Japanese Samurai warrior whom she called Takido. After some moments, she began to mutter to herself, in what could have been Japanese for all Daisy and Caroline knew. Noah sat relaxed in his seat, resigned to endure the show. Suddenly Mrs Smyth opened her eyes and stared up at the ceiling.

"I have a Mary here, a Mary with a message from the other side."

Jennifer Crooke looked out towards the audience and spotted a woman tentatively raising her hand. She tapped gently twice on the floor with her foot.

Mrs Smyth continued. "Mary is in distress. Mary is showing me … a letter? A document?"

Again, Jennifer tapped twice with her foot as she saw the woman in the audience cover her gasping mouth with her gloved hand and nod her head vigorously.

"Mary says her wishes were not followed! She says it should have been shared equally, she is showing me three … no, four fingers."

Mrs Smyth closed her eyes and sunk back slightly into her chair as the woman in the crowd took out a handkerchief and dabbed her eyes, nodding to her husband beside her as he comforted her.

Daisy and Caroline held their breath in anticipation for the next message. They did not have to wait for long.

Again, Mrs Smyth opened her eyes and stared at the ceiling. "Does anyone here recognise Charles?"

No one moved, not even Jennifer Crooke.

"Charles? Or Charlie?"

Still nothing from the audience. Mrs Smyth appeared to mutter in Japanese again and then said, "Charlotte, I see more clearly now, Charlotte."

A man got to his feet towards the rear of the hall. Jennifer tapped her foot twice and sniffed.

"Yes, yes, she sends you her most affectionate greetings from the other side. She was taken far too soon, yet her heart remains yours."

So it continued for forty minutes. Twice Penelope Smyth offered a name that was not recognised by anyone present, but more than made up for it when a name was claimed. She gave messages of joy and praise, and one or two rather cryptic messages that could have been taken in any number of ways by the recipient. As the grandfather clock struck the quarter to, Mrs Smyth's eyes opened once more, and her voice rang out clearly across the hall.

"I have a soldier here. Someone here will know Frederick. Fred, Frederick … Freddie?"

Noah had been holding Caroline's hand but could not stop her raising her other as her eyes widened. Daisy glanced at Caroline, smiling and excited.

Mrs Smyth grimaced and gasped. "He cannot breathe! Come forward Freddie, come forward so I can hear you. Whisper to me Freddie."

Caroline too struggled to breathe.

"Freddie says, you are not alone. You have someone with you who will look after you… he is showing me …. Is that a telescope?"

It was all Caroline could do not to shout out "Binoculars!"

Mrs Smyth continued, "Freddie says you will be going on a journey, lots of packages, packing crates, and keys … he is showing me keys. And a boat! A sailing boat … no, a fishing boat. There are gulls, the sky is a clear blue, I can almost feel the sand beneath my feet. Freddie, do speak up dear, what is it? A train coming? … He is fading."

This time Mrs Smyth sunk more dramatically into her seat and her eyelids fluttered. Jennifer signalled for the lights to be raised and stepped forwards to help Penelope Smyth to stand. She draped the kimono around her mistress' shoulders and led her shuffling gently out through the side door.

The guests began to make their way into the blue drawing room, following Abigail and her escort Norman. Daisy stood up to follow them. Noah squeezed Caroline's hand.

"Are you feeling alright, Caroline?"

She roused herself, now unsure of how she felt. She nodded, not trusting her voice at that moment and allowed herself to be led from their row of seats into the entrance hall.

"I think I should like to leave now, if that's alright with you Daisy?" She said.

"Of course, dear. I expect you are feeling rather out of sorts. I'm told that happens when one is the subject of a message."

Noah withheld a snort of derision, "I'll get our coats if you girls wait here for a moment."

It was only once they were on the train headed east again did Caroline feel able to talk about her experience that evening. Daisy had asked gently a couple of times over supper, but Caroline had simply shaken her head and Daisy had changed the subject. Now as the train pulled away from Dunster station, Noah put his arm around her shoulders as had become his custom.

"Had a bit of a shock this evening, haven't you old thing?" He said quietly.

Caroline swallowed. "She couldn't have known. How could she have known? About Freddie?"

Noah shook his head. "Darling girl, I know you want to believe it all. And I am not saying that there might not be a grain of truth in it here and there, but surely you noticed the signals that assistant was giving?"

"Oh yes, for the others, I did. But Mrs Smyth said Freddie couldn't breathe."

"She described a soldier who had died unable to breathe. That could have been any one of thousands caught in the gas. It could have been me had the boys not dragged me out."

"But no one else recognised Freddie!"

"And if you hadn't raised your hand, she would have changed it to Frank or Francis. Just as Charles miraculously changed to Charlotte at the beginning."

"I suppose so. And can you explain away the binoculars?"

"What binoculars? The good Mrs Smyth said she saw a telescope."

"Noah, you know as well as I do, she meant binoculars. And the keys, well I shall be leaving Quantock Cottage in a few months' time, and I shall have to pack up all of my things. And then what about the boat? She said it was a fishing boat. Not the usual 'you'll be going on a journey' kind of thing, not a steamer or a train but a fishing boat."

"And we are on the coast. Come along now, let's not be silly about all of this. Who's to say that assistant hasn't been asking questions about the people who bought tickets? Feeding the information back to Mrs Smyth, for her to throw out like bread to the gulls."

"Do you really think so?"

"I think it is absolutely possible and probably true. Try not to dwell on it, there's a good girl. Now, you're sure you don't want me to stay on board and see you to your door? It's very late."

"No, I'll be alright. You get off at Watchet. I think I would like to have some time by myself to think over what happened this evening."

"Alright. And we're still going to Williton on Saturday?"

"Yes, if you can. If you're sure you don't mind waiting while I visit the hair salon?"

"Not at all. There are one or two things I need to do while you have your trim."

As she lay in bed later, her watch as she placed it on the bedside table reading twenty minutes after one, Caroline went through Mrs Smyth's message for her in forensic detail. She had been prepared to give the Spiritualist the benefit of the doubt before the meeting and had quickly noticed the tapping of Jennifer Crooke's foot. But when it came to the message from Freddie, how could she ignore it as Noah had encouraged her to do? She fell into a fitful sleep, dreaming of a room full of packing crates full of large keys that she had to empty but which magically refilled themselves when she turned her back to swat away a group of gulls that swooped down at her. It was almost nine thirty when she got up and made breakfast the next day.

Caroline took her bicycle to the village Post Office to clear her head and purchase a newspaper. Mr Bright was his usual cheerful self, whistling a tune as he arranged his wife's freshly baked biscuits on a tray in the window.

"Good morning, Miss Munhead! I hear you were favoured with a message last night!"

Caroline was amazed at how quickly the news had reached Doniford.

"Do you mean at the séance? Yes, I recognised one of the names that was called out."

"It's a very special thing, I always say, to be comforted by those who have passed over. Mrs Bright and I were very sorry not to be able to secure tickets. Mrs Bright particularly wanted to meet Penelope Smyth, she has read so much about her."

"Really, Mr Bright, I had no idea you and your wife were Spiritualists."

"Oh yes. Mrs Bright goes to the meetings in Minehead, regular as clockwork. I go when I can. Just a penny for the paper, can I get you anything else?"

"No thank you, Mr Bright." Caroline paused as she turned to leave the shop. "But could you tell me something please? If one receives a message but doesn't fully understand its meaning, what should one do?"

"Well, Mrs Bright would advise you to pray, Miss."

"And what would you advise, Mr Bright?"

"Oh, I think if you wait long enough, everything will become clear to you. Sometimes these things take a while to work themselves out. But praying won't do any harm in the meantime." He smiled broadly, showing a missing front tooth.

Tommy found the pub in Thurloxton was most accommodating to his requirements. The landlord of The Bird In Hand was happy to have another regular guest; David and Rupert had often stayed there during the summer when they had worked on the aircraft until dusk. Tommy drove down each Tuesday and home to Minehead again on Thursday afternoons. He had given Helen solemn promises that he would not mix business and pleasure and was careful not to give any hint of his preferences to anyone. Although he was not an experienced pilot or engineer, he was welcomed by the four men as an equal. He was quick to learn the names of the various aviation parts as they were not so unlike his car engine. Much of his time was spent greasing or cleaning bits of machinery while he listened to the conversations of the others.

By his third week at the airfield the utility plane was ready to be taken out. The runway had been rolled repeatedly, the heavy rain that year keeping the ground soft and yielding to the steam road roller the men had hired for the job. The plane that was to be used as a utility carrier was a Bristol Jupiter. Originally designed with two seats, the men had removed one and modified the space to hold a lightweight trunk that could be filled with mail. Other modifications had created another small space for parcels. It was a small plane, used extensively for training pilots by the British, Polish and Swedish air forces. Tommy was curious as to how the men had obtained it but decided not to ask.

The four men drew straws to decide who would be the first to fly. Rupert drew the shortest straw and bounded off to retrieve his flying jacket, goggles and cap. It would only be a short flight, simply to try out the runway. When Rupert returned, he climbed aboard the plane and the others pulled it using long heavy ropes out onto the grass. The engine started first time and the ground crew ran back to the safety of the hangar doors to watch as Rupert started his taxi along their makeshift runway. He drove the plane to the far end of the field, turned and then paused.

"Is this the first time he's flown it?" Tommy asked, nervously shifting his weight from foot to foot.

"No. He brought her over. First time she's been out since we reassembled her though." David replied. "Don't worry, Rupe knows what he's doing."

As if on cue, the aeroplane's engine changed pitch and began to taxi again along the flattened strip of grass in the centre of the field. It picked up speed, bumping and bouncing along.

"We need to get that surfaced," muttered Peter.

The plane lifted tantalisingly clear of the grass for a second before bouncing back down again, then on the next attempt, she rose and stayed airborne. She cleared the hedge at the other end of the airfield and climbed up into the sky as the ground crew whooped and slapped each other on the back to celebrate. Then they calmed down as Rupert flew overhead. Rodney cocked his head to one side and closed his eyes.

"It's still not right. Can you hear the miss every few turns?"

The others listened and nodded.

David turned to Tommy, "We'll need to get the spark plugs out again and check the connections when she's cooled down." Tommy nodded, vaguely aware of what David was telling him. There was so much to learn and he was thoroughly enthralled by the whole experience.

After another circuit, Rupert brought the aeroplane back down to land and taxied to a stop near to the hangar door. He climbed out of the pilot seat and removed his flying cap, smoothing his hair back from his forehead as the others ran over to him.

Rodney shook Rupert's hand. "David thinks the spark plugs need another look. How did she feel?"

"Like a tiger on a chain! It's a pity we've got to be careful with the fuel, I could have stayed up there for hours." He grinned.

November brought a change in temperature to the west of England. Caroline was thankful for her fire, and on Ron's advice had taken delivery of a half hundredweight of coal which was deposited in the coal bunker in the back garden of Quantock Cottage. The first frost had gently covered the surrounding countryside at the end of October and while it only barely touched the garden of Caroline's home, Vi was adamant that the crab apples should be picked from the tree immediately. Caroline filled two buckets with the fruit and carried them to Helwell View, where she and Vi made jars of jelly and a bottle each of crab apple liqueur with some gin that Ron had bought for the purpose. He would not drink the finished beverage, but Vi would decant it into smaller bottles for sale at the Christmas bazaar.

Bonfire night was on a Saturday, and Caroline travelled to Minehead to spend the weekend with Helen and Tommy. Daisy joined them, but Noah was watching a storm approach

Ireland and decided not to join the party. He had been unsettled by the loss of several boats off the Irish coast the night after the séance and felt he should stay close to the harbour.

There was a large bonfire constructed on Minehead beach, with fireworks set up in a roped off area and food stalls selling hot chestnuts, mugs of soup and bread rolls, and oysters. Helen had been working hard over the recent weeks to convince people that Tommy had simply been caught up in the Exeter incident as an unfortunate bystander, and the agreement of the Western Omnibus Company to extend a route through Alcombe South had helped her cause no end. She had been invited to ride on the first bus, with a small number of the press and other notable town's people. Her picture had once more made the front page of the *Western Mercury*.

Tommy had not heard from Christopher since their arrests. He had noticed an advertisement in the *Mercury* for a chemistry master at the University and drew the conclusion that Christopher had been asked to leave. To his surprise, Tommy felt not hunger, but pity for the man. Now that he had something new to occupy his time, he no longer found himself dwelling on inflated hedonistic daydreams. Tommy's focus was on air transport and even when not at the airfield he spent many hours poring over engineering manuals and studying the progress of other carriers. He was even brushing up his French to follow developments in air passenger services there, though Helen still had to help him with some phrases. He had written off for a free language learning booklet he had seen advertised in the *Mercury*. He also bought overalls and boots, and raided Mrs Rich's duster cupboard for spare rags on which to wipe his hands. The ground crew at Sunray Air had accepted him without question, and he was determined to make a success of the venture with them.

After the Mayor had made a speech and lit the bonfire surrounded by his councillors, Helen re-joined Tommy and the girls.

"Who is the woman with the wide hat standing next to the Mayor?" Daisy asked.

Helen turned and located the woman. "Mrs Eliza Fletcher. She is standing for the Periton ward. A seat has become vacant, Councillor Benson died last week, you'll remember he had a bad heart and had been expected to step down at the next election."

"Is she a Conservative party member too?" Caroline was admiring the woman's fur-trimmed coat.

"Yes, as Benson was before her. It's a safe seat, absolutely no reason for her to lose it. Rather a clever woman; plays the simpleton with the men and then gets them to agree to whatever she wants."

"She doesn't sound very nice!" Caroline turned back to Helen.

"One is often surrounded by those who are not nice in politics Caro. Nice people generally get walked over. It is a good thing that she and I are on the same side, I rather think she will be useful."

Once the bonfire was well alight and cheers had gone up as the paper-stuffed Guy caught a-flame, attention turned to the fireworks. The crowds lined the Promenade behind the ropes and were treated to a 10-minute display of noise and colour. Boards had been set up to hold Catherine wheels and tubes pushed into the sand to hold the larger bangers.

As they watched, Caroline wondered out loud, "I suppose they don't have fireworks like this in Africa. I wonder if Midge misses them as well as ice cream."

"Oh Lord, I completely forgot to tell you!" gasped Helen, "Midge is coming home for Christmas and she says she has a surprise for us. She is due to arrive in Southampton on December 16, she will be staying in Pangbourne for the main event and then she is coming down to us for the New Year. I believe she'll be heading back to Tanganyika on January 8th from Southampton again. Darling I'm so sorry, I should have said as soon as you arrived! She asked me to, you know."

"Not to worry, you've told me now. I wonder what her surprise is, did she give you a clue?"

"I have absolutely no idea, but as long as it's not one of those ghastly stuffed crocodiles I shan't mind what it is. You must come over when she is here. Bring your delightful Noah too." Helen smiled sweetly.

"I shall ask Noah of course, but he might have other plans. He could be working, or even visiting his parents." She blanched at the memory of the taxidermy arranged in Captain McTimony's apartment.

"And your father will be coming down for Christmas, is that right?"

"Yes, he will catch the train on Christmas Eve morning and stay until the day after Boxing Day. In fact, I was thinking of going up a day or so before so I can travel back with him. It would enable me to deliver one or two gifts rather than pay for the postage."

"Come to us on the Thursday or Friday afterwards. I had thought about hosting a party, but now that Midge will be with us, I am inclined to keep the celebrations small this year. I am sure my father will appreciate it at least; we have had rather a lot of parties this year."

"Daisy will be there too?"

"Of course, she will. The poor thing has nowhere else to go. I may invite one or two others, but it will still be a quiet affair."

15

KEYS FOR THE PRESENT

There was no more swimming for Caroline that year. She had taken to the sea twice in October but now accepted that she would have to admire it from the beach until spring. She had heard that along the south coast, people were known to swim in the sea on Christmas day. She did not want to risk hypothermia. She had also read that another young woman had succeeded in swimming across the English Channel. Caroline considered the possibility; she did not think she would like to be in the water and out of sight of land. However, despite not swimming, she made her almost daily pilgrimage to the beach in the mornings. She breathed in the salty air and felt more awake then than after her morning splash of cold water from the bathroom sink.

Caroline's radio became her main contact with the outside world as dusk fell earlier each day. She paid two pence each week for a copy of the *Radio Times*, delivered along with provisions from Doniford Post Office, and read it cover to cover. She had particularly enjoyed a piece written about how life might be in 2050 with fast travel between continents and the clearance of much of inner London to provide more wide avenues and vistas of St Paul's Cathedral. It had reminded her of the time she spent in London with Helen, Tommy, Lady Victoria and James. She wondered where James was now; she had not heard from him since the start of the summer.

Noah called in every two or three days on his patrol of the coast. They would take tea in the kitchen and discuss local happenings such as the opening of a new pharmacy in Watchet or the escape of a man from Taunton prison who was swiftly recaptured. Caroline went to the little cinema in Watchet almost every Saturday, with or without Noah. She had missed having films available to her as she had in Cheltenham and thoroughly enjoyed gazing up at the big screen for an hour or two before doing a little shopping in the town and returning home to her armchair and her knitting.

Caroline had asked Noah about his plans for Christmas. As she had expected, he would be with his parents on the day itself and would return to Watchet on Boxing Day. However, he seemed keen to meet her father, and suggested that he might visit for tea on Boxing Day. Caroline made him promise that he would ride the train in both directions. She felt strangely excited and nervous at having both Noah and her father under her roof at the same time.

Towards the end of November Caroline received a postal order from London as payment for three of her recent canvases. It was not an insignificant sum and she was surprised when she read the accompanying note from Elsa that it was not for the whole consignment. It had been the paintings of the life model that had sold almost as soon as the buyer had been alerted to them, Elsa said. There would always be a market for them, and could Caroline send more in the new year now that she had been able to find a model? Caroline bit her lip. She would have to ask Tommy, who she was sure would agree, but she felt she should also mention it to Noah. She was not sure he would be so accommodating. To avoid the inquisition that might accompany paying the postal order into her own post office account in Doniford, Caroline took it with her to Williton the following Thursday and escaped with only a slightly raised eyebrow from the cashier.

The extra funds ensured that Caroline could purchase small gifts for all of her friends for Christmas to supplement the jars of crab apple jelly. She was careful to not be too extravagant; she did not want anyone to feel they would have to reciprocate in kind. In Williton she made purchases ready for her trip to Cheltenham. She wrapped each one carefully and placed them all into one suitcase before packing her clothes in the other. Though no snow had fallen in north Somerset, Caroline knew there had been some and much colder temperatures in the Cotswolds. The Wednesday before Christmas brought a biting wind from the east as she waited on the platform at Doniford Halt station.

Sara was waiting for Caroline at Norwood Court, with two guests. Unfortunately, she was unable to prolong the surprise as Victor was happily shouting at his building blocks in the sitting room when Caroline arrived.

"We thought if I brought Victor to see you, you wouldn't need to come all the way out to us while you're here." Annie said after the two women had embraced. Sara organised the tea things while Caroline took off her coat and deposited everything in her old bedroom.

When she joined Annie and Victor in the sitting room she had two small parcels.

"It did at least save me carrying these. Happy Christmas!"

"Oh Miss, you didn't need to get us anything. It is nice just to see you for a while."

"I have been busy improving my knitting skills and I thought you might make use of my efforts."

Victor had immediately seen the gifts and was shuffling towards Annie intent on obtaining at least one if not both of them.

"All right my boy, you shall have yours now. Would you mind if I keep mine for Sunday, Miss?"

"Of course you may. Annie, I do wish you would call me Caroline now. Miss sounds so formal."

Annie smiled, "I suppose it would be alright to, now that Sara is here instead of me. Now Victor, let's pull this ribbon, that's it, and what's in there?"

Between Annie and Victor, they shook the contents of the wrapping onto the floor.

"A hat and scarf! Oh thank you, these are beautiful! Come here Victor, let's put this on you … it's a perfect fit."

Caroline beamed with pride. She had originally attempted a balaclava helmet for the boy but had given up after several misunderstandings with the pattern. Annie's gift was a pair of mittens, which had also started out as gloves but had become equally as challenging to Caroline's novice knitting skills.

"Has my father been behaving himself with his diet?" Caroline asked when Victor had resumed playing with his blocks on the floor.

"I think so, yes. He looks so much better than when he was ill before. Sara has been talking to Mrs Monk downstairs, and she says the diet is good for everyone."

"Is she still looking after Captain McTimony?"

"She is. And I'll say if I might, that she's looking better for it too. I think it's been good for her, to keep herself busy while Mr Monk is away. Sara has also been talking to her about becoming a nurse."

"Really? Oh, but that would mean we'd need to find another maid for Father." Caroline frowned. "I'm sure Miss Kettle would miss her company too."

"It's only talk at the moment, mi … I mean, Caroline," Annie blushed. "I don't think she'll do anything about it just yet. They've too many nurses as it is."

"I see. She would make an excellent nurse though, should she choose to pursue it. And how is Jacob and the yard doing?"

"Very well." It was Annie's turn to beam with pride. "With everyone building garages for their motor cars these days, he's doing a roaring trade. His mum's been bad these past few weeks though. It's the damp, goes to her chest every winter. And they are talking about buying a lorry. Its time Ned was put out to pasture."

The next day, Caroline had two difficult visits to make. The first was to the Vicarage at St Mark's. Philip was at home when she called, and he ushered her into the sitting room where Mary was staring vacantly out of the window. Angelica was napping upstairs and the house was quiet. There were no Christmas decorations, but a row of cards adorned the mantlepiece. Philip left the two women alone.

Caroline moved one of the chairs closer to Mary and sat down. She had been rehearsing what to say on her walk there.

"Mary. I don't know exactly how you must be feeling, but I do know how it is to lose someone very close to you. I'm sorry I couldn't be at the funeral."

Mary continued to look out of the window. "It was small."

At least she is speaking now, thought Caroline. "Philip said Celestine agreed that it should be carried out as quickly as possible."

"Yes. Celestine wanted rid of the bad spirits."

Caroline wasn't sure how to respond. She decided to change the subject.

"I brought a present for Angelica. I gave it to Philip to put away until Sunday for her along with some crab apple jelly from my garden. She must be looking forward to Christmas."

Mary at last turned her head from the window and looked at Caroline. "She is too young to know what it means. Thank you for your kindness."

"Have you thought about my offer? For you to come and stay with me in the new year? I should so like to have you and Angelica for company."

"I have thought. I have thought many things since… Tell me Miss Caroline, are there black people where you are living now?"

The question caught Caroline completely by surprise. "Well, no, not in Doniford. And not in Minehead either I don't think. But why should that matter?"

Mary's face was expressionless. Caroline felt as if Mary was looking right into her soul as she spoke, her accent becoming more Caribbean as she went on.

"I thought when I came to Cheltenham with Philip that people would be different. He told me that Cheltenham was gentile. Not like Bristol, where black people have to pick up fruit on the docks and work twice as hard for the same wage as a white person. And I believed him. And I was a fool. If there are no black people, who will I go to if Angelica is sick?"

"Why, the doctor of course. Doctor Bentley lives only a few minutes away from my home and he is very much like Doctor Riley here. But Angelica won't become sick. If anything, the sea air will do wonders for her."

"You have no nurse?" Mary's expression showed her suspicion.

"There is a District Nurse, but she lives in Watchet and I rarely see her. No, if there were any medical issues Doctor Bentley would be the closest. Mary do you really think the nurse here was negligent?"

"I think she did not care." There was anger in Mary's voice now. "She did not care because Mark was not a white baby!"

"I'm sure that's not so. She did call the doctor, didn't she?"

"When it was too late! She said it was just a cough. She knew Angelica had whooping cough, she just did not care."

Caroline did not answer. What could she say? She was well aware that some people had a low opinion of Mary and those like her. Caroline's own mother had made it clear she did not approve of Caroline associating with Mary though she tolerated it for Philip's sake. And yet the great and the good of Minehead society had flocked to see the polo team from India and had seemed to willingly mingle with them and their entourage at the match.

Mary looked at her hands in her lap. Her voice had lost its edge when she spoke again.

"I should not be angry at you. You have been a good friend to me, and a good Godmother to Angelica. Perhaps we will come to you in the spring. I should like to see the sea again."

The second person Caroline wanted to see, she intended to spend only a few minutes with. She caught the tram from Gloucester Road outside the railway station and got off at the gas works. She had never been inside the works before, but did not want to wait until five when the shift finished. She found her way to the foreman's office and was relieved to see Mr Lewis senior sitting at the desk. He offered her a seat and went out to find his son. A few minutes later Bob appeared at the door.

"Caroline! You do like to surprise a fellow! How are you?"

Caroline stood up. "Hello Bob. I hope I haven't caused you any embarrassment by asking for you here. It's bitterly cold outside and I didn't want to wait around in the street."

"None at all. Sit down again, won't you? I heard your father was taken ill. I hope that's not why you're here." His concern was genuine.

"He is much recovered now, thank you. He will be spending Christmas with me; I have come to make sure he is well enough to travel, and it seems that he is. You are looking well too."

Bob began to blush. He was so happy to see Caroline again and so surprised by her visit.

"I've thought of you often." Was all he could respond with.

Caroline had known this would be difficult. She did not want to raise Bob's hopes that she might consider him more than a friend, but she did not have time to visit Stroud now since her father had decided he would finish work at lunchtime the next day. They would catch an afternoon train back to Doniford, which would also give Sara an extra day's holiday.

She said as gently as she could, "I hope you don't mind, but I won't have the opportunity to visit Lottie while I am here now, and I was wondering if I might leave a small gift for her with you?"

Bob pulled himself together. He knew how things stood. "Yes, of course. We're going to visit on Boxing Day, I can take it then."

"Thank you. It's only something small, I would have sent it by post if I'd known father would be ready to come back with me tomorrow." She stood up again and took the small parcel from her bag. When she handed it to Bob, he tried to smile as if she were not tormenting him.

"Caroline, are you happy in your new place?"

"Yes, yes I am. I am happy on my own, with my radio and the sea gulls for company."

"I am glad of that. I want you to be happy."

"And are you happy in your house?"

Bob paused before he answered. "Yes, I am happy in my house. But I should be getting back to work. Thank you for coming, it's been good to see you again."

"Good to see you too Bob. Happy Christmas." She kissed his cheek and then left without looking back.

Caroline and George arrived at Doniford Halt at just before ten o'clock the next evening. Caroline had filled the space taken up in her suitcase by gifts with more she had bought after leaving the gas works. She had not wanted to give Helen a hand-made present. George had gasped as he got out of the carriage onto the platform, the easterly wind assaulting them after the warmth of the train. Mr Evans hurried along the platform towards them, eager to help with their luggage.

"Good evening, Miss, Sir! Wasn't expecting you before tomorrow!"

"We were able to get away sooner than we'd expected, Mr Evans. Would you mind taking this one, Father? Thank you."

"Will you be alright walking? I'm afraid there's no taxi outside."

"We shall be alright, thank you. Happy Christmas!"

They bought a very small fir tree at the Post Office the next morning and wheeled it back to Quantock Cottage strapped to Caroline's bicycle. Father and daughter decorated the tree and spent a relaxed forty-eight hours together listening to the radio and eating some of the food that Vi had helped Caroline prepare before she went up to Cheltenham. As Caroline pulled the sitting room curtains on Christmas evening, she realised it was snowing gently. She called her father to see it too.

"A perfect ending to a delightful day. Thank you for having me here with you, my dear."

"I am very happy to have you here. And now, I think you are allowed a very small sherry."

Overnight the snow fell in copious amounts across south Wales and into the Cotswolds. The southeast of England was a sheet of ice and more than a thousand people were taken to hospital after slipping over. Noah broke his journey from his parents' house to Caroline's in Watchet so that he could make sure there were no stray boats out in the Bristol Channel. It would be unlikely, few fishermen deliberately put to sea over Christmas, but he still wanted to be certain. He did not want to leave Watchet with a pricking of his conscience. Satisfied that all was well, he had a pint of beer with Escott in the Angel Inn before heading to the railway station for the next train to Doniford Halt.

Caroline was by now a bag of nerves. She could never have imagined that she would feel this way about Noah meeting her father. After breakfast she had scrubbed the kitchen table and floor, and set about the bathroom before her father convinced her to leave it and have some lunch. She had the feeling he was amused by her nervous behaviour. She was elbow-deep in washing the lunch plates when there was a knock at the front door. Noah had taken to using the kitchen door when he visited, and Caroline called through to her father and asked him to see who it was. When she heard Noah's voice in the hall, she hurriedly wiped her hands on the tea towel and took off her apron.

George was pouring sherry into glasses when Caroline joined them in the sitting room.

"Noah, you used the front door!"

"I thought this was a more formal visit," he kissed her cheek and then took the sherry George was offering him. He didn't care for sherry, but he wasn't going to make a fuss. Not today.

"Shall we sit down?" George indicated they should move to the chairs around the fireplace. Caroline accepted the sherry. This was not how she had imagined the day would go. It was as if George and Noah were already acquainted.

"It seems I have no need to make introductions," she said, sipping her drink. "How are your parents, Noah?"

"They are very well, thank you. I feel I have eaten a week's worth of food over the past twenty-four hours!" he stretched out his legs. "They send you both their good wishes and have insisted that I take you to meet them as soon as possible Caroline."

"I should like to meet them. I must say you seem in very good spirits. And you, Father, are grinning from ear to ear. Am I missing out on a joke?"

"It is no joke Caroline," George replied, "though I do not think we should continue our clandestine arrangements now that you are here Noah."

Caroline looked from one to the other. "Will one of you tell me what is going on please?"

Noah stood up and went to his coat where it hung in the hall. He returned with two very small plain brown envelopes. He looked at George, received a nod of acknowledgement, and handed Caroline the first envelope.

"I didn't have a chance to make them pretty I'm afraid. And this one is only symbolic. Open it up, then."

Caroline picked at the envelope seal and after working a hole in the top, tipped it up. A key fell into her lap. She looked from her father to Noah.

"I don't understand." She said with a frown.

"I thought about burying it in a packing case filled with bran, but then realised I couldn't very well hide that from you, or bring it easily on the train." He sat on the edge of his seat again. "Do you remember those houses we've been watching being built on the other side of Watchet? The ones you said wouldn't be troubled by flooding?"

"Yes. But they don't have doors or windows yet. The rooves only went on last week."

"Which is why I said this key is a symbol only. It's not really a key to one of those houses, but as soon as they do have doors, I shall have a key to one of them. For us, if you'd like to live there?"

"You're buying a house?"

"Have bought, yes. It was rather less difficult than I expected it to be, once I'd got your father involved." He smiled at George who was enjoying Caroline's confusion but knew it would erupt into frustration if they did not get through the explanation soon.

"My dear, Noah wrote to me at the Building Society some weeks ago. He introduced himself and explained that he was interested in not only purchasing a home but also that he was … interested in you. We have since spoken on the telephone several times, and I have assisted in his obtaining a small mortgage with a bank in Williton. A reputable bank, they have several branches, but Noah preferred to use the Williton branch."

"I see. But I don't understand why you are giving me a key, Noah."

Noah took a deep breath. "Because of this." He handed Caroline the second envelope. She could feel what was inside before she opened it, and let it carefully fall into the palm of her hand. Noah took it from her and took her hand.

"Caroline, I have no idea if you will accept this. You are the most unusual woman I have known and you continue to surprise and amaze me with how you behave and think. But with your father's permission," he turned to check one final time with George who simply smiled, "I would like to ask you to marry me. One day. Perhaps a day in the far future. Perhaps we shall continue to live in the way we have been for some time yet, but I'd like you to have this ring as an understanding of intent."

Caroline withdrew her hand. She had not expected any of this. She was happy that Noah would be moving into a better home than the harbour office, but everything else was so much of a surprise she was finding it difficult to take in. George came to her rescue.

"Noah, might I suggest that Caroline wear the ring as a pendant if she does not want to treat it as a traditional engagement at this time? I understand that is what some young people do nowadays."

"Of course. Caroline, you don't have to wear the ring at all if it makes you uncomfortable. I simply wanted to take the opportunity, with your father being here. Shall I put it back into the envelope?" George had warned Noah that the decision must be Caroline's and that he should not necessarily expect her to accept straight away.

The three of them sat still in the sitting room for a moment. Two pairs of eyes on Caroline, and her eyes on the ring that Noah was holding in front of her. The log in the fire shifted and threw sparks upwards. Caroline looked at Noah.

"No. I have a necklace upstairs that I can wear it on. I am not ready to be married yet, and I know you know that. But I shall accept this as you have described, as an understanding of intent. That one day, I might be ready."

Noah returned to Watchet on the 18:15 train that evening. They had talked of possibilities, of legal matters and of practicalities all afternoon. He had a sense that there were still things Caroline had not said because her father had been present. Noah would need to clear those few things up as soon as he could once George had returned to Cheltenham, when he joined Caroline in Minehead for the new year celebrations. He took the long route from the railway station and walked out to the row of new houses. The site was fenced and padlocked, and the buildings loomed up in the dark with a few flakes of snow still falling. It had been the right time, he was convinced of that. The mortgage payments were easily within his means. George had advised him to speak to a solicitor about making a will, to cover every eventuality should Caroline not want to marry straight away. He would no longer worry that Caroline and her belongings would be washed away by a storm tide, at least when she finally decided to leave Quantock Cottage and join him at number 3 Westmorland Terrace.

As he turned towards the harbour, a row of seagulls on the ridge tiles of a cottage on the street below stood as if they were a choir and began their sonorous calls. It sounded as if they were laughing, Noah thought.

Caroline arrived at Helen and Tommy's house in the afternoon of 30 December. Tommy had got hold of some engineering plans for an aircraft and was studying them in his room. He had set up a small table with a lamp so that he did not have to keep clearing his papers away if Helen needed to work in the study. Daisy would arrive the next day, along with Noah and another guest who Helen refused to name. She showed Caroline up to the first floor.

"I'm afraid that you and Noah will have to share a room this time, we're fit to burst with guests. I do hope that won't be too tiresome for you both?"

Caroline opened her mouth as if in shock. "Helen how could you?" Then she smiled, "I'm joking! I'm sure we will manage somehow."

"I rather thought that by now it would be what you'd require, darling. It's all yours tonight in any case."

"Do I know your other guests?"

"Patience, dear heart. All will be revealed."

As they went back downstairs, the first of the guests came in through the front door.

"Midge!"

"Caroline!"

The two embraced, and over Midge's shoulder Caroline saw a thin young man with short sun-bleached hair and a kindly face. Caroline stepped back from Midge and asked, "Who's this?"

Midge looked up at the man, a big smile on her face. "This is my husband, Oliver."

Over tea in the conservatory, Midge explained how Oliver had proposed after his second visit to the compound. He had been a great support after Marie-Claire's death, Midge added. Oliver Gregson was an Oxford scholar, with a Master's degree in theology. He had been considering holy orders, but then met Midge. They had been married just three days before setting off for England, and Midge's parents had been thrilled not only to have Midge home again for a few days but also to welcome Oliver into the family. The couple had then travelled to Oliver's parents in Sherbourne in Dorset before heading down to Minehead. Afternoon turned to evening, Tommy emerged from his room and Midge and Oliver supplied answers to an almost endless stream of questions from the others.

Daisy arrived the following morning and continued the questions from the evening before. Sleet was falling and the streets were slushy, so the group agreed in unison to remain indoors and read or play cards. Noah knocked on the front door at just before five, causing a fresh round of questions this time mostly from Midge and Oliver. Helen repeatedly looked at her watch, and after the fifth time, Caroline asked, "when is the next guest due to arrive?"

"Our final guest should have been here half an hour ago. I can only assume they will be on the next train." Helen looked at Tommy as she spoke.

"I should think so. Don't worry. Now, would anyone like a cocktail?"

A taxi drew up outside the house at twenty minutes to eight. A man paid the driver and got out, carrying a large rucksack. He wore no hat, despite the inclement weather. He climbed the steps and rung the bell.

Tommy got up and went into the hall as Mrs Rich came through from the kitchen.

"It's alright Mrs Rich, I have it."

He opened the door.

"Come on in James, so glad you could make it old chap!"

"Nearly didn't. It was absolute hell getting out of Cardiff. Still, I'm here now. Sounds like there is a real party going on!"

"Leave your bag there for a moment, we can take it up once you've met everyone."

James hung up his scarf and coat and then followed Tommy into the sitting room.

"Everyone, our final guest has arrived, and not a moment too soon as I think dinner will be served any minute.

Please welcome my good friend and famous film producer, James Baker."

Tommy furnished James with a cocktail while Helen carried out the introductions. She was careful not to hint at any intimacy between James and Caroline, much to Caroline's relief. She had left out James' marriage proposal when she had told Noah of her brief acting career. Mrs Rich appeared in the doorway and announced that dinner was ready to be served and everyone took their drinks into the dining room.

It was a very good dinner. Helen surveyed her guests from one end of the dining table, watching them talk and laugh together. Tommy, sat at the opposite end to Helen, leaned back in his chair and looked at her. He raised his glass with a wink and she did the same.

Oliver was very interested in James' latest production, a film about poverty-stricken miners in the Welsh valleys. Noah and Tommy discussed engines, both in agreement that whether inside a boat, a car or an aeroplane, the internal combustion engine worked (or failed to work) in much the same way. Caroline and Midge told Daisy tales of their school days and laughed much at Helen's expense. Helen did not mind and shot back with an anecdote or two that made all three women blush to the roots of their hair.

The party left the detritus of the dinner table at a quarter past eleven and moved back to the drawing room where the fire was ablaze and the alcohol free-flowing. Caroline found herself alone with James as Tommy and Noah went in search of more ice. Mrs Rich had left them to it once the coffee had been served.

"It's good to see you again, Caroline. I have meant to write, but … you know how things are on location."

"I am happy that you are working. It sounds an interesting project."

"Social realism they call it. In years to come it will be a record of the working man. Might not make me much money now, but still. And Noah, he is your friend?"

"He is my friend, yes."

"Are you happy, Caroline?"

She considered for a moment. "Yes, I believe I am. I have been happy many times over these past three years. I was happy in Dorset, and in Cornwall, and now here in Somerset. All different kinds of happiness, but happy all the same."

"That's good. It was all I would ever want for you. For what it's worth, I think you were right not to marry me. But I don't regret asking you." He smiled.

Caroline smiled back at him warmly. "I don't regret saying no, James."

Tommy and Noah returned with a bucket of ice and Caroline excused herself. She went up to the bathroom, and when she came out, Helen was standing outside the door smoking one of her thin, dark cigarettes.

"I'm sorry Helen, you should have knocked and I'd have hurried for you."

"I wanted to speak to you. I wanted to make sure nothing was difficult for you and James. I didn't think it would be a problem, but I saw you talking together just now and then you came up here, so I wanted to be sure you were alright."

It was an unusual tenderness that Helen displayed and Caroline was touched.

"I'm quite alright Helen, really. We were simply agreeing that it would have been madness for James and I to marry."

"I see," she sounded genuinely relieved. "Is that a present?" Helen nodded to the ring Caroline wore on a long gold chain around her neck. "I don't think I've seen you wear it before."

"You would make an excellent detective you know. It's no wonder you are a rising star in politics. Yes, it is a present, from Noah. He wants to marry me."

"Darling, how wonderful! You did say yes, of course?"

"Not exactly. You see he had been arranging things with my father in secret and I was quite cross with them both when Noah proposed. But Noah calls it a ring of intention, not an engagement ring, which is why it is not on my finger just yet. He is buying a house, a brand new house in Watchet, and when I leave Quantock Cottage I shall live there with him. And we might be married, or we might not."

"Caro, you know people will talk. You will be called names. Old women will look down their noses at you and farmers will keep their cows away for fear you will curdle the milk." Helen was trying not to laugh as she spoke. "I feel it is my duty, as the eldest of us three friends, to ensure you know what you are letting yourself in for!"

"If anyone could tell me, darling Helen, you could."

They hugged, both suddenly almost in tears. Then, after a quick check in the mirror and a fresh smear of lipstick, they re-joined the party to toast the end of one year and the beginning of another.

The End

AUTHOR'S NOTE

For those of you who have read the previous two adventures of Caroline in *Catching Up* and *The Price of Coal*, you will know that I try to use true historical events to form the backbone of these stories. I enjoy researching the period, but at the same time, things do appear afterwards that are often only known or remembered by locals to the area in question. This is the case with Watchet.

It would be remiss of me not to mention at all the stationing of the British Army at a training camp above Doniford beach from approximately 1925-35. The population of Watchet appear to have been largely against the camp, particularly as the frequency of search lights and firing increased. One report mentions that three local men narrowly missed being injured by shrapnel while they were working on a house in the village.

This gave me a dilemma. Should I rewrite the novel and try to accommodate the army camp or leave the story as I was content with it and provide an explanation of sorts at the end. You can see what my decision was. This is, after all a work of fiction, and I am at liberty to arrange scenery, people and activities as I see fit. To include the camp, and realistically to include some characters from it, would have complicated Caroline's stay in Doniford unnecessarily. However, that does not mean those men and women are forgotten, or their contribution to our nation's safety diminished.

It is highly possible that in another story, they will appear. We might just need to be flexible with the dates of the camp's existence to help things along.

Mary Lay,
2022